GRIZZLY PERFECTION

ARCADIAN BEARS, BOOK SIX

BECCA JAMESON

❀ Created with Vellum

ACKNOWLEDGMENTS

This book is for all my fans who miss reading my paranormal ménages. I love you all!

PROLOGUE

"Sir, I have those books ready for you."

Without moving his head, Stephen Rimouski lifted his gaze to stare over the top of his glasses at his new right-hand man, Vinny, who stood across from his desk. Stephen lifted one hand to reach for the thick, official accounting ledger. When he lowered the volume in front of him and opened it to the last few pages, he smiled. "Looks good."

Stephen leaned back in his chair and steepled his fingers in front of his lips, tapping them several times before speaking again. "You've proven to be a valuable team player in recent months."

"Thank you, sir." Vinny was tall, over six feet, but lanky. His dark hair was cropped close to his head. His dark eyes were nearly always furrowed, serious. His skin was too pale, as though he didn't get enough sun. To most people, he looked like an ordinary enough guy, but Stephen knew better.

"I think it's time I gave you more responsibility." Stephen paused. "And more pay to compensate for your loyalty to the team."

"That would be appreciated, sir." Vinny shuffled his feet and rubbed his hands together.

Ordinarily, Stephen wouldn't consider hiring someone this uptight in a million years. But Vinny had qualities that were invaluable to the team.

When he'd come to Rimouski's office six months ago looking for a job, Stephen had hedged. But Vinny had balls, and he didn't back down. That's when he began to weave a tale so absurd and unbelievable that Stephen found himself at a loss for words, allowing Vinny to continue to dig a hole for himself. At the time, Stephen fully intended to bury Vinny in that hole as soon as he finished speaking.

Instead, at the end of a rambling tale about the existence of bear shifters, Vinny had pushed his chair out of the way and transformed right in front of Stephen's eyes.

Stephen had jumped from his seat and taken two steps back while his heart beat out of his chest. "Fuck."

The grizzly had bared his teeth, but it almost seemed as though he was laughing instead of threatening anyone. After lifting his paws to place them on the desk in a show of dominance, the bear had transformed back into a human and stood in the same spot, his hands on the mahogany surface. His expression was tight, his eyes unblinking. "Like I said, Mr. Rimouski, I believe I have a quality that would be useful to you."

Shaking thoughts of the past from his mind, Stephen stared at Vinny. There was no question the man was invaluable. As it turned out, people who could shift into a bear form possessed many other abilities Stephen was coming to rely on, not the least of which involved the fact that Vinny could scent other shifters.

What Stephen now knew was that although no ordinary human could ever be a match for him, in the course of his life, he faced a far bigger threat—shifters. Those damn animals had powers he could only dream of. If any of them found out about his nefarious dealings, they could ruin him. Which meant he needed Vinny. The man was invaluable.

The fact that Stephen now had a shifter working for his team gave him a certain level of relief, but knowing there were others out there kept Stephen on edge. On any given day, how many people did he pass in the street who weren't fully human? And how many of them could sense things that could lead to Stephen's total ruination?

Vinny had spent no small amount of time warning Stephen about the importance of keeping the existence of shifters to himself. Whether or not Vinny had been shitting him was irrelevant. Stephen would heed the admonition to avoid risking his own life testing the possibilities.

Keeping Vinny on his payroll was important. Keeping the shifter happy was also crucial.

Stephen cleared his throat. "I'll transfer funds to your account this afternoon. Think of it as a bonus for your loyal service."

"Thank you, sir."

"Have any of my men proven to be anything other than on the up and up lately?" He used Vinny to spy on his other employees.

"No, sir. Everyone I've met is a team player."

"Excellent." Stephen smiled. Damn, it was nice to have someone sensitive working for him. The man had an uncanny ability to read others and report back. "I have to leave town for the weekend. I'll be back Sunday evening. You need anything, you call my regional manager, Joe Stringer, got it?"

"I won't let you down, sir."

"I hope not. You don't want to know what happens to traitors around here."

"You can count on me, sir."

"Good. I'll call you when I get back in town."

CHAPTER 1

Nolan Osborn was running late. He was also completely out of sorts as he pulled up to his parents' house on the outskirts of Calgary. He glanced at the ominous, serious man sitting in the passenger seat and sighed. He needed to gather half his wits before he went inside. Did the guy have to be so damn...intense?

Carl Schaefer. *Officer* Carl Schaefer. The man who intended to remove Nolan from his current life and place him in witness protection. He had insisted Nolan leave with him that afternoon, but Nolan pushed back. His parents had returned from a sabbatical in Australia hours ago. Nolan hadn't seen them in eight months. He really wanted a chance to face them before he disappeared for weeks or months.

Damn his stupid job.

"Five minutes, Nolan." Schaefer pointed at his watch. His expression never changed, and he didn't make eye contact with Nolan. He continually scanned their surroundings as he had from the moment Nolan met him about three hours ago.

Nolan twisted his neck in every direction. "Come on. There's no way anyone followed us here. I'm sure it's safe. This is a welcome-home party. Let me at least have enough time to explain things to my family and reassure them."

"Five minutes. And the clock is already ticking." Carl never stopped scanning the area, his head slowly swiveling right and left as if he were a robot instead of a human. Unfortunately for Nolan, Carl *was* human. Completely human. This entire day would have gone smoother if he'd been a grizzly shifter, but he was not. And Nolan had to deal with it.

As he reached for the handle to open the car door, he hesitated. Perhaps Carl was right, and the decision to come here was too dangerous. Was he selfish for putting his parents and their friends in jeopardy like this? There were a dozen cars up and down the street. The house was filled with guests.

Fuck.

Determined to at least hug his mom and dad and speak with his two younger sisters, Nolan yanked the door open, set one foot on the ground, and lifted himself out of the car.

That was as far as he got. In fact, his right foot was still inside on the floorboard when he took a deep breath and jerked his gaze toward the house. He could see inside the front window. The living room was packed. The kitchen probably was, too. He scented about twenty different people.

But that wasn't the problem.

Son of a bitch.

Why? He lifted his gaze toward the sky and tried to keep his heart from pounding out of his chest. *Why today?* The world was seriously out to get him today. Or at least Fate. Did She think She was funny? He didn't.

He paused long enough to breathe in deeply a second time and assure himself he wasn't crazy. Nope. He didn't know who the scent belonged to that stood out over all the others. It wasn't someone he'd met before. But there was no mistaking the fact that its owner was his intended mate.

Shaking, he slid back into the car, closed the door, and stared out the windshield.

"What's the matter?" Carl asked.

"Give me a second," Nolan murmured. Deep breaths. No way in hell could he go inside. For one thing, he couldn't possibly put his mate in the kind of danger she would assuredly be in if he confronted her. For another thing, meeting her would only make the separation they were about to face worse.

"Changed my mind," he whispered as he started the engine. "You're right. It's not worth the risk."

"Thank God. Let's go."

His sister Paige was in his head in a heartbeat, communicating in the way only shifters could. *"Nolan. What the hell?"*

"Can't explain right now. Tell Mom and Dad I'm so sorry."

"Don't even try to blow me off like that. You know Mom is going to be on you in two seconds. Everyone in the house knows you just pulled up and then left."

"You sure everyone *knows?"* he asked. If Fate had even one pinch of common decency, She hadn't revealed Nolan to the woman inside destined to be his.

There was a split-second pause, and then Paige communicated again. *"Shit. Yes. Everyone,"* she emphasized. *"Why the hell are you running from her?"*

Nolan fought the urge to groan out loud as he gripped the steering wheel and hoped Carl didn't notice how stressed he was.

"Long story. Can't talk now." He needed to concentrate on

the road. It was almost harder to pay attention to his surroundings while communicating telepathically than if he'd been using a cell phone. Carl would notice his detachment any second. He took the next right turn and headed toward the highway.

"You cannot just disappear without saying anything, Nolan Osborn," Paige screamed into his mind. *"Why would you do this? Mom and Dad are waiting for you."*

"Please, Paige, I'm begging you to trust me. I have my reasons. I'll talk to you later."

"Do you even know who she is?"

"No. Tell me later. Please," he pleaded again. He tried to control the tone of his connection before he continued. *"Please apologize to her for me. This has nothing to do with her. And tell Mom I'll call her when I have a chance."*

"Nolan," Paige screamed.

"Paige. I'm not alone."

"Oh." She hesitated. *"You're with a human."*

"Yes."

"Female?"

Oh, Lord. His sister had the wrong idea, thinking he had a date. Made sense. But no such luck. *"No. Give me a bit. Apologize to Mom and Dad. Apologize to my...mate."* He cut off the connection abruptly, mostly because he was afraid his emotions were going to start spilling into the car.

Grizzly shifters did not ordinarily deny their mates like this. It wasn't possible. But somehow, he was going to have to put off this initial meeting, indefinitely.

Adriana Tarben stood rooted to her spot for long seconds. The tiny hairs on the back of her neck stood up, sending a shiver down her spine. A flush rushed across her face, undoubtedly leaving her cheeks red. She turned her gaze toward the front of the house, her eyes widening, her mouth falling open.

Every breath during the few brief seconds afforded her reinforced what she'd known the moment Paige Osborn's face lit up as she announced the arrival of her brother. "Nolan's finally here."

While everyone around them shifted their attention toward the front door, Adriana froze in her spot. Stunned was too mild a word to describe her reaction. In hindsight, Nolan had only been outside of his car for a few precious seconds, but it seemed so much longer to Adriana. Her world changed drastically without warning.

While her heart stopped beating and the breath was sucked from her lungs, Paige's brother disappeared as quickly as he'd arrived. Thoughts raced through her mind, too many to grasp at any one thought long enough to follow it.

She couldn't believe the power of Fate. Intellectually, she knew this could happen to her one day. Any day. Without warning. It had happened to so many grizzly shifters lately, including two of her brothers. But she was only twenty-three. And she was blindsided.

People around her were all talking at once, but she heard nothing. As if a mute button had been pushed, noises stopped reaching her ears. She glanced around, feeling like she'd left her body and was watching everyone move from somewhere near the ceiling.

The large family room of this ranch-style house was filled with people who were oblivious to her plight. Laughter and bits and pieces of conversation filled her ears. A few people sat on the soft beige leather sofa, but most were standing in groups. A glance toward the wide opening that led to the eat-in kitchen reinforced how damn many people were in attendance.

She had to get out of this crowded room.

Spinning on her heels, she rushed down the hallway toward the bedroom she'd been staying in for the past two months while the Osborns were on their sabbatical and her brother and his mate, Alton and Joselyn, were renting this house from them. She slid inside without bothering to turn on the light. She eased herself onto the edge of the bed, her hands shaking, her mind still spinning. The faint glow of a crescent moon spilled across the floor from the partially open blinds. It was all the light she needed. Grizzlies could see fine in the dark. Besides, she didn't want or need to see anything at the moment.

Nolan Osborn was her mate.

Where had he gone and why?

Unease replaced shock as the implications of his flight took hold of her. He would have scented her, too. Just as strongly. And then he'd fled. There was no other way to interpret that than to realize he hadn't wanted to meet her. Why?

Granted, the two of them had never met before. She had no idea what he looked like. She knew very little about him, actually. But he most likely had no knowledge of her, either. Until tonight, they had never crossed paths. She was from the small town of Silvertip two hours west of Calgary. Her pack owned and operated one of the two microbreweries in the rural town tucked away in the Rocky Mountains.

Adriana took a few deep breaths as someone else slipped into the room. She lifted her gaze to find Paige shutting the door with a soft snick before padding toward her. "You okay?"

Adriana didn't know how to respond. Paige knew her

brother had arrived and left. If she was sharp, she might even have known there was a connection between him and Adriana. She was certain she had done nothing to school her expression. Besides, she'd turned tail and fled the room hastily.

Paige cleared her throat. "My brother… He, uh…"

Yep. She knew. She'd even communicated with him. Not surprising. They were siblings. They could easily exchange information telepathically, even from a distance of many miles. Adriana said nothing, waiting on her new friend to stammer through whatever explanation she had.

The two women hadn't known each other long, nor had Adriana spent much time with Paige yet, but she liked her, and she felt confident she could trust her.

Paige reached the edge of the bed and lowered herself next to Adriana. "I don't know what to say. Nolan isn't normally like this."

Adriana almost laughed. "You mean all the other times he realized his mate was in the house, he didn't speed away without a word?"

Paige smiled, tipping her head to one side as she faced Adriana. "I don't know what his deal is tonight. He was vague and acting strange."

"So, he did communicate with you?" Adriana crossed her arms and rubbed her biceps with her palms, suddenly chilled. Hopefully, Paige would be able to give her at least something to explain away the tightness in her chest.

"Yeah, but I don't know much more. He wasn't alone. I thought maybe he'd had a date with him and then felt too weird to come inside with her."

That would explain a lot. Adriana sat up taller. "But that wasn't it?"

She shook her head. "No. He was with a human, but not a woman. A man. Maybe a co-worker or something?" Paige threw up her hands. "I don't know. I can't make any sense of it. Mom and Dad have been gone for eight months. Tonight is all about welcoming them home. Why on earth Nolan would get back in his car and drive away is a mystery to me."

Adriana's heart rate increased again.

Paige twisted her body to more fully face Adriana. She set a hand on Adriana's shoulder and gave a squeeze. "I'm sorry I don't know more. He did ask me to apologize to you. I'm sure he has some reason for all the drama and mystery. Please give him a chance to sort out whatever he has going on, okay?"

Adriana forced a small smile. "Do I have a choice?"

Paige grinned back. "I guess not."

"Does he know who I am?"

Paige shook her head, her expression tight. "No. He... didn't want me to tell him."

Adriana tried to process that. One word kept running through her mind, over and over. Why? Why, why, why?

Paige stood. "I need to go talk to my parents. I'm sure they're equally confused."

"Of course. Go ahead."

Paige hesitated. "Will you be okay? Why don't you come back out to the party?"

"I'm fine. Just need a few more minutes alone."

"I could send your brother in or his mate."

"No. I'm fine. Really. Alton and Joselyn are having a good time. I'll catch up with them later."

Paige stepped toward the door, but before she opened it, she turned back and whispered across the darkness. "This was his room, you know. When we were growing up, I mean. He moved out over ten years ago, of course, but my mother didn't change much. Some of his things are still in the closet and drawers. Whatever he didn't take with him when he went to university and then got his own home."

Adriana swallowed through her emotion. "Thank you."

Paige bit her lower lip, nodded, and slid out of the room, shutting the door again with a soft *snick*.

Adriana continued to sit in the blessed darkness, the only sound in the room the pounding of her heart. The dull roar of the party down the hall tortured her with its happiness. From one second to the next, her world had changed so drastically she couldn't catch her breath.

When she inhaled long and slow, she realized the faint scent of her mate lurked in the room. Until she'd scented him directly, she hadn't recognized his scent in the house for what it was. Her mate. But now...

Taking the gift of suggestion Paige had left her with, she pushed off the edge of the bed and headed for the closet. When she opened it, she smiled and closed her eyes.

With one hand on the door frame for support, she leaned farther inside the confined space and fingered the first item hanging in front of her. A leather jacket. It was his. Probably from high school, but it had hung here all these years, his scent still gripped in its fibers.

She eased it from the hanger and held it up to her face, inhaling slowly over and over. The potency made her sway, her legs threatening to give out. Her body came alive at the same time, her nipples stiffening and her sex clenching. She was aroused. How absurd. Who got horny for a man they hadn't even met?

She slid the jacket on. It was too big, the sleeves of the supple black leather hanging past her hands. But it took the chill away as she wrapped it tighter around her over the silk blouse she wore. Less than two hours ago, she'd gotten all dressed up in her favorite purple blouse that hung long over black leggings. She'd designed the shirt herself several months ago and loved the way it hung over her shoulders and draped across her chest. She also wore black heels.

She shut the closet and leaned down to slide her feet out of the shoes, and then her gaze landed on the dresser near the closet. The top had several framed pictures. How had she not noticed them earlier? In her subconscious, she realized they were family photos, but she hadn't examined them closer.

Now she inched toward the dresser and lifted one trembling hand to pick up the first frame. She held it in the beam of moonlight and let her finger trace over the strong features of the man smiling back at her. A younger version of her mate, no doubt, but he stirred something deep inside her anyway, making the pucker of her nipples more pronounced.

He was blond like his sister. Blue eyes twinkled as they stared back at her. He stood in the middle of a meadow, the mountains in the background. With one foot lifted onto a large rock at his side, he had posed, his elbow on his knee, his chin in his palm. Damn, his smile took her breath away.

Her mouth was suddenly too dry, and she hadn't blinked for so long her eyes burned. Staring longer would do her no good. She set the picture back on the dresser and headed for the bed. She needed to lie down, overwhelmed. So many emotions slammed into her.

This should be the best moment of her life. She'd just met her mate. Except she hadn't met him. He didn't know who she was. And she was alone with the knowledge that, for whatever reason, he hadn't wanted to confront her.

She forced herself to believe his flight had nothing to do with her. He'd been just as blindsided as she had. Maybe he wasn't ready? Maybe he'd needed time or space or something to wrap his head around things.

But that didn't add up, either. Paige said he'd been with someone. A human man. What was that about? She couldn't take this personally. After all, he had no idea who she was or what she looked like. Unless the man had an aversion to binding in general, his rejection tonight had nothing to do with her. He had something to take care of. It must have been important.

Adriana lowered herself onto the bed, curled up on her side, drew her knees up to her chest, and hugged the jacket around her tighter. Normally she was warm. Grizzly shifters ran hotter than regular humans. But a chill had taken over her body several minutes ago and wouldn't let go.

She closed her eyes, thinking how fickle Fate could be. Was it pure coincidence that she'd moved to town two months ago to pursue an art degree at the University of Calgary? Did Fate not only decide who Adriana was meant to be with but also when the two of them would meet? No one would ever know the answer to those questions.

The truth was Adriana already had a degree. In computer science. She'd been working fulltime at her family's brewery since she'd finished her education. But she hadn't felt connected to the work. She'd been bored and unsatisfied. She should have known. She'd been working at the brewery part-time the entire time she was going to school. However, the minute she finished her degree in May, she knew she'd made a mistake.

A few months ago, when she'd come to Calgary for a visit, she'd gone with Joselyn to a fashion show just for fun. And her entire focus changed from that day forward. She'd always been interested in fabrics and clothing and shoes, but she'd never pursued anything in the arts because it didn't fit with her goals. With her family's goals.

Designing outfits had been nothing more than a hobby

she played around with at home. She'd gotten her first sewing machine when she was nine and had worn out three machines since then. Her latest had cost a fortune and would last her entire life.

Everyone in the extended Tarben family who was willing and able worked for Mountain Peak Brewery. It was in their blood. There was no call for someone with an eye for fashion. So Adriana had ignored the passion and gone for the practical.

It was Joselyn who noticed her enthusiasm and encouraged her to think bigger. And here she was, two months later, living in Calgary and attending classes at U of C to start her life over again. It would take several years and a lot of work, but she knew in her heart the decision was right. She'd never been as relaxed and calm as she'd been since making this choice, leaving her childhood home and heading to Calgary.

She was a grown woman, for heaven's sake. She had never lived anywhere but home. The baby. The youngest of five. A homebody.

But not anymore. This new adventure had invigorated her.

Until an hour ago, she'd planned to find an apartment near campus, get a part-time job to help pay for her second round of education, and wrap herself up in her new career choice.

Until an hour ago...

Now? Her foundation was shaking.

She closed her eyes, inhaled Nolan's scent again, and tried to calm her racing heart.

Where was he? And why the hell had he left her like this?

CHAPTER 2

Nolan was pacing his hotel room as he made the phone call to his parents, Stanton and Oleta Osborn, two hours later. He hoped he'd given them enough time for the party to die down so they could take his call.

"Nolan?" His mother's voice came through, but in the background, he could hear many other voices too. "Hang on. Let me find someplace quieter."

He waited, listening to the rustling sounds of movement for a few moments.

The sounds died down, and then his father spoke. "Nolan. Where are you?"

"Hey, Dad. I'm so sorry. Is Mom with you?"

"Yes," she replied. "We have you on speaker. We're in the bedroom now."

He'd intentionally called instead of reaching into their minds, wanting to hear their voices but also not wanting there to be any misunderstanding in his tone and inflection. "I'm in a hotel room for the night."

"Why?"

He took a deep breath. "One of my clients at the law

firm was laundering money. A lot of money. I stumbled on the inconsistencies last night and then spent hours making sure I was right. This morning I went to the police. It's bad. I'm so sorry, but I'm a witness."

His mother gasped. "So, what are you saying?"

"I have to lie low, Mom. Until the trial."

His father cleared his throat. "How long will that take?"

"Not sure yet. They haven't even arrested the guy yet. Could be months." He rubbed his forehead as he stopped pacing to stare out the fifteenth story window at the bustling city of Calgary below. The lights twinkling all over the streets and buildings were a reminder that life would keep moving on while he hid.

"Months?" His mother's voice rose, a pitch higher than it normally was.

"I wanted to at least see you for a minute this evening, give you and Dad a hug, welcome you home. I spent half the afternoon arguing with the officer to let me stop by. And then..."

"Oh, son," his father said, "what a mess."

"Yeah." He leaned his forehead against the glass. There was no way to shake the memory of the scent of his mate from his mind. He needed to ask the hard questions now. "I communicated with Paige."

"We know. She was pissed," his mother said.

He smiled at his mother's choice of words. *Pissed* wasn't a word she normally used. It must have been bad. "I couldn't explain things to her at the time. I was driving, and the officer was with me."

"He's human," his father confirmed.

"Yes." He took a deep breath and then forced out the big question. "Who is she?" His voice was weak, thready, unsteady.

"Oh." His mother sounded surprised. "You don't know?"

"No. Paige started to tell me. I cut her off. Her scent hit me like an avalanche. I've never met her."

His father cleared his throat. "Addy is a wonderful girl. You'll be pleased."

"Addy?" He searched his mind for that name. How was someone at his parents' coming-home party he'd never heard of?

"Adriana," his mother corrected. "Adriana Tarben. She's Alton's younger sister. Her friends call her Addy."

Adriana... What a beautiful name. Someday *he* would be her *best* friend, and he would not be calling her Addy. He smiled. *Adriana Tarben...*

He swallowed the lump in his throat, hating that he had not met her tonight. "So, she's from Silvertip? What's she doing in Calgary? What does she look like? Is she mad?"

His father chuckled.

Nolan winced. "I'm sorry. This is your night. I should be focused on you. How was your trip? Was the flight okay? Tell me all about Australia."

His mother's laughter reached his ears next. "Don't be silly. We can discuss our trip another time. We're home. We're safe. The trip was great." She hesitated. "This day is no longer about us, though. Yes, she's from Silvertip. She moved here in August to start school at U of C. She's been staying here in the house for the last two months with Alton and Joselyn, but she's looking for an apartment now that we're back."

He interrupted. "U of C? How old is she?" *Please tell me she isn't eighteen.*

"Twenty-three," his mother added. "Sorry. I didn't say all that quite right. She's already got a degree. It's in computer science. But she hated it. She's gone back to school."

He breathed a sigh of relief. He was thirty-one. He

19

didn't think he could possibly start a relationship with someone who was eighteen. In fact, he shuddered. Twenty-three was far more palatable.

His father spoke again. "Would you like to speak to her?"

Nolan closed his eyes. "No. Not yet. Let me figure something out here. It's going to be difficult. I mean I told the police this morning I didn't have a girlfriend. No attachments. I don't know how I'm going to handle this." He hated for his first communication with Adriana to be by phone. It was so cold. How could he possibly express himself appropriately? His chest tightened. He needed to see her. Touch her. Kiss her.

Damn. His cock stiffened at the memory of her scent.

"Is she…" He didn't even know what to ask.

His mother's voice was gentle. "She went straight to her room when you left. Your room, actually. Paige went in to talk to her for a while. I'll go talk to her after we get off the phone."

My room… A burst of jealousy rushed through him. She had access to pictures and information. His sisters and his parents could fill her with information. He had nothing.

Hell, she had his childhood in that room…

For the first time in his life, it annoyed him that only family members and bound couples could communicate mind to mind from a distance. Until they completed the binding, he would only be able to communicate with Adriana telepathically if they were in close proximity.

His mother must have read his mind, possibly even literally, since he doubted he was blocking well.

"Honey, pull up her social media. And, well, call her. I'll text you her number."

Right. Why hadn't he thought of that? So far, he'd done

nothing but panic. His hands were shaking. It was a wonder he hadn't dropped the phone. This was so unprecedented. What the hell was he supposed to do? No way on God's green earth was he going to be able to sit in this hotel room for months on end without meeting her. He needed to figure something out. Fast. "Can she stay with you?"

"Of course," his father confirmed. "But I don't think that was in her plan. She would have moved out already if she'd found a place. She's been looking for a roommate, hoping she would meet someone at school to share the rent with. She didn't know a soul at the university when she arrived."

"Well, things are different now. I'd rather she be with you."

His father chuckled again.

"What?" Nolan stiffened. Was his request so strange?

"So possessive. You haven't even met her or spoken to her, and already you're giving orders."

Was he? He shook his head. "Of course not. I just want her to be safe."

His mother's soft giggles filled the air. "I remember when I met your father. He did the same thing. I'm pretty sure he was only about six-foot-three when I met him, but that day he grew four inches." She laughed harder. "His chest puffed out, and he got all alpha on me before I even caught his name."

"I'm not getting all alpha," Nolan contended, his shoulders squaring. He immediately released the tight muscles when he understood what his mother meant about his father getting taller.

His father spoke again. "It's normal. The impulse to protect. But, take my advice, from experience, you won't win any points if you start ordering her around right off the bat. She's a grown woman. She won't take it well. Trust me."

"Who's ordering anyone around?" Nolan knew he was getting defensive. Dammit, she was his mate. He just wanted her to be safe. His life was upside down. If anyone found out he had someone in his life who was special, she could be in danger. But even without the threat of his stupid money-laundering client, he would still prefer his woman not be living in an apartment alone. Why was that so unreasonable?

"Just a suggestion," Stanton added. "She's welcome to stay here as long as she likes, son. You know that. But I'm sure we're cramping her style."

"Her style?" Nolan stiffened again. What style? It wasn't like she was going to go out late carousing around with friends and come in drunk or bring men with her. He gritted his teeth. Did she do that before today?

"Nolan," his mother soothed, "calm down, honey. We just got here this afternoon. We don't know her well yet. Your father is simply suggesting you choose your words wisely, especially if you aren't able to meet her face to face."

He sighed. Arguing about this subject was ridiculous. He was inventing imaginary problems for no reason. When did he get so damn possessive?

When you stepped out of that car earlier and inhaled your future. That's when.

"We should get back to the party, honey," his mother continued. "Is there anything you want me to say to Addy for you?"

"Tell her... Just tell her I'm sorry."

"Okay." Oleta's voice was soft. "We'll talk tomorrow."

"Yeah."

"Bye, son," his father added. And then the line went dead.

Nolan lowered the phone, breathing heavily. He needed to get a grip on himself and fast before he fucked up the most important thing that would ever happen to him.

~

It was after midnight when a soft knock sounded on Adriana's door. She hadn't moved from her fetal position on the bed for hours. "Come in," she said as she inhaled the scent of Nolan's mom.

Oleta stepped into the room and shut the door behind her with a *snick*.

Adriana's eyes were well-adjusted to the dark, and she could see the smile on Oleta's face. The blonde-haired woman looked so much like her daughters, it was uncanny. She also didn't look old enough to have a child as old as Nolan. He had to be over thirty.

Oleta sat on the edge of the bed and put her hand on Adriana's shoulder. Her smile widened. "You found his old leather jacket."

Adriana swallowed. "I hope you don't mind. I didn't mean to snoop around. Paige—"

"Of course, hon," Oleta interrupted. She waved her free hand through the air. "Don't worry about a thing. Tear this room apart if you want. I don't think my son has secrets in here he would keep from you."

Adriana relaxed marginally.

"Are you okay?"

Adriana shook her head slightly. "No."

Oleta chuckled. "Of course not. Silly question. Stanton and I spoke to Nolan on the phone a bit ago."

Great. He's speaking to everyone on the planet...except me.

"He wanted me to apologize on his behalf."

She'd already gotten this apology from Paige.

"I was at least as frustrated as you earlier. That's why I didn't come in here sooner. I wanted to speak to him first and slap him around a bit." Adriana was going to love this woman. Her gentle hand squeezed Adriana's shoulder. "Anyway, I can't imagine what on earth the Universe is thinking today. She must be laughing hard at this twist."

That was an understatement.

"Nolan is an accountant. He owns his own firm. Apparently, he discovered one of his bigger clients was doing something illegal. He went to the police, and they put him in a hotel for his protection."

Adriana's entire body jerked. She bolted upright. "Are you serious? Is he safe?" Her heart beat rapidly.

Oleta's smile broadened. "I think so. He was with the officer when he came by tonight. He wanted to have a moment to see us before he went into hiding, but when he scented you…" She took a breath. "Honestly, I think the main reason he didn't come inside was because he didn't want to put your life in danger."

Adriana couldn't breathe. "My life?"

She shrugged. "By association I guess. He's probably worried his client will come after his loved ones when he finds out."

"His client doesn't know?"

"I don't think so. Not yet. This all happened this morning."

Adriana chewed on her bottom lip. "That's awful. How long will he be in hiding?"

"Not sure yet. He was afraid it could be months."

Adriana's eyes bugged out. "Months?" That was a long time for her to go without meeting her mate. So many possible reasons why he hadn't faced her tonight had run through her mind in the last few hours. He had a girlfriend he needed to break up with. He didn't want to bind to someone at this point in his life. He hadn't wanted to meet her in front of so many people. Dozens of thoughts. None of them included witness protection.

"Let's not get ahead of ourselves yet. He's still figuring things out. I'm sure he'll call tomorrow with more information."

Adriana nodded. On the one hand, she was relieved this had nothing to do with her. On the other hand, she was freaked out with concern for his safety. But one thought still lingered. *Why didn't he reach out to me himself?* All these messengers were making her dizzy.

"Your brother is worried about you. Joselyn too."

"Tell them I'm fine. I'll talk to them in the morning." Adriana didn't feel like hashing this out with her brother or his mate tonight. She wanted to crawl under the covers and sleep.

For a few months.

Too bad bear shifters didn't need to hibernate for months at a time. Now would be a great time to take advantage of that ability.

CHAPTER 3

Adriana took a deep breath and forced herself to leave the sanctuary of her—correction, Nolan's—room the following morning at about ten. She knew Alton, Joselyn, Oleta, and Stanton were all in the house. It was quiet. They were probably holding their collective breaths.

Sure enough, they were all four sitting at the kitchen table. She was surprised Paige and Wyatt weren't there. Or even the Osborns' other daughter, Ryann, whom Adriana had met on several occasions.

Four sets of wide eyes followed her into the room. Joselyn spoke first. "You okay?"

Adriana nodded. "I'm fine. You all look like someone died." She wrapped her arms around her waist, a chill making her shiver for the tenth time since she got up. She'd worn Nolan's jacket all night, but it would have been weird to wear it all the time, so she'd forced herself to take it off, shower, and dress. Jeans, a long-sleeved white tee, and a thick navy cardigan that was not doing enough to warm her.

Normally, she put a lot more effort into her

appearance, not because she was vain but because she truly enjoyed matching fabrics and coordinating her makeup and jewelry. Today she felt like curling up in a corner and staring into space.

"Are you cold, hon?" Oleta asked.

Permanently it would seem, but Adriana shook her head. "I'm fine," she repeated. Shifters ran warmer than regular humans. She wasn't usually cold. But she'd been shivering ever since Nolan drove away without meeting her.

She wondered if any of them had spoken to Nolan this morning, but she didn't have the guts to ask. Mostly because she couldn't stand the idea of him continually talking to other people without contacting her. It was absurd to feel so much frustration, but she couldn't avoid it.

"We left you a plate of food," Joselyn stated as she rose from her seat and padded toward the microwave. "I'll heat it up for you."

Adriana took a seat at the table, trying not to shake or think too hard. *He'll call when he can.*

"Coffee?" Oleta asked.

"No, thank you."

Joselyn pulled the plate from the microwave and brought it to Adriana. "Addy doesn't like coffee. She's more of a tea person." She spun back around and pulled a mug from the cabinet.

Were they all going to dote on her, walking on pins and needles all day? Or for months for that matter? "Look, I'm fine," she repeated for the third time. Eventually, she would believe so herself. "I'm sure you all have a lot to do. Don't worry about me. I have homework to do, and I need to find an apartment."

Did she? Was finding an apartment still on her list of

priorities this morning? Yesterday she'd been determined to get up early and go visit a few. But that was before she'd met Nolan—or *not* met Nolan.

Stanton glanced away, and Oleta pursed her lips. Now what? No one said a word. She decided she wasn't about to ask more questions.

Joselyn set a steaming cup of tea on the table and lowered into the chair beside Adriana, tucking one foot under her. "You could stay here, you know. You don't have to move into an apartment. I mean, at this point, maybe it would be better."

Adriana took a sip of the too-hot tea and then picked up her fork, knowing she needed to attempt to eat the scrambled eggs and sausage they'd left for her. She glanced at Joselyn, who fiddled with the corner of her placemat.

"Jos has a good point," Oleta added, her voice too happy. "You could stay here. You're family now. You were practically family before we even met you. This house is plenty big. This way you won't have to worry about having to break a lease later."

Stanton nodded, his arms folded across his chest. "She's right."

They all had a point, but something was off. Everyone was way too excited about this plan. Even Alton was nodding agreement. Adriana was twenty-three years old. She'd never lived on her own or even with a roommate. She'd taken classes online from her childhood home through Athabasca University. As the youngest of five kids, she was the baby in lots of ways. She was the only one still living at home for the last few years.

Moving out had been huge. Coming to Calgary had been huge. Finding an apartment hadn't been a priority for the last two months because Alton and Joselyn insisted she stay with them. But now that the Osborns were home, it was time to move out. They didn't need a house guest when they'd just returned from their sabbatical.

Joselyn and Alton definitely didn't need her under foot any longer. They'd only been bound together for eight months. They needed privacy.

Alton spoke next. "Or you could move in with us. You know we'd love to have you."

Adriana set her fork down and glanced around at every face. What was going on? She felt like she was at an intervention. "What on earth are you all trying to convince me of? I'm just going to find a roommate near campus like I planned. No one was concerned about the idea yesterday. I don't see how it's any different today. Nothing has changed."

Except my mate is at a hotel somewhere hiding.

"We don't even know how long this witness protection thing might last, is all," Alton said. He was seated at Adriana's other side, sandwiching her with his mate. "Could be weeks. No sense moving all your stuff and promising someone you'll room with them and then moving again."

Adriana frowned. "The word I got was months. And I'd rather carry on with my life in the meantime. Besides, even if it was only a few weeks, that doesn't mean I intend to rush into anything." Jeez. Even if she met Nolan today, it didn't mean she would drop everything, pack her stuff, and move into his home. These things took time. Didn't they?

She glanced at Oleta, who was frowning while fighting a smile at the same time, her lips tucked between her teeth. Joselyn's eyes were wide, her mouth open.

Adriana picked up her fork and took another bite, her skin crawling from the secret club meeting she was interloping. The club of bound couples who knew things those who hadn't yet met their mate did not.

"It doesn't work like that," Alton stated slowly. He reached out to set a hand on Adriana's forearm.

She rolled her eyes. "Whatever. I'll handle it. Stop treating me like a kid." She could talk to her brother that way. She meant the words for everyone in the room, but she looked right into Alton's eyes to make sure she didn't blatantly insult all of them.

"You're my sister. We've always been close. I'm just trying to help."

"Yeah, well, news flash. I'm old enough to make decisions." In truth, she was being stubborn. She knew it. She didn't even have the finances to move in with a roommate. She had dug her heels in on the subject weeks ago because she wanted her independence—from her parents, her brother and his mate, and now Nolan's parents. Any roommate would do. She'd get a job. Work evenings. Whatever it took to make it on her own. This conversation was over.

"So, what is everyone else doing today?" She forced herself to resume eating her breakfast in the silence that followed her question.

The house phone rang several seconds later, making Adriana flinch.

Oleta pushed from the table and rushed to grab it from the counter. She answered, but her gaze was on Adriana. Of course, the woman already knew who it was. And it was obviously Nolan. He could reach out to his mother telepathically without needing modern phones. He could not, however, reach out to Adriana. They weren't immediate family. They would only be able to communicate in their minds in close proximity until after they completed the binding.

She shuddered. The thought of binding to someone made her nervous for so many reasons. Most importantly, at twenty-three she had just moved out of her parents' home for the first time and was looking forward to finding herself and enjoying her newfound freedom. In addition, it was nerve-wracking to consider binding to someone who had yet to make an appearance.

Adriana must have blocked out whatever greeting Oleta made into the phone because suddenly she was holding it out toward Adriana. "We'll give you some privacy."

Adriana's hand shook as she reached for the cordless while everyone else jumped up from the table and fled the room. It wasn't necessary. She would take it in her room anyway. *In Nolan's room.* She rose on wobbly legs and gripped the phone at her side while she made her way down the hallway and shut herself in Nolan's childhood bedroom.

She half-considered opening his closet and sitting in the back of it to inhale his scent while she spoke to him for the first time. But it wasn't a walk-in, and she would look foolish if anyone came in. Instead, she headed for the window, too fidgety to sit on the bed.

When she finally lifted the phone to her ear, she heard his voice. "Adriana?" Deep. Sexy. Nervous. Kind. Scared. So much emotion in that one word. And she loved the way he said her name, enunciating it in a way that sent a chill down her spine.

"Hi." Breathy. Short. It was all she could manage to utter.

She heard him exhale as if he'd been holding his breath the entire time she sought privacy. "I'm so sorry about last night."

"I heard. Are you okay? Is this thing with your client serious?" About twelve more questions were on the tip of her tongue, but she forced herself to stop before she sounded like a fool.

He sighed. "I don't know yet. Maybe the police are being overly cautious until they arrest this guy. I'm hoping I can come out of hiding after they pick him up."

"Really?" Her voice rose, and she stood taller. How long could it possibly take to arrest someone?

"I might be overly optimistic. No one has insinuated I could leave this hotel room even to go downstairs yet, but I don't see how big of a deal it will be before they even pick him up. He doesn't know anything is in the works until then."

"So, they haven't located him yet?"

"No. I don't think he's hiding. I don't even think he has a clue anyone is onto him. I think he just happens to be out of town for the weekend."

"Oh." Several seconds of silence.

"Adriana..." Her name again from his lips sounded so exotic. She shivered as if he'd spoken the word into her ear. "The timing of this absolutely sucks."

"Why didn't you come inside last night?" She needed to understand.

"I didn't want to put you in any danger. The officer who was in the car with me wasn't happy with the plan at all. It was bad enough that I was putting the rest of my family in danger by showing up. When I got out of the car and caught your scent..."

Her breath hitched.

He hesitated. "I panicked. If this guy decides to take revenge out on me, he won't have any problem finding my family. I can't change that part, but he has no idea there's anyone special in my life, and I'm not about to give him any reason to think so."

For no reason at all, the weird conversation from earlier suddenly made more sense. "Did you tell your parents to encourage me to remain living here?"

He exhaled. "Yes. I guess they weren't discreet about it."

She chuckled sarcastically. "Definitely not. It was like an intervention in the kitchen. Between your parents and my brother and his mate, I felt like they were urging me to go to drug rehab or something."

"I'm sorry. I didn't mean to go behind your back. When they told me you were looking for an apartment, I freaked out a bit."

"Why?"

"Because I'd like you to at least be safe long enough for me to meet you."

She tried to read his tone, but since she didn't know him, she wasn't sure if he was kidding or serious. Probably some of both. "You said this guy the police are after doesn't know I mean something to you. Why would he come after me?"

"Just erring on the side of caution."

She schooled her voice in the same manner as him, trying to hide her intonation, but also not sure if she was joking or dead serious. "Are you truly worried about this idiot coming after me, or are you opposed to me moving into an apartment in general?"

A few seconds of silence passed before he responded. "Both?"

She rolled her eyes, knowing he couldn't see her. "God, save me from overprotective men."

He chuckled. At least that lightened the mood.

She let her shoulders relax a bit.

She wasn't sure how she felt about Fate chaining her for life to a man whose first action as soon as he met her was to try to keep her sequestered somewhere. Too much?

His voice was deeper when he spoke again. "Will you do this for me?"

She smiled. "No."

His breath hitched.

She decided to hold on to her independence a little longer. It didn't seem prudent to let Nolan think he could easily boss her around. "By your own logic, I should move out this afternoon and never even stop by to visit." *Argue that one, big guy.*

"What?"

"If they haven't arrested your client yet, then he isn't paying attention to you or your family. The sooner I get out of the house, the better. By the time he starts snooping around, he won't find any connection between me and your parents." She felt pretty damn good about herself. But Lord, why was she arguing about her living arrangements with an overprotective man she hadn't even met?

"Adriana…"

"Yes?" She poured that syrupy sweet word out in several syllables.

There was another long pause while she assumed he dug around in his brain to come up with another argument.

In truth, while she waited for him to think, she got a little miffed. She was done with this subject. If he kept pushing, she would end this conversation fast and move on with her life. Could she do that?

"Do me a favor."

"Maybe." Her defensive walls went up.

"Give me a few days to figure something out. Something we can both live with." He schooled his voice, a mix of concern and stubborn persistence.

She stiffened. "Nolan, I'm not staying here with your parents. They just got back in town yesterday, and I'm sure they'd like to have their lives back in order. They don't need a stranger moving in and getting in their way."

"My parents don't need privacy, Adriana. They've been

bound to each other for over thirty years. And you're not a stranger. Maybe you were yesterday, but not anymore. As far as they're concerned, you're already their daughter. They would do anything for you."

She knew he was right. She felt their support already. Even last night when his mother came in to comfort her, Adriana had felt her love. At this point, she was continuing to argue her point on principle. Half of her wanted to see how far she could push him.

Lunacy. The situation was so farfetched it had already turned into the opening scene for a made-for-television movie. "I'm also not moving in with my brother. He *did* just bind to his mate, and they definitely don't need me living in their space."

"Two days. Give me two days." Did he realize he didn't ask? His words didn't lift at the end in the form of a question. He was bossy. Damn alpha grizzly shifters.

She swallowed. Half of her wanted to continue to dig her heels in and make sure he didn't think he could steamroll her for the rest of her life. The other half thought it was hotter than hell that he cared so much about her safety. "Okay." *Don't make me regret this.*

He blew out a breath. "Thank you." Was he really worried? Or was he really that domineering?

"Can we change the subject?" This was her first conversation with the man she was destined to spend her entire life with, and so far all they'd done was argue over a topic when she knew full well they were grappling over control, setting the tone for the rest of their lives. She may have only been twenty-three, but she'd taken psychology at her university. She recognized this disagreement for what it was.

"Excellent idea. Tell me everything about you." His voice was far more upbeat.

Already she liked this side of him better. "Okay. How about the short version? Leave a bit of mystery."

"Gotta start somewhere." Yes, she liked *this* Nolan much better.

"Born and raised in Silvertip."

He interrupted her. "Youngest of the five children of Allister and Beth Arthur. Twenty-three. Thick brown hair I'm dying to run my hands through. Big brown eyes that seem to stare right at me when I look at them, even on social media. Computer science degree from Athabasca University. Worked at Mountain Peak Brewery with your pack and family until August. Decided your heart wasn't in it. And then you came to Calgary to pursue a degree in art with an emphasis in fashion."

A huge grin spread across her face as she listened to his litany. "What do you need me to tell you? You know me better than I do. I guess we can hang up now."

He laughed, the sound reaching into her soul and making her stomach drop. She hadn't met him in person, and already he made her sit up and take notice in a physical way.

She was aroused.

"I did my homework. What else did I have to do all night?"

She chewed on her bottom lip. She hadn't looked him up at all. But she had something better. She'd slept in his childhood room. The same room she was standing in now.

His voice dipped and softened. "Now, tell me something no one else knows about you."

That drop in her stomach plummeted. A flush spread from her face down her chest. "Mmm."

"Come on. There has to be something."

She didn't have many secrets. After all, she'd lived with her parents until two months ago. She hadn't even gone away to school like her siblings and friends. She was super close to her mom and told her nearly everything. Except one thing.

"Adriana?"

Did she dare blurt out the thought on the tip of her tongue to a man she'd never met? It seemed like the perfect opportunity. If she was truly destined to be with him for life, she would have to tell him sooner or later. If it broke the ice and gave him a tiny piece of her soul, maybe it would be worth it.

"Hon?"

More stomach dropping. "I'm a virgin."

Silence.

No. Not silence. Breathing. Short, sharp breaths. Panting. Like he'd been running for an hour.

She shouldn't have told him. She wished she could take it back, most especially because she wanted to see his face. This silence was deafening and made her squirm and regret her hasty decision. A knot formed in her throat, and she couldn't swallow over it. Sweat beaded on her forehead and not from heat. Embarrassment and humiliation.

Was he still on the line? No way in hell was she going to be the one to say the next word.

"Adriana... Baby... My God. I'm so..."

What?

"Humbled." He cleared his throat. His voice was cracking. "You took me by surprise."

"You asked me to tell you something no one else knows." Did she sound defensive? She still felt uncomfortable with her reveal. She could kick herself.

"I did. And... I wish I was there in the room with you."

"I'm in your room. I've been sleeping in your bed for two months."

He groaned. "Do you know what you're doing to me?"

What? She turned from the window, leaned against the wall, and eased down until she was sitting on the floor, her knees at her chin, her hair falling around her in a curtain. She had the urge to hide even though no one could see her.

"Adriana?"

"I…" She cleared her throat. "I can't read you. I don't know what you're thinking." That was the truth. And it was driving her crazy. "I don't know what your tone means. I'm sorry I said anything. I feel stupid now."

"Oh, baby, don't. I'm sorry I'm not right in front of you. I'm glad you told me. It means the world to me. I'm so turned on right now I can't form coherent sentences. Please forgive me. I know I'm botching this."

He was botching this? She begged to differ. A tear fell down her face, maybe from emotional overload and lack of sleep. But also from embarrassment. "You must think I'm a freak."

"Not at all. Baby, that's so…" Did he choke on his words a bit, too? They were still cracking. "Dammit." The sudden harsh expletive made her flinch.

She held her breath. Could she have made a bigger mess of this?

"Okay." He sounded calmer. "So." One word sentences. "I'm." What the hell? "Look." His words were growing in strength, but they made no sense. He was totally flustered.

Slowly she switched from horrified beyond belief to something far calmer. She could almost breathe.

He blew out a long breath. She could picture him pacing. He was winded when he next spoke. "Wow. I didn't expect to feel this powerfully about you."

Okay. That was a good thing. Right?

"I thought I could hold you at arm's length while I waited for this trial. I mean we haven't even met. How hard could it be? I told myself a thousand times during the night it would be all right. As long as we didn't meet, you would just be some elusive woman I would meet when this was over. A phantom. A mystery."

She slowly smiled as she listened to him ramble. He wasn't nearly as demanding now that she'd shaken his world up a bit. Suddenly her ridiculous declaration didn't seem like such a bad idea. Not if it brought Nolan to his knees. Flustered Nolan was a lot more palatable. Human. Well, shifter.

Her heart rate increased. The chill she'd felt for twelve hours loosened its hold. She felt a stirring deep inside that was new to her. Foreign. He did this with his endearing rambling. He might have also started the process with his commands if she were perfectly honest. But this side of him squeezed her heart.

He was truly honored and humbled.

And he was still speaking, though she realized she might have missed some of his words in her reflection. "Today. Like now," he stated firmly.

She jerked her attention back to his words. Damn. She'd missed something important. "I'm sorry. What?"

He chuckled. "I know it's crazy, but I'll figure something out."

"Figure what out? Nolan, I think you lost me."

"I'm going to send someone to get you."

"What? And take me where? I told you I was going to spend the day looking for an apartment. I wasn't kidding. That's still the plan—"

"Adriana." He stopped her mid-sentence with one word. "Yes?"

"I want you to come here."

"To the hotel?"

"That's what I'm saying. I'll send someone to pick you up, someone I can trust. Someone who can keep you safe."

"But I thought you weren't supposed to have any contact with your family or friends."

"Technically you aren't family or friend. No one will know. I need to see you face to face."

"Okay." She glanced around the room. The last thing she'd expected was to meet him today. She was suddenly extremely nervous. How weird would it be to meet him? And in his hotel room. Was she ready for that? Was he asking her to come there so he could sleep with her? Would he bind her to him today?

So many questions raced through her mind, but she didn't voice them.

She thought she heard him snap his fingers. "I know the perfect person. Hopefully, he's not working today. Can you be ready in ten minutes?"

"Ten minutes?" Her voice squeaked. She pushed herself hastily to standing and rushed over to the mirror above his dresser. She hadn't done much of anything to herself this morning. She'd showered, but she hadn't expected to meet her life partner when she'd failed to fix her hair or put on much makeup. Ten minutes?

He was silent for a beat or two while she switched to full-on panic mode.

"Okay," he continued, as if he'd been away from the phone. For all she knew, maybe he was. "His name is Reid. He's going to pick you up."

"Reid? Who's Reid?"

"One of my best friends, who also happens to be a bodyguard. I just texted him. As luck would have it, he finished a job two days ago. He's available, and he's going to help us."

"A bodyguard?"

"Don't worry. That's just who he is. Or what he does. Whatever. Nothing will happen to you in his care."

How had this day taken such a sharp right turn so fast? "Nolan, I'm not ready."

"Ready for what? To meet me?"

"Yes. I mean no." She shook her head, trying to find brain cells and gather them into coherency. "I mean I'm in jeans and a T-shirt. My hair's a mess. I'm not wearing makeup. This is not how I want to meet you." Her gaze darted around the room as if she could possibly find something to make this all better in seconds. There was no way in hell.

"Adriana, I don't care what you look like. I've seen hundreds of pics of you. You're gorgeous. You don't need makeup and fancy hair. Just come."

"I was cute last night. Why didn't you come inside last night?"

He chuckled. "Stop worrying. You're perfect. Hang up and go answer the front door. Reid will be there any minute."

She inhaled long and slow and then jumped into first gear. "'K. Bye." She ended the call, raced from the room, and slammed into Joselyn in the hallway.

Joselyn grabbed her by the elbows to steady them both. "What's wrong? What's the rush?"

Oleta stepped into the hall from the front room. She was wiping her hands on a kitchen towel.

"Nolan is sending someone to pick me up. Like now. Like right now." She raced into the hall bathroom and stared at the mirror. "Oh, God. I look awful."

Both women stepped in behind her, smiling. She could see them in the mirror.

Oleta took the phone from her hand. "You're fine. Perfect. Nolan isn't a fussy guy. He wouldn't even notice if you got all dressed up and primped for two hours. You'd look the same to him."

The doorbell rang.

Her eyes widened. She was going to hyperventilate. For like the third time in twelve hours.

Oleta patted her arm. "Why didn't you tell me it was Reid? I didn't realize he was in town."

Apparently, Reid was a close enough friend of Nolan's that his mother knew him well. Male voices came from the front room. Stanton must have let him in.

Adriana grabbed the side of the sink with both hands and closed her eyes, forcing herself to take deep breaths.

Huge mistake. The biggest mistake of her life. She froze, head down, oxygen no longer her main concern.

Oh. My. God. No. No no no no no. This could *not* be happening.

She was going to faint.

"You're going to be fine." Joselyn's voice was filled with mirth. "He's just your mate."

Adriana jerked her gaze up to meet Joselyn's in the mirror. What did she mean by that?

Joselyn frowned. "You okay? No reason to panic. Sounds like Nolan has it all worked out. Whoever Reid is, I'm sure he's reliable and safe or Nolan wouldn't have sent him."

Reid was anything but reliable or safe. Adriana knew that from the bathroom without seeing him.

He might have been Nolan's best friend and a bodyguard who could protect anyone from anything. But that's not all he was.

He was also her mate.

CHAPTER 4

Reid continued to nod at whatever Stanton was saying, hoping he wouldn't be required to add to the conversation or comment because there was no way he could form words or even breathe. His mouth was dry. His heart was pounding. His hands were shaking. He stuffed them in his pockets to keep anyone from noticing how unhinged he was.

What the hell was going on? He'd gotten a text from Nolan who asked him if he was free and begged him to please go pick up his mate and bring her to him.

It was a Sunday. Reid had intended to spend the day vegetating in front of the television watching any sport he could find. He'd been on a lengthy assignment for a dignitary for two months. It had ended Friday night. Reid hadn't recovered.

And now this?

He was so confused that his brain wouldn't function. He'd hung up the phone with Nolan ten seconds ago as he approached the front door.

His best friend. The one who called him and quickly

explained his plight. He was in witness protection. His mate was at his parents' home. Could Reid please pick her up and bring her to the hotel for a while?

Something was seriously messed up with this situation. Either he was losing his mind or Fate was playing a cruel joke on him.

He wanted to reach out to the woman in the hall bathroom and communicate with her, but at the moment he wasn't sure he could do so without alerting the entire room to the insanity of this situation. He didn't have enough faculties to properly block everyone else in order to concentrate solely on...what was her name?

Seconds ticked by, but they seemed like hours. Was Stanton moving around in slow motion? What he needed was for the world to freeze. Come to a complete halt, just until he could make sense of his life and take a few cleansing breaths.

He jerked out of his weird trance when he realized the woman he was there to pick up was approaching. When he spun around, he found her bottom lip pinched hard between her teeth and her huge brown eyes wide. She subtly shook her head.

Was she getting the same weird message from Nature he was getting? Was she as shocked as him?

It seemed that way.

Thank God someone had vocabulary, because otherwise things would have gotten far more awkward superfast. Oleta closed the distance and wrapped her arms around him. "So good to see you." She grasped his biceps next and turned to face the stunning woman with thick brown hair that hung in long waves down her back. Really long. He had the urge to twist his hand in it, pull her head back, and kiss the life out of her.

He shook the image from his head and forced himself

not to look directly at her, settling his gaze on the wall behind her instead as she stuffed her arms into the sleeves of her coat.

His hands were still in his pockets. No way in hell could he touch her.

What the absolute fuck? The Universe was tipped on its axis in a way that made him think he's stepped from one dimension to another. This could not be happening.

"Reid Terrance, this is Adriana Tarben. Adriana, Reid."

Stanton—God bless him—stepped past Reid and opened the front door. "Let them get out of here, Oleta. Addy doesn't want to stand in the living room making pleasantries. Any second now Nolan is going to start shouting at us in our heads if we stall progress. I don't want that kind of wrath," he joked.

Oleta laughed.

There were two other people in the room Reid didn't know. A man who looked a lot like Adriana. And that man's mate.

Reid turned around, pulled his hands from his pockets, and gripped the open door. "We'll catch up later?" he said to Stanton. "I want to hear about your trip. I'll call you." *If I'm still alive after your son gets his hands on me.*

"Sounds good."

Reid didn't look back at Adriana as he rushed down the front steps toward his SUV. He didn't need to. He could tell she was right behind him. And they wouldn't even look funny to the four people watching them. After all, they were on a mission. To get Adriana to her mate ASAP.

He rounded the car, not even bothering to open the passenger door for her. Normally, he would never be so unchivalrous. His mother would scold him for fifteen minutes if she saw his behavior. There was a good chance Oleta Osborn would chew him out the next time he saw her too. But for now, his actions were out of self-preservation.

Get in the car. Start the car. Drive a safe distance away.

Don't look at her. Don't breathe. Don't say a word.

Just drive.

He repeated some form of that mantra over and over in his head, making it truth. He knew Adriana was in the car. He knew she had put her seat belt on somehow. He knew she had shut the door. He knew she was also not breathing any more than necessary.

How he managed to follow his own chanted directions was a mystery. He remembered nothing when he thought back. But somehow, a few minutes later, he was a safe distance from the house. He pulled into a fast food parking lot outside the residential neighborhood, managed to steer the SUV into a spot, and shut off the engine.

Thank God the windows were tinted so no one could see inside. The SUV was his baby. It was totally decked out with all the bells and whistles. It was also bulletproof. He used it on every mission. But it could not keep him safe today. The biggest danger was *inside* the SUV.

Nolan Osborn, his best friend for over a decade, was going to kill him.

Finally, he turned to face his mate.

She was staring at him, her cheeks flushed, her hands twisting around each other in her lap. Those gorgeous brown eyes were wide with shock. She swallowed. "I'm so confused."

He blew out a breath. "You and me both." He lifted both hands to run them through his hair, not caring that he left it in disarray. Though perhaps he should care, since women had often told him he looked hotter that way.

"Now what do we do?" she asked in her fucking sweet voice that went straight to his cock.

He couldn't tear his gaze off her. After avoiding her entirely from the moment he first saw her, now that no one was there to witness them, he couldn't get enough of her. "I have no idea."

She looked like she might cry. When she released her lip, it started trembling.

On instinct, he lifted his hand, intending to cup her cheek and soothe her.

But she jerked back a few inches. "Don't."

He pulled his hand back, nodding. "You're right." He tucked both hands under his thighs.

Seconds ticked by. "Nolan's waiting on me." Her words were monotone, like that fact no longer interested her as much as it had ten minutes ago.

"How long have you known him?"

She closed her eyes slowly. "I've never even met him."

"What?" Reid's voice hitched. His text conversation with Nolan had been brief. His phone conversation had also been short. Somehow Nolan had left that detail out. Reid had grasped the gist of the convoluted situation. Nolan was in witness protection. He'd met his mate. He wanted Reid to keep her safe. Apparently *met* was a loose term.

"Last night."

"What happened last night?"

"His parents had their homecoming party."

"Right, I was invited."

"Why didn't you come?"

"I just got off a long case. I was exhausted. I figured I would come by and see them sometime this week. I didn't feel like making nice with a bunch of people." Now he wondered what would have happened if he'd shown up. "Wait, I'm confused. Nolan didn't come either?" How did the two of them know they were supposedly mates if they hadn't met? Maybe this was a good sign. Maybe they were mistaken.

"He came. He just didn't come inside. He was with one of the officers on the case. He intended to stop by quickly, see his parents, and then leave. Instead, he scented me and didn't come in."

Reid tried to process this information. "Did you scent him too?"

"Yes." The one word was breathy. She held his gaze.

"Is it possible you were mistaken?" *Please say yes.*

She shook her head. "No."

He rubbed his brow with two fingers. "How... How did you feel?"

Her voice dipped so low he almost couldn't hear her. "Like this."

After shifting his body to face front, he stared out the window. His phone vibrated in his pocket. He didn't bother to pull it out. If it was Nolan, he didn't want to know what he had to say right now. If it was anyone else, they didn't even rank on his short list today.

He put the car back in drive and pulled out of the parking lot. They rode in silence for several minutes, both of them breathing so heavily it reverberated around the car. Stress. Anxiety. Confusion. He could feel waves of the same emotions coming off her to match his own.

He drove away from the suburbs, heading toward the city. The police had chosen a hotel in the busy metropolitan area. With each passing mile, the buildings got taller, and Reid's anxiety grew incrementally to match as if there were a correlation between the two. As he pulled into the hotel parking lot, his nervous tension doubled. What was he supposed to do? Leave her with his best friend? Fight for her? And more importantly, what did she want him to do?

The last thing he wanted to do was alienate her by making the wrong choices. If he said the wrong thing, he could lose her. But what was the wrong thing? They'd exchanged so few words that he didn't know enough about her personality to make a judgment call.

He turned off the engine and faced her again.

Damn, she was beautiful. Those deep brown eyes would melt any man. And her hair… He wanted to run his fingers through it. He wanted to wrap it in his fist and angle her head so he could take her mouth. The drive had been excruciating, and his dick was so hard from breathing in her pheromones for so long he wasn't sure he could walk properly.

She squirmed as he stared at her, his hand on the back of the seat, inches from touching her cheek. She was aroused too.

He'd dated a lot of women in his life. Many were pretty, funny, cute, smart… None of them made him feel the way he'd felt since the moment he stepped into the Osborns' home. This amazing woman and all that she was slammed into him like a punch to the gut.

She was scared out of her mind. Her hands were shaking, and she kept wringing them in her lap.

"I have to come up with you. I can't let you go alone. It's not safe." He glanced around, remembering the reason he was with her in the first place. How stupid could he be? He needed to pay closer attention to their surroundings. Someone could have followed them. It wasn't likely since Nolan's client hadn't been arrested yet, but Reid recognized the importance of keeping Adriana safe. His task had new meaning.

"Should we tell him?" she asked.

He'd asked himself that same question about a dozen

times in the last ten minutes, and he had no answer. He needed to let her make that decision. "It's up to you."

"Me?" Her voice squeaked. She glanced at her lap, her thick hair falling around her shoulders like a shroud. "My brain is racing. I can't concentrate on any one thought. This is insane. Like a nightmare."

His heart seized. He hated how torn she must feel. Half of him wanted to grab her by the biceps, kiss the hell out of her, and turn around and drive to the other side of the country. But he wouldn't do that to her. She needed to make this choice on her own. Whatever twisted game Fate was playing this morning, he would love to ring Her neck —if She were a tangible being.

He needed to talk to someone, find out if this sort of thing happened to other grizzly shifters. He'd never heard of anyone meeting two mates and having to choose between them. Something was out of line in the Universe.

"Do you think it's because Nolan and I met last night but didn't act on it?" Her head lifted, her eyes wide again as thoughts organized in her mind. "I mean maybe it's unnatural for mates to meet and walk away. Maybe it leaves one or both of them vulnerable, like open, or available to another because they didn't do what Fate intended."

He eased his hand forward and lifted a lock of her wavy hair, letting it run through his fingers. "That's like saying there's a vindictive God. I don't think Fate operates that way. Not intentionally at least."

"Why me? What am I supposed to do? Choose?"

"I don't know, Adriana. I'm as confused as you are."

Suddenly, one of her hands jerked up to wrap around his at the side of her head. Her hair was still tangled between his fingers, but she pulled his palm to her cheek and tipped her head into his touch. Her eyes slid closed as she pressed firmly against him.

He held his breath, luxuriating in the feel of her cheek. So smooth and soft. Her skin was several shades darker than his. He'd been born with jet black hair and a pale white complexion that did nothing but burn when he was exposed to the sun. Against her perfect features, the contrast was stark but made his cock jerk again.

When she tipped her head farther and placed a gentle kiss against his palm, he had to hold back a groan. She released him to lift her face. "This is not fair. Someone's going to get hurt. And I'm worried about your friendship."

He couldn't argue with her logic. She was absolutely right. There was no way he and Nolan could come out of this intact. They had never fought in all the years they'd known each other. They'd met at U of C thirteen years ago and been thick as thieves ever since. Other than the occasional disagreement during the years they'd shared an apartment, they'd been like brothers.

Reid valued his friendship with Nolan above almost anything in the world. His own parents were older and lived on the other side of the country in Ottawa. He rarely saw them. He'd left home at eighteen to attend U of C and never returned except to visit on holidays.

Nolan's parents had treated Reid like their own son from day one. In recent years all of them had been busier with their own lives and spent less time together, but like families everywhere, they always came back together.

This… This was going to ruin everything. Unless… "We won't tell him." He tugged his hand back and sat up straighter, rubbing his palms on his thighs. "It's simple. He met you first. I'll bow out. You two already had a connection. It should have been him. You're right. I bet we never would have felt the connection at all if Nolan hadn't driven off last night. The two of you would have completed the binding before I ever met you, and we never would have known about this." He lifted a hand to wave it back and forth between them.

Her face went white. "That's a horrible plan. It's not fair to you at all. And besides, I couldn't keep a secret like that from my mate." She shook her head. "No. Let's go up to the room together and face this like civilized human beings."

He blew out a breath. "I'm not sure we *are* civilized right now, and we're way more than human. That's the entire problem."

"Okay, but do you have a better plan? You want to just drop me off with Nolan and drive away? How's that going to work out for you?"

It wasn't. He would pull his hair out while she was in that confined space with his best friend. "Nolan's going to kill me." He reached for the handle of the door and opened it. A blast of cold air entered the car. It was an unusually chilly day for late fall. In fact, it felt like the dead of winter all the sudden. Was that the actual temperature? Or was it Nature's way of chilling his heart?

CHAPTER 5

Adriana couldn't seem to draw in a full breath. It felt like something was pressing on her chest, keeping her from getting enough oxygen. She unbuckled her seatbelt as Reid rounded the back of his SUV and twisted in her seat when he opened her door.

He didn't reach for her or take her hand, for which she was grateful. The one and only contact they'd had told her everything she needed to know. Reid was her mate. There was no doubt. The current that flowed between them when she set her cheek on his palm was palpable. She knew he felt it too.

It had been a gamble, an impulse. Perhaps a horrible decision. But she'd needed to know. And now she did. As she followed him to the front door of the hotel, she pulled her coat tighter around her shoulders against the cold wind whistling between the buildings.

Reid wasn't even wearing a coat, and he didn't appear to notice the cold. He wore black jeans and a tight black V-neck sweater that hugged his pecs to perfection. It should have been illegal.

Maybe she and Nolan had it all wrong, and the moment he opened the door to his room, they would realize it had been a mistake. Was it possible Fate's true plan was to put Adriana in Reid's path, and She'd chosen this convoluted plot to align the stars?

That seemed ludicrous. There were better ways. They could have run into each other in the grocery store or something. If Fate had that much power, She wouldn't need to create a love triangle to get Her way.

Reid said nothing as he led her toward the bay of elevators. The hotel was busy and accommodated a lot of guests. It was also one of the nicer hotels in downtown Calgary. Several stories high. The perfect place to hide out.

When one of the six elevators opened, Reid set his hand on her lower back to guide her inside. Instinct. It warmed her that he was so polite. His mother raised him well. He opened doors and guided his dates around like a gentleman. And it was second nature. He didn't even know he was doing it. The best kind of man.

Was he hers?

They rode in silence to the fifteenth floor. When the doors slid open, Reid reached out with a hand to ensure they didn't close before she got off. Yep. Total gentleman. And then his hand was on her back again, the warmth seeping through all the layers of her coat, her cardigan, and her tee.

"I should leave you here," he stated as they approached the door. "You deserve to have some time alone with Nolan."

She shook her head. "Not fair to any of us. We'll face this like adults, tell him everything, and see what happens." She lifted her face to meet his gaze. His brow was furrowed. He was scared.

She was too. "I won't come between the two of you. If

54

your friendship gets in the way, I step out. You have a history. I'm not part of that. I wouldn't be able to live with myself if anything happened to destroy your friendship." She had no idea if she could follow through on her threat, but she needed to voice it at least.

Every inch of her was secretly hoping when Nolan opened the door to his room, she would meet his gaze and they would both realize there had been a mistake.

On that thought, she caught his scent in the air and drew it in deep. She was not going to get her wish. The door several yards in front of them on the right opened, and a man who could only be Nolan stepped halfway into the hall. His smile was wide. His eyes—an unusual shade of blue that reminded her of the ocean—danced with excitement.

He didn't even glance at Reid. Understandable.

She had visualized meeting this man a thousand times last night. In none of those scenarios had she been half as nervous as she was now. She forced a warm smile but knew it didn't reach her ears and wasn't fooling anyone.

Nolan either didn't notice or ignored her reaction. He reached out a hand, cupped her face in the same way Reid had done in the car, and licked his lips. "Wow."

She swallowed over the lump in her throat, realizing he had no idea his world was about to be upended. She was the common denominator here. She could feel the pull toward both men, the one in front of her and the one at her side. They couldn't feel the same draw between them.

Freaky weird. And totally unfair.

"Come in." He released her to step back, holding the door open farther. Finally, his gaze moved from her to Reid. "I can't thank you enough. Can you come in a second? I need to ask a huge favor of you."

A favor? Adriana stiffened. She definitely wanted Reid

to come in, and Nolan had made that first task a lot easier, but what was this favor?

Her plan had been to be the first to speak, to clear the air. But Nolan started talking so fast, she couldn't stop him. He closed the door and pointed at the sitting area of what she now realized was a suite. "Have a seat," he aimed at Reid.

Meanwhile, he turned toward Adriana and reached for the sleeve of her coat. "Can I take your jacket?"

The chill she'd been experiencing off and on since last night hadn't gone away. She'd rather keep the coat on and wrap up in it tighter, but that would be incredibly weird and rude. So she unzipped the front and shrugged out of it while Nolan waited. She needed to get the upper hand in the conversation. "We need to talk, Nolan. There's a problem."

He chuckled as he draped her coat over the back of one of the two kitchen chairs that flanked a small table. "Just one? Because by my count, we have about a dozen problems, and they keep growing the more I think." There was a twinkle in his eye, and she hated knowing she was going to snuff it out in a few seconds.

He was physically completely different from Reid. Where Reid was white with nearly black hair and green eyes, Nolan was blond with the same hair and eyes as his sister, Paige. His skin tone was almost as dark as hers, rare on someone naturally blond. He had the sexy good looks of a movie star. But the best part was he didn't seem to know it.

No one had taken a seat, and Adriana watched as Nolan slapped Reid's shoulder and grinned like it was Christmas morning. How long would he continue to look like that? Or even remain on speaking terms with his best friend?

The two of them were close in height, though Reid

might have been about an inch taller. Maybe six five. Adriana was kind of small for a grizzly shifter at five six, so they both towered over her in a way that sucked the air out of her lungs and made her take a step back.

There was way too much testosterone in the suite, and if she thought being near one of them was potent, the combination of their scents was making her knees weak. How the hell was she supposed to choose between them? This was beyond insane.

"It's good to see you," Nolan said to Reid. "You were on that last assignment for weeks."

Reid shot Adriana a glance. He looked as uncomfortable as she felt. She once again took in his tight black V-neck. His jeans were sinful too, fitting him to perfection.

She realized she'd let her gaze roam down to his thighs and jerked her head back up, sliding from Reid to Nolan.

Nolan's body was turned slightly toward Reid, so she had a side view of his ass. His damn fine ass, also encased in jeans that molded to his butt so well her mouth watered. His shirt was an off-white button-up that was perfectly ironed and tucked into his jeans. Stylish. Perfect for a first date, which essentially this was. The look was even rounded out with loafers. She wondered if he'd dressed to impress her, or if there was a chance this was his usual lounging around on a Sunday afternoon attire. Not likely.

"Yes. Thank God, it's over. The woman I was working for was driving me crazy." Reid opened his mouth as if he intended to continue, but he stopped himself, glanced at Adriana again, and then cleared his throat. "I should go. Let you two get to know each other."

"Reid…" She started to contradict his plan, but Nolan spoke over her.

"Can you stay a minute? I was hoping to enlist your services further."

Reid narrowed his eyes.

Adriana nearly choked. She had no idea what Nolan was going to say, but she needed to get his attention and put an end to this madness. "Nolan, we need to talk."

He turned to face her, his expression drawing in, his mouth lifting on one side. "You think?" he teased.

For a second she thought he had figured out something was off, but then she realized he was simply pointing out that they didn't know each other and yet they were destined to spend eternity together, so talking would be a great start. But *were* they destined?

Adriana stepped closer. She set her hand on Nolan's forearm and schooled her voice. "Will you please sit down?" She gave a tug, trying to lure him toward the couch.

Luckily, he followed and took a seat next to her.

Reid took two quick strides toward the armchair and lowered into it, his gaze on Adriana. "Let me," he said.

She shook her head. "No. This needs to come from me." She turned her body to more fully face Nolan and rubbed her hands on her thighs, shivering as if the room were cold.

Nolan's face fell. "Shit. What's the matter?" He glanced back and forth between them. "Did someone follow you here?"

Reid shook his head. "No. It's not that."

"Nolan," Adriana said almost harshly.

He met her gaze again and swallowed hard.

"There's no easy way to say this, so I'm just going to do it."

He didn't move.

She couldn't imagine what he must have been thinking.

"I have the same connection with Reid that I have with you."

For a heartbeat, no one moved or spoke. It was like the world froze and then jerked back into rotation. "What?" His gaze darted to Reid and then back again. "What do you mean?"

"She means that the second I showed up at your parents' house, we felt the same bond the two of you felt last night."

Nolan's back straightened. He blinked a few times while his head turned back toward her. He lifted a hand and ran it through his hair.

She wished she knew him better, at least well enough to anticipate what he might do or feel, but she didn't know either of these men. All she knew was that she wanted both of them. Equally. And she was losing her mind.

There was no doubt. Her body was on fire. For both men. Insanity. Her breasts were swollen to the point of being sore. She had to clench her legs together to keep the throbbing need at bay. Though it was possible she was getting the opposite result.

"That's crazy. Whoever heard of such a thing? Adriana?" He lifted a hand, albeit unsteadily, and cupped her face again. His thumb stroked her cheek gently.

An unbidden tear welled up in her eye and escaped to run down her other cheek as she tried to control the grip her emotions had on her heart.

His face changed several times while he processed everything. At least she never saw anger among his emotions. His voice was lower, too steady when he spoke again. "You feel the same exact connection to both of us?"

"Yes." It was true. It was also eating her from the inside. She wanted to run from the room. She also wanted to be held, and she didn't care who held her as long as they chased away the chill and assured her everything would be okay.

"Reid?" Nolan looked at his friend again.

"I'm so sorry, man. You know I had no control over this any more than you did. It just happened. I offered to drive away. I feel like a shit, as if I slept with your girlfriend behind your back or something."

Nolan winced.

Reid rushed to speak again. "Figure of speech. That didn't come out right. Believe me. I didn't let my feelings take control of my actions. We drove here in near silence."

"You offered to leave? You weren't going to tell me?" Nolan closed his eyes and let his hand slide from Adriana's face to her neck.

"I have no idea how to process this, but I won't lie about it." She set her fingers on top of Nolan's against her neck. Somehow, she drew strength from him. "No matter what happens, I want you both to know, I'm going to be an open book here. The most important thing is your friendship. I won't come between you."

Nolan flinched. He drew his hand back slowly and stood. "Jesus, what a clusterfuck." He stepped back, putting some distance between them and then turning around to face the window. She doubted he was seeing anything outside, but he wasn't missing anything. The window faced an alley between buildings so that the only view was of a brick wall.

For a long time, no one moved. The room was silent. Adriana figured Nolan needed time to process. He was about fifteen minutes behind on the news headline.

He didn't turn around, but he finally spoke. "Reid, Adriana needs a place to stay."

"What?" Reid's voice was off.

Adriana stared at Nolan's back. "Nolan…" What was he talking about?

"That's what I was going to talk to you about. The reason I asked you to stay a minute." He turned around and leaned against the window. His mouth lifted in a smirk. "Adriana's stubborn. She wants to get her own apartment. She refuses to stay with my parents or her brother. I was hoping she could stay with you. I know she'd be safe with you."

Reid was so stiff he looked like a wax statue.

Adriana licked her perpetually dry lips. "Nolan."

He finally looked at her. His face was too schooled. "It's the perfect idea. Reid's a bodyguard. He keeps people safe for a living. You're right about my parents. If you stayed with them, someone might notice and figure out you were mine." Suddenly he threw up his hands and laughed, too hard. "Of course, now we don't even know if that's true."

Adriana had no idea how to react to this weird outburst.

Nolan pushed off the wall, ran a hand through his hair, and rushed across the room toward the kitchenette. He yanked open the fridge, grabbed a bottle, and turned back around. "Anyone else want one?" He lifted what she realized was a beer as he asked.

Neither of them spoke or moved.

He shrugged and twisted the top off before taking a long drink. Still holding it loosely in his hand, he leaned against the small table and crossed his legs casually as if he didn't have a care in the world. He jerked his attention to Reid. "You should bind to her."

Reid shook his head. "Nolan, no one is suggesting anything like that."

"I am." He took another drink. "It's the most logical solution. If she's caught with me while I'm waiting for this

61

damn trial, she'll be in danger. I don't want to spend months worrying about her. It could be a long time before I can even devote myself to another person. She deserves better. You bind to her. That solves everything. I won't have to worry all the time, and she'll be safe and loved." Another drink. The bottle was almost empty.

Adriana didn't know how to react. She didn't know this man. She didn't know anything about his temperament. She needed Reid to handle this.

Reid stood. He didn't take a single step, but at least he put them eye to eye across the small room. "No one is binding to anyone, Nolan. I know this sucks. It stinks. I don't have all the answers. I don't even have all the questions. But I'm not binding myself to your mate. That's crazy. You found her first. I wouldn't have even noticed her in a crowded room if you'd bound to her last night."

Nolan shook his head. "There's no way I would have taken that step last night. She's…young."

Adriana gasped during his pause and then let out a long breath when he added that last word. If he'd blurted out that she was a virgin, she might have taken him up on his offer and left with Reid. That was a private detail she'd shared in confidence last night. No one but him needed to know about her lack of experience.

Though she had no idea what this latest development meant. At this point, she didn't want to bind to either of them. Ever. They were already clawing at each other from across the room.

Nolan chuckled again. He lowered his face toward the floor and spoke in a calmer voice. Too calm. "All I'm saying is that it doesn't matter who met her first. Technically, you met her first. All I did was scent her from my car. From the goddamn street. I never even saw her. There're no other reasonable options here. I need you to keep her safe. She needs a place to stay.

"No matter how altruistic anyone's intentions might be, if the connection you two feels is half as strong as the one I feel, then there's no way in hell you could live under the same roof and not bind. You wouldn't even last a day. I give you three hours, actually. So, please, take this gift. I won't hold it against either of you. I'm trapped here for the foreseeable future. I bet after you complete the binding, I won't even feel the connection anymore. I'll be fine. Just…go."

Nolan shoved off the edge of the table, tossed his bottle across the room to make a perfect basket into the trash can, and padded into the bedroom. With a soft snick, he shut the door behind him.

Adriana thought she might literally vomit. For one thing, she felt horrible and responsible for this insanity. For another thing, she couldn't stand the distance he'd put between them. She'd only met him minutes ago. She wanted to be with him. Next to him. Touching him.

She wanted him to hold her. Not walk away.

She also wanted the same thing from Reid, who made no move to help her out in any way either.

"Fuck," Reid muttered under his breath.

She took deep breaths, but once again felt like her lungs were crushed.

Reid inhaled deeply, closed the distance between them, and leaned over to kiss her forehead. He squeezed her arm briefly and then backed off. "I'm going to the bar in the lobby."

"What?" He was going to leave her here?

He reached for the door, turning back to face her. "He's a great guy. The best. I promise he didn't mean anything he said. He's just frustrated. Go to him. He's hurting. I'll wait downstairs. You can get my number from him if you need me, or Oleta has it too. I won't leave. I promise. When you're ready, call me, and I'll take you wherever you want to go." Reid opened the door, slid out of the room, and left her sitting in the cold, silent room.

It wouldn't take long for Nolan to sense that his friend had left and Adriana had stayed. Even through the closed door, he would know that.

She stared at it hard, willing him to come out. The last thing she wanted was to go after him. But she tried to imagine this thing from his perspective. His hands were tied. Although sarcasm had oozed from his lips, she had no doubt he'd meant every word. He intended to martyr himself to keep her safe.

But that's not how this was going to go down. He might have shown her he could be incredibly bossy and domineering, but he wasn't going to get his way on this issue. Not today.

Today he was going to get his head out of his ass and help her figure this out. Because she didn't have the answers, and she sure wasn't going to deal with this dilemma on her own.

Nolan Osborn was about to meet his match.

CHAPTER 6

Nolan rubbed both temples with his fingers, staring unseeing out the window of the hotel suite's bedroom. When he'd arrived last night, he'd thought the rooms seemed large and roomy. Today they had shrunk to nearly suffocate him.

His mate was on the other side of the door behind him. He'd waited his entire life to meet her, to finally know firsthand the feeling shifters got when they "knew" she was the one. He hadn't honestly expected it to happen so dramatically and with such certainty. That was rare for his species, although seemingly more common lately.

After spending the night in a combination of pacing and lying restlessly on the bed, he'd known he had to see her. Hold her. Touch her. If nothing else, he wanted to capture that feeling again. Remind himself it was real and not a figment of his imagination.

The last thing in the world he'd expected was for her to show up experiencing the same stomach-dropping sensation with another man—his best friend.

It's not her fault. He kept reminding himself of this fact over and over like a mantra he needed to memorize. She didn't ask for this problem. Neither did Reid.

The door opened softly behind him as he knew it would eventually. Her scent was stronger as soon as she was in the room sharing the same airspace. Not that it mattered. He could scent her from down the hall when she stepped off the elevator. His entire body had come to attention, heat suffusing him at the thought of seeing her—only to be doused with a bucket of ice water when she and Reid lowered the boom.

He needed to speak. "I'm sorry. I shouldn't have raised my voice," he told the window.

"Don't apologize. You have every reason to be angry."

"I'm not angry," he said as he turned around to face her, leaning against the window sill. "Okay, maybe I am," he amended, "but not at you. And not at Reid either. In my rational mind, I know neither of you asked for this any more than I did last night."

She nodded. Her arms were wrapped around her middle as if she were cold. He took her in fully for the first time. Thick chocolate hair hung in long waves down her back, cascading haphazardly over her shoulders. She was stunning even though he knew he'd given her only a few minutes to get ready before Reid picked her up. He hadn't cared that he didn't give her enough time to primp or put makeup on or change clothes or style her hair. He'd wanted to see her as soon as possible.

And he wasn't sorry. The woman in front of him didn't need extraordinary grooming measures to knock the socks off any man. She might have been wearing minimal makeup, but otherwise, he knew in his heart this was Adriana Tarben. The real Adriana. Not the one he'd seen on many pages of her social media—often dressed like a model with perfect hair and makeup and jewelry. No, this was the day-to-day woman he would wake up to for the rest of his life. Or would he?

Her eyes were wide again. Deep brown orbs that called to him. Made him want to rush across the room and take her in his arms. She looked like she needed exactly that, but he wasn't sure he should go there. Not yet. The more he touched her or even breathed her air, the harder this was going to get.

He prayed he was right about her binding to Reid. Surely if he let her go and she and Reid completed the binding as soon as possible, the strong connection he felt to her would be severed, and he would feel a sense of peace. If not? Well, fuck.

Letting his gaze roam down her body, he took in the rest of her. She was almost a foot shorter than him, small for a shifter. She wore a form-fitting white T-shirt that probably looked sexy as shit in its simplicity when it wasn't covered by the thick navy cardigan she had on over it, with the sides pulled together as if she were standing in the cold. Even with her arms crossed to keep her sweater closed and metaphorically shut out the world, he could detect the outline of full breasts.

Her sweater hung long, down to her thighs. Her jeans were worn and hugged her body perfectly in the way of well-loved clothing.

He jerked his gaze back up to her face to find her soaking in his details in a similar fashion. He smiled. "This is not how I envisioned the day going."

"I know." Her voice was soft. Kind. Soothing. It washed over him every time she spoke, luring him to get closer. He gripped the windowsill at his sides to keep from moving.

"Where did Reid go?" He knew his friend would not have left the hotel. For one, he wouldn't abandon the job he'd been asked to do. For two, he wouldn't be physically able to walk away from Adriana.

"Hotel bar."

Of course. "I'm being an insensitive ass."

"You're being human."

"Ah, but I'm not human. None of us are. At least not fully. We know how this works."

"Do we?" She cocked her head to one side. "How many shifters do you know who met more than one mate in the same weekend?"

"None." He sighed. He needed to reach out to someone, ask for advice, get help. But who? He didn't want to include his parents or anyone else in this mess yet. Not until he understood it better himself.

She stepped closer, hesitantly. Her eyes were bright with tears, and when one broke loose to run down her cheek, she lifted a hand to dash it away with the tips of her fingers. "Sorry. I'm not usually this emotional. I'm exhausted from lack of sleep. My stomach's in knots. And it feels like an electric current is zapping my brain every few seconds with mixed messages."

It occurred to him this could not be easy for her. In fact, it would be worse. Weirder. Unimaginable. He was still struggling to understand how it was possible for his best friend to have the same deep feelings for the woman he knew in his heart was his. Meanwhile, Adriana was theoretically experiencing a link to more than one person. Yep, he was an ass.

"Come here." He lifted a hand and motioned her forward with his fingers.

She swallowed, her brows coming together as she considered the ramifications of getting any closer. He let his guard down enough to open his mind to her. If he could find a way not to block her, he might be able to delve into her brain too. Understand better. Help her.

He needed to remind himself this wasn't all about him. Others were suffering too. The woman he should be safeguarding and protecting against the world was standing several yards away in pain, and he was just watching her. "Please, Adriana. Come here."

It seemed prudent to let her come to him. He could encourage her with words, but she needed to approach on her own. After all, in the end, the decisions were hers. He'd never been more impotent in his life. The frustration he'd felt earlier about ensuring his stubborn mate was safe had increased tenfold since she'd arrived.

Seeing to her physical safety was only a fraction of his job. He needed to take care of her emotional safety at the same time. And he'd set that aside for the last half hour to wallow in his pity party.

He didn't want to scare her or make her think she didn't have her own free will, but dammit, he wanted her in his arms of her own accord. A protective instinct kicked in. Perhaps it was combined with a bit of the dominance he knew was his nature, but he needed to find a way to balance those two and quick. He'd learned that morning that ordering her around would get him nowhere fast. She would dig her heels in every step of the way if she thought he was dictating her moves.

Did she realize Reid was cut from the same cloth? He was no less domineering with his women than Nolan. Possibly even more so. It was one of the things they had in common. It made him smile inside.

Damn, this was fucked up.

He could concede and go to her, but that idea still didn't seem like the best path.

She exhaled slowly and inched forward.

Thank God.

Her body was shaking when she stepped into his personal space.

He reached out, wrapped his hands around her biceps, and tugged her the last few inches until she was pressed against his chest. Closing his eyes to commit this moment to memory, he wrapped his arms around her body and lowered his face to her hair. The floral scent of her shampoo combined with her personal pheromones called to him like a siren.

Home.

There was no doubt in his mind she was his. His heart beat too fast.

After a few seconds, she released her crossed arms, closed the gap, and flattened more fully against him. Her small hands eased up his back as she hugged him fiercely. Her deep inhales told him she was also processing their connection. "It's so powerful," she whispered against his chest.

"Yes."

"Why is this happening?"

"I don't know." If only he had the answer to that question.

He wanted to kiss her senseless. Toss her on the bed and climb over her to stake his claim on her body and her soul. But that wouldn't be fair to anyone. Confusing her further would do no good. It wasn't as if he needed to taste her in order to be more certain. There was no doubt in his mind.

And he sure couldn't sleep with her.

Did Reid also know she was a virgin? Surely not. The fact that she'd told him had been a random coincidence. He was sure she didn't run around announcing anything of the sort to other people. In fact, he reminded himself, she'd specifically told him he was the only person who knew that about her.

It occurred to him that he hadn't returned the favor. He owed her a secret.

He rubbed his hands up and down her back while he considered his next words carefully. Nothing came to mind that was tangible. Instead, he gave her the next best thing, a glimpse into his vulnerable side. "I'm scared out of my mind, Adriana."

"Me too." The words caught in her throat, choked out as she tipped her head back and set her chin on his chest. Her expression was pained and so serious.

They needed to lighten the somber mood. They couldn't stand there all day shrouded in sadness as if someone had died. "Let's take a step back. Get to know each other. Pretend like we're normal humans on a blind date."

She smiled. "I'd like that."

"I should call Reid. Tell him to come back."

She shook her head, shocking him. "No. I'll talk to him later. Let this be your afternoon."

He held her at arm's length, seeking her eyes for information. She was an open book. She didn't have secrets.

"Reid and I have never dated the same woman before."

Her smile broadened. "Well, I've never dated two men at once either."

"How many men *have* you dated?" he asked as he took her hand and led her back to the living room area.

"Not many. Enough to know this is different."

He lowered onto the couch, pulling her down beside him. "Talk to me about this new degree you're pursuing. Why did you change your mind?"

She twisted around in the corner of the couch and

tucked her legs up under her. She even pulled off her sweater.

That last part might have been a mistake since her tight, fitted, white T-shirt drew his attention to her chest, but he forced himself to keep his gaze on her eyes as they lit up. Her career change excited her.

"When I got my computer science degree, I guess I was doing what everyone expected of me. Everyone expected me to fall in line and work for the family brewery." She shrugged. "It didn't occur to me that I might like to do something different."

"And fashion? When did that come into the picture?" He was trying to imagine her in a designer gown or runway dress. Something didn't quite add up. Yes, he'd seen several pictures of her in fashionable attire on social media, but the woman in front of him was not superficial.

She must have read his mind because she answered the unasked question. "It's not so much myself. I'm not high maintenance or anything. Don't get the wrong idea. It's more that I have vision. I like to dress other people. I have an instinct when it comes to knowing what will suit someone. I used to change my Barbies' clothes all day long. I even made them different dresses when I couldn't find what I wanted at the store."

She lit up further while she spoke, and her passion was palpable. He loved it. At some point, he had angled his body to the side, drawing one knee up to face her. With the hand he'd draped over the back of the couch, he reached forward to pick up a lock of her hair. So soft.

He hadn't meant to interrupt her, but she leaned into his touch, her eyes sliding shut. "What about you. Why accounting?"

He chuckled. "I have no exciting tale to tell about that. I was good at math, so I took the obvious route. While you were playing with Barbies, I was lining up numbers I guess."

"Who's the bigger geek?"

"It's a tossup." He grinned. Damn, he really liked her.

For a long time, he simply stared at her, soaking in her beauty, the flush on her cheeks that replaced the chill she'd had earlier.

"Now what do we do?" she asked.

"I have no idea. I wish I could say the right thing, but I don't know what it is. You need to leave here with Reid. Please don't argue with me on this. He has a condo not too far from campus. Stay with him. He's a professional bodyguard. Nothing will happen to you in his care."

"You're sure about that?" She lifted a brow.

It took him a second to catch her meaning. Words got stuck in his throat. He took a moment to regroup, and then he sighed. "I'll admit, I'm probably going to lose my shit when you leave. But the police are surely going to pick up my client this afternoon, and then I'm really going to be hiding. Even if it means losing you, I need to know you're safe at all times."

She didn't move.

"Please, Adriana. Do this for me."

"Leave here with your best friend? A man I'm clearly also connected to? That's what you want? I'd almost be willing to go back to your original plan of staying with your parents at this point. This is so jacked up."

He forced another smile. "But you're right. If this guy decides to go after me, he'll do anything to find me. I don't want him to know I have anyone important in my life. Stay with Reid. Stay away from my parents and my sisters. Pretend you never met me."

A tear slid down her face. "I don't know how long we can keep this weird...triangle going."

"That's why I'm not asking you to. Follow your heart. If it leads you to Reid, do it. He's a great guy."

She shook her head. "He said exactly the same thing about you."

Nolan smiled. "Not surprising." He eased his hand from her hair to the back of her neck. "Do what feels right. I swear I will never fault you for whatever choice you make. You deserve happiness. If that means I have to let you go, it will be okay."

Another tear. She wiped it away.

"No tears, baby." His voice dipped too low. Too soft. His heart squeezed tight. "Will you do one thing for me?"

She nodded.

"Let me kiss you." He glanced at her lips as she licked them. When she drew the corner of the bottom one between her teeth, he leaned forward.

She released her lip, her mouth falling open. And then she closed the last few inches to set her lips over his.

His eyes slid closed even though he had wanted to watch her expression. He couldn't help it. He needed to go inside his head more. Feel every sensation. Store it for later…or forever. So soft. Gentle.

He tipped her head to one side and traced the seam of her lips with his tongue until she opened for him. When she let him inside, her hands grabbed his waist. Her fingers dug into his hips through his jeans, desperation evident in her grip.

His cock jumped to attention, but he ignored it, lifted his other hand to cup her cheek, and deepened the kiss. He tasted every inch of her mouth, devouring her. This kiss might have to last him a lifetime. He would never forget it.

Adriana Tarben was his. No matter what happened after she left this hotel suite, he would always know she had been his at least for one day.

Later, if she bound herself to Reid, would he know it immediately? Would something sever between them, breaking the connection? Would he bolt awake in the night and know she was no longer his?

He didn't know the answers to any of those questions, but he would have to take this gift, cherish it, and let her go.

And pray Fate knew what She was doing.

CHAPTER 7

Reid did his best to keep his focus on the road and not on the woman next to him. He kept two hands on the steering wheel and held it with a death grip, causing his fingers to ache before he pulled the SUV into the Osborns' driveway.

Adriana hadn't said much, and she'd spent the majority of the trip staring out the passenger window with her arms crossed, closed off from him.

He knew he needed to give her space, and since physical space wasn't possible, he would do his best to give her all the emotional distance she needed. For now.

When he turned off the engine, she faced him finally. "Thank you."

"For what?" He furrowed his brow.

"For letting me have some time. For agreeing to let me move in with you when I'm sure it's the last thing you want to do today."

He flinched. "Adriana, that's not true. I'm humbled that you're willing to come with me. You're the most important person in my life, having moved to that spot this morning without warning and before I even knew you existed. I promise to do everything in my power to make sure you're comfortable and happy. We're going to ride this train together. You're not alone."

She nodded, though he was pretty sure she swallowed back tears. Finally, she sat up straighter and took a breath. "I'll pack as quickly as I can."

He reached across and grabbed her hand before she could open the door. "There's no rush. I'm going to talk to Stanton and Oleta while you do what you need."

She cringed. "I don't even know them. They seem so nice. I can't believe I just met them yesterday and today I have to dump this insanity on their laps."

"You don't have to dump anything. I'll do it. You pack."

"That's not fair to you. I should be with you at least."

He shook his head. She was exhausted. He knew she hadn't slept well last night, and she had stepped into a different dimension in less than twenty-four hours. All three of them had. The least he could do was take some of her burden off her plate. "I've known them for over a decade. They're like parents to me with mine living on the other side of the country. None of this is your fault, nor is it your problem alone."

She nodded consent again. He didn't get the feeling she usually liked to relinquish control over her world so easily. He sensed a fighter under the exhaustion. The fact that she would move in with him told him she was feeling defeated. Worn out.

When he'd come back to the hotel suite half an hour ago, he'd exchanged a shit-ton of information with Nolan, both verbally and silently. Adriana had encouraged them to communicate. She'd offered to wait in the hallway or the bedroom.

They had both adamantly declined the suggestion, and

they had intentionally not shared very much behind her back. It didn't seem fair. Life was super unfair today.

Nolan had stared Reid hard in the eyes as they were leaving, however, gripping his arm tightly. *"This will not tear us apart. I refuse to allow it to. Keep her safe. Do whatever feels right."*

Reid had swallowed hard, nodding at his friend. *"You know I will. You also know you're like a brother to me, and I will not destroy that bond for any reason."*

"Reid?" Her sweet voice shook him from his thoughts. "Shall we go inside?"

"Yes." He jumped down from the SUV, rounded the hood, and opened her door. Nerves forced him to take deep breaths.

Half of him was shitting bullets, worrying about how he would tell Nolan's parents something they weren't expecting to hear. Half of him was hoping the two adults could be of some help. Maybe they knew of someone else this had happened to. Maybe they could shed some light on the insanity.

Reid had been close to them for over a third of his life. The fact that something could threaten that relationship drove him crazy.

Stanton opened the front door before they stepped onto the porch. He held it open wide, ushering them inside with a wave of his hand. "How did it go?" He directed his question at Adriana.

She pursed her lips.

Reid cleared his throat. "Adriana's going to stay with me for a while. Let's sit down in the kitchen and talk while she packs."

Stanton nodded, though it was obvious from his furrowed brow that he was concerned.

His mate stood behind him. She tucked her hand under his elbow and leaned into his shoulder. "I'll make coffee."

Ten minutes later, the three of them were sitting at the table sipping hot coffee, while Adriana had disappeared into Nolan's childhood room to gather her belongings.

She wasn't comfortable with the arrangement, however, which she kept telling Reid silently. *"I should be with you."*

"You should pack."

"I feel like I'm hiding."

"And I feel like I'm protecting you. Nolan agrees. Pack." Did she growl at him when he issued that command?

"Talk to us," Stanton stated.

Reid took a deep breath. "Something strange has happened, and I don't know what to make of it. I'm hoping you can help."

Oleta leaned forward. "What is it? Are you okay?"

Reid nodded. "Nothing like that."

"Let's hear what he has to say, hon." Stanton took his mate's hand and squeezed it.

"Somehow, Fate has lost Her sense of humor, or She's not playing with a full deck today, because it would seem that Adriana is as connected to me as she is to Nolan."

Oleta's mouth opened, but she hesitated before speaking. "What do you mean?"

"I mean when I stepped into your house this morning, I knew she was mine as strongly as Nolan knew the exact same thing last night."

Oleta gasped. She set a hand on her throat and glanced at her mate. "Is that possible?"

Stanton continued to look at Reid. "What does Adriana say?"

"She feels an equal pull toward both of us."

Stanton nodded slowly. He set his free hand over his

mate's, holding her steady with both hands, sandwiching hers tightly. "That is a problem."

"Yes. Have you ever heard of such a thing?"

"No. I can't say that I have. Not among grizzlies anyway."

"What do you mean?" Reid cocked his head to one side.

"It's happened among the wolves. Lots of them."

"We don't have any wolf shifters around here," Reid pointed out.

"Right, but there are several packs of them in Montana. And in Oregon. Paige's mate, Wyatt Arthur, met them a while back while he was in the States helping them make sense of their unusual weather patterns. He and his brother, Isaiah, spent quite a bit of time there."

"Arthur... That's one of the families that owns a brewery in Silvertip, right?"

"Yes. I'm sure he would be happy to fill you in on the details of how binding works among the wolves if you ask him. I don't know enough about it to speak, but Wyatt is knowledgeable."

"I feel bad that I haven't met Wyatt yet. He and Paige completed the binding months ago. It's inexcusable." He wasn't kidding. He did feel bad about the oversight.

Stanton smiled. "You've been on a lengthy assignment. We've been out of the country. Paige was in Silvertip when they decided to bind. They've been there ever since. It's not like you were intentionally avoiding them."

Reid smiled. "Good point. They were here last night, weren't they?"

"Yes, but they went back to Silvertip this morning. Early. I'll give you Wyatt's number."

Oleta spoke next. "What are you planning to do? I mean the three of you. Nolan must be out of his mind."

"Yes. I'm sure he'll call you later. He was..."

"I understand." Stanton sighed.

Oleta twisted to face the hallway. "Poor Addy. How is she doing?"

"She's upset. Confused. Stressed. You name it." *Addy…* For some reason the name didn't suit her. Not in his mind anyway.

"She doesn't want to stay here with us?" Oleta suggested.

Reid faced her. "The three of us hashed out every possible short-term solution, but the reality is you're safer without her under your roof, and she's safer if no one ever finds out she has a connection to Nolan. That's why he called me in the first place. He asked me to keep Adriana safe, and that's what I intend to do. Not going to try and tell you this isn't complicated, but it's what Nolan wants."

"What does Adriana want?" Oleta asked, using her full name.

Adriana appeared at the entrance to the kitchen, dropping a backpack on the floor and then rubbing her arms. "Adriana wants to go back in time and find something else to do last night so that she never met either Nolan or Reid yet. There's some mix up with the powers that be."

Oleta released her mate's arm and pushed from the table. Seconds later she was across the room, enveloping Adriana in a hug. "I'm so sorry, you sweet, dear girl. What a mess. You must be exhausted and wrung out." She released Adriana's body to grab her biceps and hold her at arm's length.

"I'm confused more than anything." She stood taller, pulling her shoulders back. "I want you to know I won't do anything to intentionally hurt your son."

"Of course not, dear. We all know that."

"If I thought there was a better option than staying with

Reid, I would jump on it in a heartbeat. But this is what Nolan wants, so I'm going to stay there. In his mind, this is the lesser of the evils, so to speak. He's afraid my presence in your home is worse than me leaving, and he wasn't willing to budge on the idea of me finding another place to live with a random roommate. Hopefully this trial won't take long to get to court, and the three of us will be free to figure out what the Universe is suggesting."

"We're here for you," Oleta said. She twisted around to face Reid. "Both of you. I don't have the answers, but I know you'll make the right choices. When the time is right, you'll know."

Reid hoped Oleta was right. At the moment it seemed hard to believe since the time was right *now*, and they *did* know. What they knew didn't make a bit of sense though. How could one person belong to two mates?

It was impossible for Reid to fully grasp. Every time he forced himself to think about their predicament, all he could come up with was that Adriana was mistaken. Reid was certain she was his. He knew it to the bottom of his soul. But then he took one look at Nolan and knew his best friend felt the exact same way. He'd seen it in his eyes when they first arrived, and the sentiment was confirmed the moment Reid came back up to the suite.

And then there was Adriana. She was the link. He had to believe her when she said she felt the same pull toward both of them. Who would make something like that up?

The answer wouldn't be found in one of them mistaking their instinct. It was something bigger. Something bigger than any of the three of them could possibly fathom yet.

Reid knew one thing—patience was his only option. He needed to focus his energy on keeping Adriana safe and let time sort this insanity out for them. He had to believe eventually something would happen to solidify who was truly meant to bind to Adriana. Either she would realize it definitively one day, or one of the two men would lose the strong connection.

Was either of those scenarios possible?

He had to believe so in order to get out of bed each morning and face the day.

Stanton pushed from the table and headed for the kitchen counter about five seconds before the home phone rang. He returned with it in his hand. "It's Nolan. He wants us to put him on speaker." After connecting the call, he set it on the table. "Hey, son. We're all in the room. Your mom, Reid, and Adriana."

"Good. I wanted to update you. The police stopped by to let me know they picked up my client. When we hang up, turn on your television. It will be all over the news."

"That big?" Stanton asked.

Reid stiffened, setting his elbows on the table as Oleta and Adriana came closer.

"Huge. I have to admit, I didn't grasp the enormity of this case. When I went to the police yesterday with my findings, I thought I was turning in some random guy laundering a bit of money. Apparently, it's much bigger. The name my client has been using with me was an alias. The police knew the name. A red flag went up. His dealings with me were the last in a series of events that finally gave the police enough evidence to arrest. His real name is Stephen Rimouski."

"I've heard the name," Reid said.

"Not surprising. He owns a lot of property north of here and many other businesses and high-rises under other aliases. Not going to get into the details, but now I see why the police yanked me into witness protection yesterday."

Oleta lowered herself back into the seat she'd vacated minutes ago. "Why do the police think your life is in danger?"

"Arresting Rimouski isn't good enough. A lot of people work for him that wouldn't want to see him convicted. They'll do anything to ensure he's acquitted."

Reid sucked in a breath. "Including eliminating anyone set to testify."

"Exactly."

Adriana had inched closer to the table, and she set a hand firmly on Reid's shoulder, squeezing. He reached across his body and set his palm on top of her fingers, though he doubted the gesture would be reassuring. He wasn't sure she even realized she was leaning on him for support.

Stanton cleared his throat. "I think we need to alert the Arcadian Council."

"Yeah." Nolan sighed. "That thought crossed my mind. So far I'm not aware of any shifters being involved. If I'd run into even one officer working on the case who was grizzly, I would have let him or her handle it, but I haven't. Better to keep the council informed. Just in case."

Adriana swallowed her nerves. This was serious. The Arcadian Council was their governing body. They operated out of the Northwest Territories. She hadn't met any of the forty members, but she was aware they could and should be called into any crisis situation. If things got hairy, they might be able to step in. In most instances, the council didn't like to interfere in human affairs unless it was absolutely necessary. Considering the seriousness in this case, she agreed. But the thought of taking that step made things even more real. And scary.

"I'll make some calls," Stanton responded.

"Thanks. Anyway, I'm not going to be able to keep

using this phone. Too risky. The police will move me later today and give me a burner phone. Dad, I can keep in touch with you and Mom, thank God. Reaching out to Reid and Adriana is going to be more difficult. I won't tell any of you where I am, and you won't be able to call me."

Stanton flattened his hands on the table, spreading his fingers. "Anything you need me to pass on to Reid and Adriana at any time, you let me know."

"I will, Dad. Love you all." There was a hitch in Nolan's voice that Reid had never heard in all the years they'd been friends.

"Can you take me off speaker and let me speak to Reid for a minute?"

"Of course." Stanton grabbed the phone and tapped the screen before handing it to Reid.

Reid's body was trembling as he held it to his ear.

Stanton and Oleta quietly went out the back door to sit on the deck.

Adriana leaned her face in and pointed to the hallway, mouthing that she was going to finish packing. He doubted she had anything more to pack but nodded all the same. It was possible Nolan would say things to Reid that were better kept from Adriana for the time being. Not that Reid had any intention of keeping secrets from her, but some things might require a bit of finesse.

"I'm here," Reid finally stated into the phone.

Nolan sighed. "This is the biggest clusterfuck of my life."

"Agreed." Reid tried to chuckle, but it came out choked.

"Listen, I'm going to forward Detective Carl Schaefer's information. He's in charge of this case. If anything happens, call him."

"Okay." Reid took a breath. He'd never heard Nolan sounding so serious.

"I need you to promise me something," Nolan continued.

Reid shook his head even though Nolan couldn't see him. "You know I'd do anything for you. You know I'll keep her safe. I'll guard her with my life. You don't even have to ask because she means as much to me as she does to you."

"Reid," Nolan interrupted.

Reid halted his rant, his ears ringing. He knew what his friend was going to say.

"She's not safe as long as she isn't bound to someone."

"She's safe enough. She doesn't need to be bound to anyone as long as I don't let her out of my sight."

"You can't guarantee that."

"Of course I can."

"You going to go to class with her?"

"Yes. Sure. If that's what it takes."

Nolan sighed. "Listen to me."

"No. Don't say it. We'll get through this. Pretend we're human and she's dating two men. People do that. As long as neither of us is having sex with her, she can date whoever she wants. There's no verbal commitment."

"You're rambling, and you aren't making any sense."

"I'm not going to bind to Adriana so you can martyr yourself. It's not fair to any of us. We'll wait and see."

Another sigh. "Okay, how about this, if there's ever evidence of clear and present danger, then you do it. Do it to protect her. Do it to keep her alive. Don't let someone take her and leave her vulnerable because you were too stubborn to bind to her. You'll hate yourself later. All the posturing will be for naught if she's kidnapped or something and has no way to reach out to either of us. Promise me."

Reid rubbed his temples with his free hand. "Okay." He

had no intention of binding to Adriana while Nolan was in hiding. It wasn't fair. It would take away her free will. She couldn't make informed choices if she only "dated" one of them and had occasional phone conversations with the other. And hell, "dated" was an inappropriate term for what they were about to do—live together.

Reid also recognized the gravity of the situation. He understood where Nolan was coming from. It would give him comfort to know that in a crisis Reid wouldn't leave her vulnerable. And he was right. Reid never intended to be put in that position, but he would promise his friend anything that would give him peace of mind. "You know I won't let anything happen to her."

"Even if you have to bind to her to ensure her safety."

"Even then." *I just won't let it come to that.*

"Thank you. I'll sleep better knowing she's in good hands." He paused, catching his breath. "Can I speak to her?"

"Of course." Reid pushed from the table. "Give me a second." He lowered the phone to his side and headed down the hall.

Adriana was sitting on Nolan's bed in his childhood room. She lifted her gaze as Reid held out the phone. "Your turn." He smiled as warmly as he could and then left so she could speak to her other mate, shutting the door behind him as he returned to the front of the house.

Her other mate…

Fuck.

CHAPTER 8

Adriana put the phone to her ear. "Hey." She fell back against the bed.

"Hey." His voice. Damn. All she needed was to hear his voice about once a day to be reminded what they had.

"Are you okay?"

"Yeah." He sounded anything but okay.

"When are they going to move you?"

"Not sure. In a few hours, I think."

"Will you still be in Calgary?"

"Don't know that either."

"I'll be fine. I don't want you to worry about me."

"Be smart. Please. I know you like to assert yourself and be all self-sufficient, but this is serious."

"I'll be fine, Nolan. The guy doesn't even know I exist. You worry about lying low and keeping yourself alive."

"I'd worry less if you would bind yourself to Reid and move on with your life."

"We're not discussing this again. No one is binding to anyone while you wait for this trial."

"It could take months."

"Then we wait months."

He exhaled sharply. "I hate this."

"You and me both."

"I'll call you when I have an opportunity."

"Okay."

"Bye, Adriana." He ended the call before she could speak again, leaving her name as the last thing she heard from him. So much feeling came out in that one word. She'd never heard her name from anyone's lips with so much emotion in it.

Nolan Osborn, you better come back to me.

Heaving herself off the bed, she joined the others in the living room. "I'm ready to go."

Reid stood from the couch and crossed the room. He picked up her backpack from the kitchen floor. Her suitcases were already missing from the hallway. He must have put them in the car while she'd spoken to Nolan.

This was the craziest thing she'd done in her life. Crazier than quitting her job at the brewery just months after finishing her degree to move to Calgary. Which reminded her that she needed to reach out to her parents. What was she going to tell them?

She gave Oleta a hug and followed Reid outside. "I'll follow you in my car." She pointed to her cherry red Honda Accord.

He shook his head. "Leave it for now. We'll get it later."

"Why?" She didn't want to put herself in a situation where she relied on him.

He opened the door to his SUV and turned to look at her. "I'm stressed and tired right now. I just want you in my SUV. We'll figure out your car another day."

She nodded and climbed inside, equally stressed and tired. He was right. It would only add to their tension if he had to worry about her following him. And she wasn't sure she had enough brain cells to avoid an accident. It didn't escape her notice that both Reid and Nolan had a bossy side that might push her over the edge, given enough time.

As soon as he had her settled in the front seat, he rounded the hood. Those were the last few seconds she would have without his constant potent scent smothering her. Tempting her. Taunting her.

Sure enough, as soon as he climbed into the SUV and shut the door, she inhaled nothing but Reid. Potent. Her mate.

One of them anyway.

"Have you communicated with your parents?" he asked as he started the engine.

Was he a mind reader?

She almost chuckled. Yes. He was a mind reader. And chances were she was doing a piss-poor job of blocking him completely. Even if she hadn't specifically communicated her last few thoughts with him, he could pick up on the gist of her concerns if he tried to delve into her mind.

"Not yet. I can't imagine what I'm going to say."

"Will Alton tell them? I mean at least about Nolan. He was here last night. He knows, right?"

"Yes. I don't think he would share my secrets. He'll let me handle it. Besides, if he'd told them anything, they would have reached out to me themselves by now."

"Good point." Reid drove.

Adriana worried. He didn't say anything, but he had to be thinking the same things she was thinking. How was this going to work? The connection between them was already so palpable she couldn't imagine how they could avoid binding. It would be a challenge to get through the drive to his condo, the evening in his home, the night... But weeks or months?

She shuddered and closed her eyes, trying not to pay attention to what happened to her body every time she inhaled. She wrapped her arms around her middle, totally aware of the pressure against her bra from her swollen nipples and the throbbing of her sex against her jeans.

All her life she'd heard people speak about what happened when two grizzlies met and completed the binding. Few people told stories that matched what she'd experienced in the last twenty-four hours—even half of what she'd experienced to be precise. Most shifters dated and got to know each other and fell in love and decided to bind.

The binding could be powerful. Or perhaps it always was. No matter how close the couple was before the binding, they would be united so tightly afterward that separation was inconceivable. Grizzly shifters didn't have breakups. They didn't usually marry in the traditional sense unless they decided to do so for the purpose of fitting into human society, but their connections were stronger than humans. Divorce or any type of separation was unheard of.

Lately, relationships between grizzlies had been crazy weird though. People had been meeting and knowing instantly more and more often. She'd been skeptical, until yesterday. Now she understood what her brother had insinuated he felt for Joselyn. And then there was Paige and Wyatt. Now she got it. But none of them had met two people.

She really needed help figuring this out.

Half the reason she was reluctant to contact her parents was because she was embarrassed, as if something was wrong with her for feeling a connection to two people. What would people say? Was she some horny crazy woman who was being punished for some unknown transgression?

What did she do to deserve this?

Or maybe the fact that she hadn't given herself to any man was exacerbating the draw toward more than one man. Though that seemed ludicrous since it could have happened at any point. Why now?

"Adriana?"

She startled, realizing the car was no longer moving. Reid grabbed her hand. It was kind of dark. She glanced around to find them in a garage. "Guess I spaced." She hadn't paid attention to anything as he drove. She had no idea where they were in relation to the university or the city or the suburbs. Lord.

He smiled. "You were a million miles away. I wasn't sure if you were sleeping or worrying."

"I was inside my head."

He gave her hand a squeeze and exited the SUV.

She opened her door and climbed down to follow him toward the rear of the SUV. She looked around outside. His was an end unit in a row of four condos. While he grabbed her suitcases, she picked up her backpack and put it over her shoulder. She followed him to the back of the garage and into a downstairs media room where he turned to punch several buttons on an alarm pad before they climbed the stairs to the main level. She wasn't surprised he owned a fancy security system, considering he was in the business of keeping people safe.

The main floor was bright and spacious. Inviting. "Nice." She set her bag down in the open kitchen area and draped her coat over a chair while Reid put her suitcases next to the stairs. "How old is this? It looks brand new."

"About a year. I'm the original owner. I even got to pick out the colors, appliances, tile, paint, everything." He approached her and grabbed her hand. "Come on. I'll give you a tour."

She threaded her fingers with his, more aware of the electric current running between them than the surroundings. It was difficult to focus on his condo with him touching her. And it was going to be nearly impossible with his scent all over the place. It filled her lungs with every inhale.

Yeah, this was a bad idea. Horrible.

And yet, she didn't have a plan B, and she'd promised Nolan she would stay with Reid. How whacked was this situation?

She forced herself to focus on the condo. The kitchen had a lot of natural light coming in through the sliding glass doors off the dining area and several windows. The cabinets were white. The counter a black speckled granite. The appliances were black. The floor was done in tiles swirled with black, gray, and white. His kitchen table was a glass-topped oval with white chairs. Modern. Sleek. Inviting.

When she turned around to take in the living room, she found a similar color scheme. Black leather sectional with gray carpet and a giant whitewashed entertainment center. He liked his electronics. The television was enormous, and there were several other pieces of equipment she couldn't identify. Gaming stations or something, she assumed.

The designer in her went into overdrive, imagining everything she could do with the space to make it look less like a model home and more like people lived in it. *This is not your condo*, she reminded herself.

Reid tugged on her hand, and she followed him down a short hallway. "Bathroom. Office." He pushed doors open and pointed inside.

When he spun her around and headed for the stairs, he released her to grab the suitcases.

She followed him upstairs. There was an inviting landing with a black, plush leather chair next to a small round table. It looked like the perfect place to read. She could do homework there.

Reid used his foot to kick a door open. "Guest room." He nodded across the hallway. "Guest bath." And then he backed through another door and set her suitcases on the floor. "Master."

She followed him inside. Spacious. Lots of natural light streaming in like the kitchen below. "You're fond of black and white." It needed color.

He chuckled. "I guess I got carried away."

She smiled. "It's modern." His king-sized bed was unmade, which was about the only thing out of place in his condo. She gasped sarcastically, setting a hand over her heart. "You didn't make the bed." A jumble of black sheets and pillows and even a black comforter lay haphazardly on top.

He gave her a playful shove. "I rushed out the door when Nolan called. Making the bed didn't seem like a priority at the time."

She flushed. What a morning. "You have an aversion to colors?" she teased. The dresser, four-posted bed, and end tables were also black. The carpet was the same gray as the living room. She could go crazy for days in this home with a credit card and carte blanche.

"Not really. It's more like I was afraid to do it wrong, so I never decorated at all. It needs a woman's touch."

"You think?" She grinned. Was it possible she could be that woman? "Let me guess, the bathroom is a mirror image of the kitchen."

"Pretty much." He shrugged. "I'll take you shopping. You can make changes."

She swallowed. That sounded so…permanent. They had no way of knowing if they would be together when this was over. She had no business decorating his condo. But she didn't say anything.

"You must be starving. We haven't eaten since breakfast. Unfortunately, there's no food in this house. I haven't had a chance to shop since I got home from my last assignment. We can head to the grocery store or order out."

She considered the options. "I know you didn't ask for the inconvenience of having a house guest and didn't get up this morning expecting a roommate at the end of the day. I also can't contribute much to this arrangement. I'm on a thin budget paying tuition and eating up my savings. But," she lifted a finger and smiled, "I can cook."

His expression was serious as he closed the distance between them. He set his hands on her shoulders and stared into her eyes. "You're not an inconvenience, so stop that. And I also don't want you to worry about finances. This is totally out of your control. I make plenty of money to live comfortably. You worry about school and leave the rest to me."

She frowned. "I'm at least going to get a job. I've applied to a few on campus. Easier to manage."

He shook his head. "Now's not a good time for you to have a job. It makes it harder for me to keep track of you."

"You don't have to keep tabs on me twenty-four seven, Reid. I'm a grown-up."

He furrowed his brow. "It's not about how old you are, Adriana. It's about safety. Even if it seems like overkill, I'm going to stick to you like glue for the time being. Besides the fact that I want you to stay safe and alive, Nolan would kill me if I let you out of my sight."

"Whoa." She stepped back, breaking the contact with him and leaning against the side of the bed. "You can't go everywhere with me. I have classes and studying."

He stepped closer until he was once again in her space. It was hard to breathe when he got that close to her. And when he touched her... "I'll do my best not to hover too close or draw attention to you, but you have to let me do my job."

"I'm not one of your usual clients, Reid. Don't you think you're overreacting? I mean now that I'm not at the Osborns', that Rimouski guy won't even know I exist. I'll be fine. Although it will be difficult for me to get to class tomorrow since you insisted I leave my car at the Osborns'."

"You're right. You're not one of my clients. You're so much more. So, don't argue with me on this. You won't win."

"Don't you have to work?" It suddenly occurred to her how messed up this was. As long as Reid followed her everywhere she went, he wouldn't be doing his regular job.

"I just finished a case. I have employees. I'll assign everything to them while we deal with this threat. I can manage my job from home. My guys will fill in any gaps."

"Have you thought of everything?" She tried to sound lighter, but it was tough because he was now standing so close his knees were touching hers.

When he reached for her hands with both of his and lifted them to press them against his chest, she stopped breathing. He was so muscular, a byproduct of his job or vice versa. She'd been able to see how huge he was all day. Broad shoulders, firm abs, a damn fine tight ass. But touching him like this? This was different.

His brow was furrowed again. She wanted to reach up and rub her thumb over it to smooth it out. She hated knowing she was responsible for putting it there in the first place. As usual, he must have read her mind because his face relaxed and he smiled. He wrapped both her hands in one of his against his chest and lifted the other to tuck a lock of hair behind her ear. His thumb grazed her cheek.

Her heart pounded at the intimate contact and the way he looked at her.

His thumb lowered to her lip, tracing the bottom one softly. His voice was deeper when he whispered, "Did he kiss you?"

For a moment she didn't know who he was talking about. But then she realized he meant Nolan. "Yes." They were not going to have secrets. That much she needed to promise herself. She couldn't imagine a stranger arrangement, but she would not keep things from either of them.

She thought Reid was going to kiss her too. Wasn't that why he asked? Did he want to level the playing field or something? Keep things fair?

But that's not what happened. Instead, he lowered his hand, stepped back, and slid his other hand into one of her, tugging her to follow him. "Let's order something to eat. We'll hit the grocery store tomorrow sometime."

She followed him back downstairs, her lip tingling from his touch. Her legs were wobbly too. Her entire body seemed to have only one thought, making it difficult to walk properly. She would have preferred if he'd pushed her back onto the bed and kissed her rather than stepping away and dragging her from the room.

But what was she thinking? She needed to get control of her emotions and fast. Otherwise, this was going to be a disaster. She couldn't let this thing between them take flight. It wasn't fair to any of them. She needed to keep her distance, physically and emotionally.

"Pizza? Chinese? Mexican?"

"You have Mexican places that deliver?"

He grinned. "We're in the city. We can get whatever we want. If they don't deliver, a service will pick it up."

"Huh. They don't do that in Silvertip. Then again, we don't have many restaurants in Silvertip, so what would I have delivered?"

When he reached the island in the kitchen, he hauled her closer, grabbed her waist, and angled her so she was leaning against it. He was crowding her again, which was both hot and domineering. When he got in her space—this time with his legs on either side of hers, trapping her against the island—she had trouble thinking.

He tugged a drawer open next to her hips and pulled out a pile of menus. "Anything you don't like?"

"I'm not picky."

"Excellent." He fanned out several like playing cards. "Pick one."

She grabbed one from the center, not looking. Her gaze was on his face. He was in a playful mood. She liked it better than his business slash serious mood. It didn't matter what he ordered, as long as he continued to talk to her so she could get to know him.

He set the stack of menus on the counter, cupped her face with both hands, and met her gaze.

She stopped breathing while he looked at her. "You're killing me."

"What did I do?" She lifted both brows.

His smile spread. "You came into my life. That's all it took."

Her cheeks burned with a flush. "The feeling is mutual."

"You have no idea which menu you picked."

"Nope. Surprise me."

"Okay." He released her again.

It felt like a game of Ping-Pong. Every time she thought he would close the gap and kiss her, he stepped back. Eventually, she would melt into a pile of goo on the floor and hit her head when her legs gave out.

"You go sit on the couch. I'll order something. Later, maybe I'll teach you the exciting concept of grocery shopping online. Then we won't even have to waste time roaming the aisles."

She rolled her eyes. "I'm aware that grocery stores deliver these days."

"Have you ever done it?"

"Well, no. The one and only store in Silvertip doesn't deliver. I'm just saying I'm familiar with the concept. Don't want you to think I'm some small-town girl."

"You *are* a small-town girl," he teased.

"Okay. True. But I'm educated."

He pulled her hand to his face and kissed her knuckles. "I can see that. Never doubted it."

When he stepped aside, she made her exit. Not that it was a far distance nor did it block her view of him. The living room and kitchen were all one big room. But she wasn't sorry he'd asked her to go sit on the couch. At least that way she couldn't fall when her legs gave out.

She picked a spot on the far corner of the leather sectional and tucked her legs under her. And then she watched him moving around the kitchen.

He popped open a laptop on the counter, clicked a few keys, and then closed the lid again. When he lifted his gaze, he asked, "Done. What would you like to drink? I don't have much food, but I do have some beverages. Soda? Beer? Wine?"

"Wine? What color?" Her nerves would surely calm if she had a glass or two of wine.

"I have both red and white."

"White would be great."

He spun around, opened the fridge, and grabbed a chilled bottle. What a Boy Scout. The whirr of an electric corkscrew filled the silence, and the next thing she knew, he was seated next to her pouring two glasses of wine.

It all happened so fast she didn't have time to put her brain cells back in order before he scrambled them all again with his proximity.

"This is never going to work," she murmured.

"What?" He looked confused as he handed her a glass.

She waved her other hand through the air. "This. The entire arrangement. I should be doing homework, not playing house. I have classes in the morning, and I'm worried I won't be able to concentrate with you cluttering my mind. I can't think when you're in the same space as me."

He leaned back, turning his body to face her and setting his hand on the back of the couch behind her, not quite touching her. "I'll stay in the back of the room. You won't even know I'm there."

"What room?" Did he think if he went to the kitchen or even upstairs, his pheromones wouldn't continue to torture her?

"Your classes."

She'd just taken a sip of the wine and nearly spit it across the distance between them. "My classes." She shook her head. "No. Hell, no. You can't come to my classes with me. For one thing, I'd look like a fool, and you'd draw attention to me. For another thing, I would flunk the entire semester."

He chuckled. His hand slid down to reach for a lock of

her hair. He fingered it casually, staring at it. "We'll figure it out." His mood switched again. She was going to get whiplash.

Then again, if he felt anything similar to how she felt, it wasn't shocking. She couldn't keep up with herself either. She kept switching from convincing herself to stay away from him and clear her head to wanting to throw herself at him and damn the consequences. Except, that was only two moods. He seemed to have more.

"When you order groceries, get more of whatever shampoo you used. I love the scent." He leaned closer, lifted her thick hair to his face, and inhaled. "Vanilla or something."

"Yes." Her voice was breathy. "We can't do this." She reached for the front of his shirt as she spoke and fisted the soft material in her free hand. She needed more contact with him. Now. Like a drug addict, she needed to press against him.

She closed her eyes, took deep breaths, and released her fist to flatten her palm on his chest. She concentrated on the rise and fall with every heartbeat.

Reid took her glass from her hand and leaned away from the couch. She imagined he set it on the coffee table. And then his hands were in her hair, threaded in both sides, tipping her head back. "Look at me."

She opened her eyes.

His gaze was serious again.

Whiplash.

"Deep breaths."

"You do realize any breaths only make this worse."

He grinned. "You've got me there. But we're grown adults. Pretend we're human. Pretend we're dating."

"And not exclusive. And living together? Do you realize how ridiculous that sounds?"

He set his forehead against hers. "Yes. But we have no other option. Between the two of us, we'll have to come up with enough self-control to wait this out."

She jerked free, shaking him off, and jumped to her feet to put several yards between them. "Wait it out?" She set her hands on her head, feeling like a lunatic as she paced farther across the room.

Reid didn't move from the couch.

Her voice rose to hysterical. "Between the two of us? Between the two of us, we aren't even playing with a full deck, Reid. If you're half as aroused as I am, we won't make it until dark before we sleep together. And then what? How will we keep from binding? It's a slippery slope."

She couldn't catch her breath. She wasn't exaggerating. She wanted him. She wanted him to strip her naked and take away the edge that had been simmering all over her body since she first scented Nolan last night. That high-level arousal only a shifter with their mate would feel had doubled that morning. By now, she seriously thought she might need a straitjacket.

Reid stood.

She faced him, dropping her hands from her hair and fisting them at her sides. "I can't stay here." She threw her hands up in the air next. "What am I even talking about? If I left, the problem wouldn't even go away. I only felt marginally less needy last night in Nolan's bed, and at the time I hadn't even met him or you." She was still shouting.

Reid didn't move. Thank God. Was he humoring her? Did he not feel the same pull?

"Even if I went back to the Osborns' or to a hotel or a stranger's house, I would still be unable to calm down or sleep. I have no idea how I'm going to shut my mind down to rest for an hour tonight. Months? That's inconceivable."

She slapped one hand over her forehead and twisted around to face the back of the condo.

In far fewer steps than ordinarily would be necessary, she raced toward the sliding glass door and yanked it open. The rush of cold air was welcoming. She stepped outside, slid the door closed, and gasped for oxygen. His scent was watered down outside, at least. As she moved across the small deck, she took long breaths.

It was too cold to stand outside without a jacket, but she didn't feel it even though she was easily colder than most people. She felt like flinging off her sweater and tossing it to the deck. Actually, what she wanted to do was shift and go for a long run in her grizzly form.

But that wasn't going to happen. After twenty-three years of running in her natural form almost any time she wanted right out the back door of her parents' home, she was now restricted. Grizzlies didn't have that luxury in the city. And this condo was definitely in the middle of Calgary. She didn't even have total privacy.

At least Reid's condo faced an easement. There was a copse of trees behind his property. But there were no fences or anything else to keep the other occupants of the row of condos from seeing her if they stepped outside. Luckily no one was outside at the moment.

Ignoring the outdoor table and chairs next to the grill on the deck, she lowered herself to sit on the edge, her feet on the first of three steps that led down to a grassy area. More deep breaths. She was grateful he left her alone. He didn't come outside, nor did he probe her mind.

Surely he also needed space and time.

How the hell was this going to work out?

CHAPTER 9

Reid stood by the window, watching his mate suffer in silence. He understood exactly how she felt, and he couldn't blame her. It wasn't natural to deny the call of mates. Her sexy little body had driven him insane all day, and it was only getting worse as the hours ticked by.

She was right. This was not going to work. No matter what he told himself, he couldn't keep his hands off her. He wanted to fuck her so badly it hurt. His cock had been stiff for hours. His heart pounded. His palms were sweaty.

What other options did they have? She was right about another thing—separating wouldn't fix the problem. Even if they lived in two separate homes, they would suffer just as much. Maybe the desire would ease a bit to allow them to breathe without inhaling the essence of the other, but only marginally. Their plight would infiltrate their dreams.

Reid would give anything to be able to unzip his jeans and jerk himself off. He didn't think it would take the edge off, but he would do it if he could. But he wouldn't leave her alone outside to take care of such a carnal need. He needed to get a grip. He needed to be strong for her. She needed him.

His chest clenched as he watched her sink to her butt at the edge of the deck and lean her elbows on her knees. When she put her forehead against her palms, he swallowed the pain he knew she felt.

The doorbell rang.

Damn. The food.

He turned around, rushed across the room, and opened the door. Thank God he'd paid online, because he didn't think he had enough sense to count money. He thanked the delivery guy and rushed back across the room to find Adriana still in the same location.

Jesus. He was a wreck. How could he protect her with his brain jumbled like this? He was not in the right state of mind to keep her safe. But the thought of turning her over to someone else's care brought bile to his throat. Nolan wouldn't go for it anyway.

He set the paper bag on the table and leaned a hip against the glass door again. He ached for her. Even through the glass, he could feel her stress. He felt it too. It was palpable. And it would only get worse.

Denying one's mate was inconceivable. Doing so while remaining in a confined space with them was beyond imagination. And yet, he was going to manage this somehow.

He watched her for half an hour, not bothering her until he finally opened the door and stepped outside. She would be freezing.

He eased up next to her, sat on the top step, and wrapped his arm around her to pull her against his side.

She'd been crying, which broke his heart, and she wiped her tears on the back of her hand and leaned into his chest. "I'm sorry. I'm being a bitch about this."

"Don't apologize. You have a right to be freaked out. I'm in the same boat, babe. I feel the same things you do."

"You're controlling it better." Her voice hitched on a hiccup.

He kissed the top of her head. "Only externally. On the inside, I'm slamming you against the wall and ripping your clothes off." Yeah, that probably wasn't a helpful thing to say.

She giggled though, the sound vibrating through him and doing nothing to ease the throbbing in his cock. Setting a palm on his chest, she tipped her head back and met his gaze. "I'd like to see you try."

He lifted a brow in confusion. Was she challenging him?

She shook her head. "That came out wrong. What I'm trying to say is that I wouldn't let you do that even if we were mates and Nolan wasn't involved."

"Pardon."

"Not this soon anyway. I'm not that kind of girl."

He stared at her. "What kind of girl? The kind who has sex with her mate?" What was she saying?

"The kind who has sex…" She bit her lower lip hard enough to make him wince.

He couldn't even blink. He opened his mouth finally to lick his lips. "Uh…ever?"

She shook her head.

Still not sure he understood, he asked the question straight out. "You're a virgin?"

"Yes. And ordinarily I wouldn't share that with anyone, even you, but since I told Nolan last night, it only seemed fair."

"You told him that?" Why would something like that come up in conversation?

She nodded. "It slipped out. He asked me to tell him something no one else knew about me."

Reid's mouth was so dry, he thought he might choke. *Fuck me.* That revelation did nothing to calm his cock. *Nothing.*

After a few seconds, when he was finally able to communicate in the English language, he spoke. "I'm humbled. Thank you for sharing with me. It means the world to me." He squeezed her tighter. If he didn't change the subject, he was liable to slide to his knees in front of her and make a fool of himself. *Deep breaths.* "The food came."

Her stomach grumbled. Perfect segue.

He smiled. "Guess I should feed you." He pushed to standing, pulling her up with him. Luckily, her hysteria had temporarily passed, and she followed him inside.

After the reprieve from inhaling each other's pheromones, they managed to sit at the table and eat Chinese food right out of the containers like any normal couple would do. They used chopsticks and passed the cartons back and forth, not bothering with plates or utensils.

When they were done, and the mess was cleared, it was dark out. It wasn't late, but it was dark. The darkness made their world shrink. Reid couldn't quite imagine going to bed and calming down enough to relax or sleep. And he had yet to discuss their sleeping arrangements.

He led her upstairs silently, not touching her.

When they reached the master bedroom, she finally brought up the elephant. "You brought my stuff in here. I should sleep in the guest room."

He knew she was right, intellectually. But he didn't think he could stand having her across the hallway. He needed to feel her during the night. Not physically, but at least know she was in the room. Listen to her breathing. Smell her sweet scent. Know she was okay.

She shot him a look. "I'm in your home. You're planning to follow me to school tomorrow—" she lifted a scolding finger, "—which I still intend to discuss in the morning. You can't expect me to also sleep with you. Let me have my space."

He considered her request, knowing he was frowning. Was he being unreasonable or greedy? "You're right."

She blew out a sigh of relief. "Thank you. Between you and Nolan, I don't feel like I'm entitled to my own opinion." She grabbed one suitcase and pulled it toward the door.

He took the other, following her. When they reached the room across the hall, he stopped her with a hand to her forearm. "You're always entitled to your opinion. Yes, we're both rather dominating. But it's only because we care, and we put your safety first, even above your wishes."

She lifted up on her tiptoes, kissed his cheek, and shoved him toward the door. "Get out. Let me study for a while and then sleep."

He backed out the door, which she shut in his face, and then leaned against the frame for a moment. This was going to be the hardest test of his life. Failure seemed imminent.

After listening to her move around for a few minutes, he headed for his own room. It was seven in the evening. Not even close to bedtime. He closed his door anyway and grabbed the remote, hoping the television would drown out at least some of his problems. He reached into her mind. *"If there's anything you need, just ask or come across the hall."*

"Okay. Thank you. I'll be fine."

"The alarm is set. Don't leave the house for any reason."

"Yes, master." Her sarcasm made his cock harder again.

Reid propped himself up at the headboard and started flipping through the channels, though he didn't have any idea what passed by because he wasn't paying attention. When his phone buzzed in his pocket, he muted the TV and pulled it out, assuming the unknown number would be Nolan. "Hello?"

"Hey. You okay? Adriana?"

"About as you would expect. It was a rough day for both of us. She's in the guest room. I'm in my room."

A few seconds of silence. "I'm sorry that pleases me."

"Yeah. I know."

"Is she agreeable to letting you follow her around tomorrow?"

"Not at all." He chuckled. "But we'll work it out. I find it's easier to act first and catch her off guard. When I give her every detail ahead of time, she has too much time to think and then argues with me."

Nolan laughed. "I can see that."

Reid changed the subject. "You safe?"

"Yeah. I'm in a new location. I have a burner phone. I'll call you on it when I can. Don't call me. I'll call Adriana when I hang up with you."

"What do the police think? I haven't watched the news."

"It's a giant mess. This guy is huge. He's squandered away millions of dollars in offshore accounts over decades. I'm betting I'm not the only person who will need protection until we can testify. He probably has a different accountant for every alias. It's just a matter of time before the police can find other witnesses."

"What a fucking idiot."

"No kidding. I guess he thought if he had an accountant, it made him look less suspicious. But he didn't count on me having a brain, I suppose. He's a relatively new client. Until a few days ago, I didn't notice anything out of the ordinary, and then some numbers didn't add up."

Reid smiled. Nolan certainly was sharp. No much got by him. That's how he'd ended up in this situation. "How are you going to handle your other clients?"

"Luckily this isn't the time of year when everyone needs me desperately. I have my computer. I can work from anywhere. Not many people need an appointment in October. I can put them off. Reschedule."

That was good. At least he wasn't going to lose his job.

"What about you? I'm keeping you from working."

"Don't worry about it. I have guys. They can handle things."

"It's a lot to ask."

"Don't forget, I would do it even if you didn't exist. She's important to me. I won't let anything happen to her." *As long as I can keep my dick at bay and not lose sight of what I'm promising.*

"You'll do whatever it takes, right?"

"You know I will."

"Even if it means you have to bind to her and cut me out."

"Nolan…"

"I mean it." His voice rose. "Promise me."

"I promise you it won't come to that."

"Fine, but if anything suspicious happens or you hear from me that I'm afraid for her life, you'll bind to her, right? I don't want you to hesitate and risk her life. There could come a day when she needs the connection."

"Yes. Nolan, stop talking so morbidly. We're going to figure this out."

"Okay, just so we have a plan in place, let's establish an easy, quick, communication. One word that will tell you the situation has gone FUBAR if I text it to you." He paused. "Rope."

"Rope?"

"Yeah, as in bind. It wouldn't mean anything to anyone else, but it gets the message across to you."

"Okay. Got it. Rope." Reid prayed he never received that message, because the option to bind to her without letting her exercise her free will and choose between the two men was not on the table. If it came down to it, Reid wasn't sure he could go through with it. But how could he not?

What if he didn't bind her to him and she was taken from him, and he had no way to communicate with her? The thought of her in harm's way because he was too stubborn to bind her to him made him grimace.

All he could do was pray the situation never came up.

Adriana was trying to concentrate on her assignment when her cell rang. She picked it up, saw it was Nolan, and smiled as she connected. "Hey."

"Hey. You okay?"

"No. What kind of question is that?" She laughed. More like forced herself to laugh.

"I just hung up with Reid."

"You called him first?" There was a moment of silence before she put him out of his misery. "Just kidding. Don't worry. I know you need to speak to both of us. But don't spend all your time with Reid plotting my every move. It won't bode well for either of you."

"Adriana, I don't want you to spend all *your* time arguing with Reid about your safety. Do what he says.

Please. If I have to worry about you on top of everything else, I'll lose my mind."

She stiffened. *Do what he says?* "I'm not a child. I haven't been obedient since I was like ten years old. I can take care of myself. I need my car, and I need to go to class."

"Where's your car?"

Ah, so Nolan wasn't in on the scheme to leave her Honda behind. "At your parents' house. Reid wanted me to leave it there. I feel a bit trapped." That was an understatement.

"You don't need a car right now. Let Reid drive you."

She pinched the bridge of her nose. "Listen, I don't want to spend every second arguing with you."

He sighed. "I'm sorry. I don't want to either. But my gut tells me to be cautious."

She hoped she could get him to be reasonable. "Nolan, the police picked Rimouski up today. I was already with Reid. No one has any idea I even exist. Why are you so convinced someone is coming after me?"

"I don't know, but I feel uneasy. That's the only way I can explain it."

She suddenly had a new thought in her favor. "Hey, my car isn't helping by sitting at your parents' house. If someone decided to watch your family members, they would start with your parents. They might wonder why there's an extra car there. What if they run the plates?" She was exaggerating. No part of her believed anyone would bother to go to that much trouble, but she hoped it would help her cause. *I need my car. I need my independence.*

"Aren't you the detective," he teased. "You're right. I'll have my dad move it."

"Move it where? How about here? How about you stop trying to control my entire life?" She didn't mean to be a bitch, but this situation was totally overboard. Both of the men she felt drawn toward were bossy and controlling. That wasn't going to happen. At the moment, pheromones aside, they were competing for last place.

"Okay."

Okay? That was it? He was going to "let" her have her car? There had to be a catch.

Wait for it…

"But that doesn't mean I want you to drive around on your own."

Of course. She rolled her eyes.

"Adriana…" His voice was softer. It got to her in a way she knew it would for the rest of her life. All he had to do was say her name in the particular fashion that he always did, and she would melt.

Maybe if she could get him to call her Addy instead, she wouldn't become a total pile of goo every time he said her name. "You know, my close friends call me Addy."

"That's nice."

"You could be one of my friends," she added.

"I could be your mate. Anything is possible. But no matter what happens, I love your name. It's beautiful. Sexy. Mysterious. Let me have this." His voice was deeper as he finished speaking, as sexy and mysterious as he proclaimed her name to be.

She shuddered, shaking the feeling from her mind. She needed to get back on track. She cleared her throat. "Whatever. Fine. Listen. Here's the thing. I realize you're both older than me. Significantly. I get that. But I'm not eighteen or sixteen or twelve. I'm twenty-three. And yes, I've been living with my parents until a few months ago. But they haven't questioned my whereabouts or my driving skills or anything else for about five years now. I'm a capable adult." Maybe she was going overboard. Again. Maybe she shouldn't dig her heels in so hard on this issue. But she was afraid if she let either of these men steamroll her now, they would do it for life.

And what was she even thinking? They weren't both going to be in her life. Just one. One domineering man. Perhaps she should open a spreadsheet and keep a tally of how often each of them bossed her around. Then at the end of the month, she could pick the one with the least infractions. She almost laughed out loud.

"I'm not questioning your ability to take care of yourself, hon. I'm not worried about you. It's the other guy I'm concerned about. The man is powerful. He has billions of dollars. I have no doubt at the snap of his fingers, even from jail, he can get someone eliminated from this earth, and the body would never be found."

She shuddered. He was right. Why did he have to be right? "Okay. I'll let Reid take me to class. But I want my car here at his condo in case I need it. You never know. If someone did come after me, wouldn't you want me to have the ability to escape?"

He chuckled. "You sure you aren't studying to be a lawyer? I thought it was fashion."

"Ha ha."

"Please, hon. Do what Reid says. He knows how to keep people alive. I want you to be one of them."

"Okay."

"Now, tell me about your classes."

Joe Stringer stared hard at the man in front of him who the boss had put in charge of several aspects of their operation. He had no earthly idea what Rimouski saw in this guy or why he felt he could trust him, but Joe certainly did not.

The guy was gangly and uptight as if he was hiding something. His expression was always serious. There was something about him that put Joe on edge, and Joe was usually a good judge of character.

But the reality was Rimouski put his faith in Vinny, so Joe's hands were tied. When he'd gotten the call about an hour ago that Rimouski had been arrested, Joe had gone into protect mode. They'd discussed the plan all of them would follow if anything like this happened. And today was that day.

They were prepared. They would get their boss out on bail ASAP and return to business as usual while Rimouski obliterated anyone who dared testify against him.

Joe reluctantly handed Vinny a thick file. "This is a comprehensive list of people who have dealings with the boss. Find everyone on this list."

"Find them?" Vinny lifted a brow. "That's it?"

"Yep. That's it. If you can find them, they aren't the problem. It's the ones you can't find we need to worry about."

Vinny nodded sharply. "Ah. Got it."

"Rimouski is very powerful, as you well know. Everyone in that file works for him in some capacity. If the police have taken the boss into custody, there's a rat or two. I need to know who those assholes are so we can take them down."

"On it."

Joe watched as Vinny strode from the room. Was there a chance in hell he could find all those people? Joe had no faith, but at least the task would keep Vinny busy and out of Joe's way while he worked on figuring out what to do next to help his boss from behind the scenes.

No one working for Rimouski wanted to see him caught or sent to prison. It would mean their complete ruin. That was one of the aspects of Rimouski's life he had complete control over without saying a word. His men were loyal. Because if they weren't, they would lose everything.

CHAPTER 10

By Tuesday Adriana was frazzled beyond belief. Two days of having Reid drive her around and sticking to her like glue was more than a shifter could tolerate—a shifter who knew the man always in her space was her intended mate. Her damn Honda was even in his garage, but he had balked every time she suggested he let her drive it.

Yesterday Adriana had met with two members of the Arcadian Council. Daunting was a mild word for the encounter. Charles and Laurence had come to Reid's condo. The two of them often handled any matter that took place in or near Calgary. They were serious and distinguished. Powerful. She hadn't found herself afraid of them, but she felt chilled the entire time they spoke.

At over six and a half feet tall, it wasn't that they were larger than most grizzly shifters, but they had an aura about them that made them seem more formidable. And that was a good thing. Adriana simply wanted her and Reid and Nolan to be not dead when this was over.

The council members took notes as Reid gave them the details, and then they left, promising to look into the situation and keep their ears and eyes open. Even though she'd exhaled a long sigh of relief after they left, she was glad they were involved. It gave her peace of mind.

But that was yesterday's drama. Today she needed to call her parents. She'd put it off long enough. Maybe they could help. Maybe they couldn't. Either way, leaving them out of the loop wasn't fair. Every day she waited to speak to them it would get harder and harder to do. Their feelings would eventually be hurt. Especially her mother's.

She waited until evening, sequestered herself in Reid's guest room, and placed the call.

Her mother picked up on the first ring. "Adriana. How are you? I was beginning to think you'd fallen off the face of the earth. You don't usually go this long without calling," she joked.

"Sorry, Mom. I've been...busy." She took a deep breath, intending to continue, but her mother spoke again before she could gather her thoughts.

"I'm not surprised. You always did jump in with both feet when you set your mind to something. It shouldn't shock me to find you deeply involved in school and your studies. I hope you're not trying to do too much, honey."

"Mom."

"Don't even try to convince me you're calm as a cucumber over there in Calgary. I know you better than that. Have you opened your own fashion show yet? Perhaps designed something for the princess of some foreign country?" She giggled.

"Mom," Adriana said with more force, her voice cracking.

"What?" Beth Tarben's voice fell. "Is something wrong?"

"No. Well, yes. I mean, I don't know. Depends on how you look at it."

"Tell me." Now her voice was softer. Kind.

She needed to blurt out the gist and move on. No sense breaking it down into pieces. "I met two men over the weekend. Both of them seem to be my intended mate. I've never been so confused in my life. And I put off telling you because I feel like a freak." There. Done. Not nearly as bad as she'd visualized.

Her mother hesitated a moment, her breath hitching. "You went out with two men?"

"No. Not exactly. I didn't go out with either of them."

"But you like them?"

"Mom, I don't think you're hearing me correctly. I'm quite certain I'm meant to bind with both of them."

"Bind? You can't bind with two people, honey. You must be confused."

Oh, she was confused all right. No denying that fact. "Yeah, I'm super clear on that. And yet, I'm telling you I'm equally attracted to both of them. I could really use your help and support right now. Don't overanalyze this."

"Honey, I'll always support you, no matter what. But I'm not following."

"I met Nolan Osborn Saturday night at his parents' homecoming party. I mean, scratch that, I didn't meet him at all. I scented him from inside the house before he decided not to get out of the car and face me. The following morning I met his best friend, Reid Terrance. I got the same vibe. The same tight feeling in my stomach that insisted he was my mate."

"Wow. I don't even know what to say. Have you seen them again?"

Have I ever. "It's complicated, but the short version is that Nolan is a witness to a huge crime, and the police are keeping him hidden. I've been staying at Reid's place for the past three days. He happens to be a bodyguard."

Her mother inhaled sharply again. "Lord. Why don't you come home?"

"Mom, you know I can't do that. For one thing, I'm in the middle of my semester, and I refuse to let this situation get in my way. For another thing, neither Reid nor Nolan would ever let me do that. They're...overprotective."

"They know you're attracted to both of them?"

"Yes. They're best friends. It wasn't as though I could have kept this a secret. When I'm with either of them, I can't breathe. It's like the air is sucked from my lungs. It's that potent. It's not like I could ask Alton or Austin or even their mates about how they felt when they met since both couples met when they were very young." Adriana let her voice drift off.

Beth sighed. "There's certainly no denying the fact that several grizzly shifters have met lately and known instantly they were fated. Paige and Wyatt are another example. You know I was very young when I met your father, so it's hard to relate, but I can say that moment when I knew was precise and I'll never forget it."

Adriana smiled. "You were fourteen," she remembered.

"Yes. It was as if I met him that moment and hadn't known him prior to that day. He'd known. He says he'd known from a ridiculously young age. But for me, it was a specific instant. That rush of excitement that made my body come alive and a tight knot form in my belly." She sighed.

Adriana knew if she could see her mother, she would find her face filled with the bliss of the memory. She whispered her response. "Well, take that overwhelming rush of excitement and multiply it times two. I know it's crazy. But I know what I'm feeling."

Deep breaths. "Honey, I'm so sorry. I can't imagine the confusion. I don't even know what to say. I've never heard of such a thing. Even though there have been a number of mates meeting and instantly knowing they belonged together lately, none of them met two shifters at once. I've never heard of having to choose."

"Yeah, well lucky for all of them. Fate thinks She's making a funny apparently. I'm just sorry She's doing it with my life. I can't sleep. I'm frustrated. Shaking. Having trouble eating. Can't study. I'm worried. I don't understand why this is happening to me, and I feel like I'm in limbo waiting for the Universe to make Her intentions known with far more clarity.

"Every hour that goes by I think something will change. Every morning I wake up hoping I won't feel the connection to one of them." Adriana sucked in a sob, even though she'd been trying hard to keep herself together while she spoke to her mom. "Meanwhile, I'm also scared out of my mind worrying about which one I will lose this connection to. I don't want to choose, but I can't visualize losing either of them. It's maddening. If I picture no longer having this connection with one or the other, I start to shake. I'm losing my mind."

"Oh, honey. That must be incredibly draining. You want me to come there for a few days? Maybe another set of eyes will help. Maybe if you had someone to talk this out with."

She didn't want to explain to her mother how much danger Nolan thought she was in. Her mother didn't need that added stress. But it also meant she didn't want her mother to come to Calgary. "No. Nothing will change things. It's not like you could talk me out of my attraction to one or the other. It's hard to explain. It's just there. I fear it will never end. It's like I'm stuck in a groundhog day, and I have to get it right before I'm permitted to find out who I'm meant to be with. But why? What did I do to deserve this insane turmoil?" Another sob, this one louder. Tears fell down her face. She hated sharing this with her mom. She hated how torn her mom would feel. Maybe she shouldn't have called.

"Honey, what can I do to help?"

"Could you maybe ask around a bit? See if this has happened to anyone else? Maybe if someone has been through it, they can offer advice or at least let me know how long it took for them to figure out who their real intended mate was."

"Sure. I can do that. Let me speak to your father this evening. See what he thinks. Maybe he knows someone."

"The Osborns said that Wyatt and Isaiah Arthur met several wolf shifters who have had this happen in Montana. But I have to be honest, that doesn't make any sense to me. I don't see how there's a correlation. Who cares how the wolves choose their mate? What matters here is that grizzlies don't operate this way. Not normally." Adriana slumped back against the pillows on her bed, curling onto her side. She could sense another long cry coming on.

Why had she called her mother like this? She'd known it would set her off. She had cried at some point or another every day since Saturday night. She closed herself off physically and emotionally from Reid every evening and let herself feel the emotional overload, silently fighting back the tears, or at least keeping the noisy sobs at bay. The last thing she needed was for Reid to catch wind of her silent turmoil and try to comfort her. She was afraid of where that might lead. She didn't have the willpower to keep him at arm's length if he got in her space.

Besides, she'd put on a brave front so far, trying to convince both men she was stronger than reality. She wasn't willing or ready to let that go yet.

She could sense Reid across the hall from her. His walls were down enough for her to know he was concerned. She hadn't blocked her emotions well while she spoke to her mother. She needed to end this call. "Mom, I need to go. I have a lot of homework."

"Homework? You can study under these circumstance?"

"I don't have a choice. I'm in the middle of my classes. No way am I going to drop out at this point. I find a way to compartmentalize part of every day, pretend this isn't happening to get my work done. It would be worse for me if I didn't have school. Sometimes it seems like that commitment is the only thing keeping me sane."

Her mother gave a soft chuckle. "You call this sane?"

Adriana smiled, wiping her tears off her face with her fingers. "Fair point, but as sane as I can be."

"I'll talk to your father, ask around, see what I can find out. Hang in there. There must be an explanation. You'll figure it out when the time is right."

"Thanks, Mom. I love you. Give Dad my love too."

"I will, honey."

Adriana ended the call and dropped the phone to the mattress, still lying on the bed in a curled ball on her side. She hugged her knees to her chest.

"Adriana? Hon, you're putting off an incredible level of stress. Talk to me." Reid's voice in her head was soothing.

"I'm okay. Promise. Just called my mom. It was...tough. Give me a minute to regroup. I'll be fine."

"I'm sorry, babe. Do you need a shoulder? I'm right across the hall, and yet miles separate us."

"No. I can't deal with you in my space all the time, Reid. And I don't mean that to sound insulting. It's just so stressful. You being in this room would only compound my anxiety. Don't take it personally."

"I get it. I won't come in there, but babe, I need you to know

I'm here for you. Anytime. I don't care what time it is. You can even wake me if you want. Don't ever think you're alone in this. You're not. I'm here. Reach out if you want me to come. Or come to me if you prefer. Don't shut yourself off to deal with this alone."

Suddenly, she needed to face him, at least long enough to make sure he fully understood. She uncurled herself from the ball on her side, swung her legs off the bed, and stood. Two seconds later, she was through the door and across the hall, leaning into the open doorway of Reid's bedroom.

He lifted his gaze, his face lighting up.

She grabbed the door frame. "Don't get all excited. I just wanted to make sure you understood me completely when I told you this."

"Told me what?" He cocked his head to one side. He'd been sitting on his bed against the headboard, a book in his hand which he dropped to his lap.

"You don't get it. You can't. It's not the same for you. I'm sure you spend at least a fraction of every day wondering what the hell is wrong with me. And I don't blame you. You're only attracted to one person. How can I expect you to understand that the person you desire also feels a connection to your best friend? I can't. That's my burden alone. It's a lonely place to exist. I'm tired. But I don't have a girlfriend to chat about this with. And you can't fully grasp it.

"Talking to my mom almost made things worse. She can't get it either. I'm sure she thinks I've lost my mind, and she was placating me. I feel like anyone who finds out will pat me on the back condescendingly and try to figure out a logical explanation for something so illogical it can't be explained away. I get it. I hear myself tell this saga, and it sounds absurd even to my ears."

"Adriana..." There was pain behind his eyes and in his voice. He hated that she was hurting.

She did too. But it wasn't avoidable, and neither Reid nor anyone else could fix it. "Addy."

He lifted a brow. "What?"

"My friends call me Addy." Why had she picked this moment to tell him that?

"But Adriana is such a beautiful name. I love it."

She rolled her eyes as she shoved off the door frame and turned around. Just as fast as she'd appeared in his doorway, she was back in her room with her door shut. Of course he liked her name. It rolled off his tongue like silk. It went straight to her sex every time. Just like when Nolan said it.

They didn't use the same tone, but both men made her panties wet when they spoke her name all the same. She loved it. She didn't know why she felt the need to request that they call her Addy in the first place. It wasn't what she really wanted. Maybe she was testing them. They both passed. As usual.

Dammit. When would something happen to make one man stand out as far less appealing than the other?

She leaned against the door for several moments, trying to catch her breath. She didn't know what had her so on edge this evening. Could have been the chat with her mom or maybe the trip across the hallway to put Reid in her line of sight again. Not her brightest move. She should have remained sequestered.

She didn't easily have the ability to test Nolan on a daily basis, but she could push Reid's buttons. Something had to give one of these days.

Something never did. All she saw every time she looked into Reid's eyes was compassion and empathy. She was right. He didn't fully understand her plight. But she was also wrong. He did the best he could to step into her shoes. He couldn't try harder if he wanted to. He was a saint.

And she was the worst devil imaginable.

Taking a deep breath, she forced herself to put her unimaginable problems on the back burner. She needed to get some work done. She was behind. She had sketches do for her design class in a few days, and she was way behind.

Five minutes later, she sat cross-legged in the center of the bed with her sketch book open and an array of pencils next to her. She closed her eyes, took a deep breath, and visualized what she wanted her next design to entail.

A dress, mid-thigh, cut low between the breasts, loose skirt, filmy, slit up the sides, sexy…

She grabbed a pencil and went to work, her hand flying across the page. Instantly she lost track of time. She didn't know if minutes or hours went by, but she was on her third sketch when she became aware that she was not alone.

She jerked her gaze to the doorway to find Reid standing there, head cocked to one side, brow furrowed.

"Hey," she murmured. "Everything okay?"

"That's what I was going to ask *you*. I was worried. You left my room kinda frustrated, and then I haven't been able to read you since."

"Sorry. I've been in a zone." She held up the drawing, though she had no idea why. He couldn't possibly find it interesting.

He stepped closer, surprising her by taking it from her hands and staring at it closely. "This is amazing," he whispered as he flipped back through several pages. "And then you turn these into real three-dimensional designs?"

"That's the plan." She smiled, feeling a little giddy that he admired her work. Most men would wonder what the point was.

"Let's go," he said as he handed it back, a twinkle in his eyes.

"Go where?" She was shocked. They never went anywhere.

He wiggled his eyebrows. "You'll see." He backed up slowly, challenging her to follow him with a smirk.

Fine. She'd take the bait. She pushed her supplies aside and slid off the edge of the bed. After stuffing her feet in her favorite cute suede ankle boots, she followed him from the room.

He didn't say a word, but he was standing at the door that led downstairs to the garage. "Grab a coat."

Still intrigued, she pulled her coat on over her sweater and headed down the stairs behind him. "Where are we going?" she asked his back.

He spun around at the bottom of the stairs, making her almost crash into him. But his hands were on her waist, steadying her when he spoke, their eyes almost level since she was still two steps from the bottom. "So many questions. Trust me."

"Okay..." Her heart beat faster, partly from him touching her, partly from the look of excitement in his eyes, and partly from the intrigue of whatever he had planned. Anything to break up the monotony that had become her stupid life.

She climbed into the passenger side of the SUV, thinking how insane it was that her own car was also in his garage parked next to his. Even though he hadn't permitted her to use it, she felt like an old married couple having it there, like she lived with him.

Did she?

She watched out the window as he drove, sitting on her palms to keep from fidgeting. They headed away from high-rises and the campus toward the north. Soon they were past the suburbs and driving in a less populated area.

That's when it hit her. She sat up straighter, eyes wide, as she turned to him. "Are we going to run?"

He shot her a grinning glance and winked.

"Oh. My. God. You have no idea how good that sounds. I haven't shifted in weeks. It's so hard to do so in the city. In Silvertip I could shift any day of the week and lope off behind my parents' house. Calgary put an end to that luxury."

"Then it's your lucky day." He set a hand on her thigh and gave a quick squeeze before releasing her to grip the steering wheel. It was enough to send an electric current running up her thigh and across her sex. She shivered, squeezing her legs together.

She spent hours every day fighting the attraction. It was going to be tough keeping him at arm's length while they ran. Shifting was invigorating. It made her feel alive. That scared the hell out of her at the moment.

When he pulled off the highway onto a side road and then off that street onto an even sketchier dirt road, she got excited.

Half of Reid's mouth was lifted when he pulled the car over. "If I had known how energized you would get from the idea of shifting, I would have taken you every day."

She grinned, jumped down from the SUV before he could round the hood, and met him on his side. Before he could react, she grabbed his biceps, lifted onto her toes, and kissed his cheek. "Thank you. I needed this so bad." Stepping back, she closed her eyes, inhaled to ensure they were alone, and let the shift wash over her. Thirty seconds later she was on all fours, pawing at the ground next to him. *What are you waiting for? Let's go,* she communicated.

Reid shook his head as he watched Adriana bolt into the woods. It was clear he'd been correct to assume she needed to shift and run free. Nevertheless, he was shocked by how animated she was. A side of her he'd not yet seen.

He hurried to shift and took off right behind her, working hard to stay in her wake. She was gorgeous in her grizzly form. Her thick brown hair looked to be the same shade in her bear form, equally thick and lush. The brief glimpse he'd gotten of her eyes before she bolted told him she was playful when she shifted. Excitement danced in her brown eyes.

There was no need to run right on her heels. She was safe. There was no other human or shifter in the area. He would be able to scent them. But he didn't like her straying too far from him anyway. He could blame it on a desire to protect her. The truth was far different. He liked to be near her.

The last few days had been a bag of mixed blessings. On the one hand, planting himself within yards of Adriana at all times was sheer torture. Her pheromones made his brain foggy and his cock constantly alert. He had trouble concentrating and never fully relaxed even at night.

But it was more than that. Being with her was a pleasure. He enjoyed her. She was funny and cute and smart and sexy all at the same time. Her scent was intoxicating in human form and made his knees wobbly now that they were in grizzly form. Because he genuinely liked her.

And that scared him to death. Every day he fell harder for her, making him scared out of his mind at the prospect of eventually losing her.

It was painful not having more of her, not being able to

hold her and kiss her and make love to her. Not having her in his bed. Physically painful. But nothing matched the thought of no longer having her in his life at all. He'd give up ever having sex for the promise of keeping her within reaching distance for the rest of his life.

She surprised him by how hard she ran. Pent-up energy had needed an outlet for a long time. A few times she doubled back, literally running circles around him. She was playful like a cub. It was impossible not to smile inside.

When they finally turned back toward the car, her gait slowing, he stared at her from an angle. He was falling hard. He was going to get hurt.

Shocking Joe to the core, Vinny showed up at his office again after only two days of searching. "Found a potential problem, Mr. Stringer."

"Really. So fast?"

Vinny narrowed his gaze.

Perhaps it was time to give him the benefit of the doubt. "What'd you find?"

"I should have worded that differently. It's what I *didn't* find." He handed Joe a piece of paper. "Nolan Osborn. Accountant. Met with Rimouski on Friday. Hasn't been back to his house since I started looking for him on Sunday."

Joe sat up straighter. "You're sure?"

"Yes. Kept a close eye on his place around the clock. The man hasn't been there."

"Fuck." If that was the truth, Joe needed to find Osborn as soon as possible. If he knew something and already went to the police, it would make things that much harder. Not impossible. Just harder. "Can you find him?"

"Of course."

God, he hoped Vinny didn't disappoint him. If he even smelled like he wasn't on the up and up, Joe would have him removed from society without even consulting with the boss. Joe narrowed his gaze. "What's your secret, Vinny?"

Vinny frowned, his gaze never wavering. "No idea what you mean, Mr. Stringer."

Joe chuckled. "Oh, I think you do. To be this close to Rimouski's inner circle after only a few months on his payroll, you either have to be sucking his cock, or you know something. And since Rimouski is currently unavailable for blowjobs, I'm going with the latter."

Vinny's gaze narrowed more than usual. "I don't know anything special, Mr. Stringer. I'm just a guy the boss hired to work for him."

Joe chuckled again. "Yeah, well I've got a beachfront property in Saskatchewan I'm selling if you're interested in that too."

Vinny's brow furrowed, his aggravation palpable in the room. "I won't let you down. It's in my best interest as well as yours to get the boss out of custody. Why would I jeopardize my job?"

Why would he? That was the million dollar question. Joe sincerely hoped he never found out.

CHAPTER 11

By the weekend, Reid was slowly losing his mind. He was cohabitating with a woman he was certain was meant to be his mate, and they had spent six days skirting around each other. It was unnatural, and he wasn't sure how much more of it he could take.

He had intentionally not even kissed her. Even though he knew Nolan had kissed her, he hadn't taken advantage of the opportunity yet. *Yet* being the operative word.

It was a two-sided problem. For one, if he closed the distance between them and let his mouth settle over hers, he didn't think he would have the willpower to stop at just a kiss. But more importantly, he was afraid after he let his mouth touch hers, his level of arousal in her presence would shoot up sky high and put him in a worse predicament than he was already in.

He knew Adriana was walking on the same eggshells. Half the time she even looked a little frustrated with him, as if she would prefer he make a move. Maybe to save her from having to do it.

They were sitting at the kitchen table eating the

amazing enchiladas she'd cooked when she suddenly wiped her lips with her napkin, pushed her plate away, and set her elbows on the table. *Shit.*

"This thing isn't as powerful for you."

He flinched. What was she talking about? "What do you mean?"

"I mean your unbelievable willpower leads me to believe you aren't as interested in me."

He dropped his fork, not intentionally. It clattered to the plate. "Are you insinuating I'm not as attracted to you as Nolan is? Or not as attracted to you as you are to me?"

"Me. I'm talking about me. I can't judge Nolan. I've only met him once, and it was like ten years ago at this rate. This has been the longest week of my life."

"You and me both." He reached across the table to grab her hand and held it between them. "You're wrong. I'm dying a slow death."

She lifted a brow. "Really?" The word was laced with sarcasm. She jerked her hand free and pushed from the table to pace back and forth in front of the sliding glass doors, the darkness of night behind her. "You drive me to school. You wait outside my classes like a stalker. You sit with me in the evenings while I study or watch TV. And then you make a hasty retreat to your bedroom. It looks so easy."

"Easy?" His voice rose. "You think it looks easy?" He scooted his chair back, but he didn't stand. He was afraid of how he might react if he approached her.

She made a deep frustrated sound that came from her chest and turned to face the window. "I can't take it anymore."

"Take what?" He stood slowly, knowing it was a mistake.

"The stress. The pressure. The scent of you all over this

condo. The constant consuming need to touch you." She set her forehead on the glass and moaned. "I have to get out of here before I lose my mind, Reid. The only relief I get is while I'm in class, and it's only marginal then because I can still scent you in the hallway."

"And you think it's not the same for me?" His voice rose. He hoped he didn't sound angry, but he wanted there to be no doubt he agreed with her. He felt every bit as intensely as she did.

She shook her head against the window. "No. I don't."

He took two long steps toward her back, and then he plastered her body between his front and the window before he could stop himself. He grabbed her hands, threaded his fingers between hers, and lifted them up to flatten them on the glass above her head.

She sucked in a sharp breath.

His cock had been stiff for days, even when he was sleeping, even right after he masturbated in the bed or the shower, even when she was in class. But now...pressed against the small of her back, it was about to explode.

He lowered his face to bury it in her thick hair, inhaling her shampoo. He'd smelled the faint vanilla scent all week and kept himself from getting high on it. However, at her inference, his control snapped. He nudged her hair out of the way and set his lips on her ear.

She shuddered, a small moan escaping her lips. Good. He could smell her arousal. It was the same thing he'd scented all week, but stronger. Not because he was closer, but because she was more aroused.

He teased her earlobe with tiny touches of his tongue before biting down on it gently and then releasing it. "I've never been so fucking turned on in my life. One minute with you sends my arousal higher than all other sexual encounters I've had combined. And that's without touching you."

She whimpered, tugging her hands slightly. But he didn't release her. He wasn't about to release her. He'd snapped completely now. She'd challenged him, and he was going to give her what she wanted. She would not doubt his attraction to her again.

He kept talking even though her body went limp and he had to hold her up with his torso against her. "I can't sleep. I can't think. It's hard to swallow. I've jacked off in the shower twice a day since Sunday. I lie in bed flipping around because you're across the hallway and not in my bed."

She opened her mouth, but he stopped her.

"No. Listen to me. Don't talk now. When your shower runs, my damn vision blurs knowing you're naked in that hall bathroom and I've never seen your sexy body. When you lick your lips or bite that bottom one or purse them or even talk, I'm mesmerized. When you stand in my kitchen in your bare feet cooking, it's all I can do to keep from swiping the food onto the floor and flattening you on the island."

Another whimper. And her pussy was so wet. He didn't need to touch it to know. He could smell it.

"I want to strip every inch of clothing off you, spread you open, and taste that sweet cream always dripping from your pussy. It's like a drug. And I'm an addict." He took a deep breath. "So no. You're wrong. I'm far more attracted to you than you can imagine. I've been exerting a level of self-control I didn't know I had. But I'm kinda done. Now I need your lips on mine."

She started to turn around, but he held her firmly, his chest pressing hers against the window. He could see her hooded expression in the glass. She was aroused like a woman in the throes of passion who was about to come.

Several deep breaths. He needed some semblance of control, or he would go too far.

She twisted again. This time he let her, releasing her hands so she could wiggle around against his body. And then his cock was lodged against her belly, and her hands were on his hips. Her eyes were dilated. Her mouth open.

He cupped her face, angled her head slightly to one side, and claimed her mouth in the way he'd dreamed of for six days. He didn't ease into the kiss. He took. He licked the seam of her lips to demand entrance, and she readily gave it up for him. If he thought her pheromones all over his house were bad, nothing compared to tasting her. His cock throbbed at the idea of tasting her all down her body. He would probably die if he had the chance to lick her clit or drive his tongue into her pussy.

He wouldn't do anything like that. Not tonight. Not in the near future. Possibly never. But he wanted to be absolutely sure she knew how much he burned for her. After tonight, there would be no doubt.

As he kissed her, he knew he wanted one more piece of her. He wanted to feel her softness beneath his palms. When her hands flattened on his back and smoothed upward until she wrapped them around his neck, he released her face to trail his own hands down her sides.

The moment he cupped her breasts, she moaned into his mouth. And then she shocked him by sucking his tongue. He wasted no time grazing his thumbs over her nipples, feeling the hardness of those peaks through her thin shirt and bra. One of the many damnably sexy shirts she'd worn all week that fit her perfectly and showed off her assets because she'd designed them herself and had an eye for what was attractive on every fucking body type. Today's selection was a dark brown blouse that had forced his attention to her breasts several times.

She rose onto her tiptoes, her mouth no longer actively participating in the kiss.

Yes. Damn. Yes.

To drive his point home—though he had no idea what he thought he needed to prove to her—he pinched her nipples between his thumbs and forefingers.

She gasped into his mouth and broke the kiss, panting, writhing in his hold.

He slowly released the pinch, smoothing his hands away from her breasts to hold her upright at her sides.

She lowered her forehead to his chest, her eyes closed. Hiding?

He set his chin on her head and breathed deeply for a long time, trying to catch his breath from the hottest sexual encounter of his life. No clothes were removed. No groping below the waist. No sex at all. And yet, he'd never been more turned on with any woman.

Yeah, this had probably been a mistake because it would hurt that much worse when Nolan came out of hiding and claimed her. Reid had no idea why Fate was torturing him like this. She was a cruel bitch. But he also knew in his heart this was a fight he would not win.

He would not even attempt to win.

She was his. No doubt about it. In the absence of another person also claiming her, he would have bound to her last Sunday before darkness descended. But the Universe had something else in mind. He only hoped he would one day understand Her freaky reasons.

◈

Adriana couldn't breathe. No matter how many times she inhaled, it didn't seem like enough oxygen filled her lungs. She also couldn't face Reid's gaze. It would destroy her resolve.

It would destroy *her*.

She shouldn't have taunted him. What was she thinking? Had she truly been concerned about how much he felt for her? More likely she'd simply needled him into taking things to the next level because that's what she wanted. Perhaps she'd subconsciously absolved herself of any guilt by forcing him to take the next step so she didn't have to.

She got what she asked for. And then some.

For as horny as she'd been since moving into Reid's condo, she'd had no idea how much worse it would be if they kissed. How was she going to manage now? Tonight? Tomorrow? She grabbed his T-shirt in her fists and wadded the material against his abs. Half of her wanted to pound into him with those fists. Damn him for making her feel so much more. The other half wanted to hold him more firmly against her so he would never let her go.

His hands worked their way up her back until they fisted in her hair in a similar fashion to how she fisted his shirt. Did he have the same thoughts? Hopefully, he didn't want to punch her, though she couldn't blame him if he did. Gradually, his hands flattened, tangled in her hair but holding her tight. "You gonna doubt me again?"

"No." She shook her head against his chest, loving the feel of his rock-hard pecs against her cheeks. Strength. Protection. The very things she fought against. "I'm sorry."

He chuckled. Thank God. "I'm not."

She lifted her face. She couldn't hide forever. She knew a flush covered her cheeks. She was embarrassed about her outburst and the way she'd completely lost all her faculties in his arms. She forced a smile. No, it came naturally.

His fingers, threaded in her hair, gave a tug, forcing her head to tip back more. "Woman…"

She grinned wider.

And then his phone rang.

It was on the kitchen table, but the ringtone was the one he'd set for Stanton. They both froze for a moment, and then Reid let go of her and spun around to take the call.

Adriana lurched forward too, grabbing the back of a kitchen chair to brace herself.

Reid didn't even lift the phone. He simply tapped the screen and put Stanton on speaker. "Stanton?"

"Good. I caught you. Is Adriana with you?" He sounded winded. Out of breath. Scared…

"She's right here. We're on speaker." Thank God Reid didn't take the call in private and try to hide anything from her. She would have killed him.

"Nolan's been compromised. He reached out to me telepathically. He's on the run, and he left his phone behind."

Adriana froze. Her body tightened with fear. *Oh God. Please God. Don't let this be happening.*

"What happened?" Reid asked.

"He was in his hotel room when three men approached his door. He scented them and grew concerned when they didn't keep moving down the hall. When he looked out the peephole, he knew they were after him. They looked like thugs. One of them was holding a keycard. Nolan panicked."

"Shit. Please tell me he got away." Reid flattened his palms on the table and leaned in closer, his stress palpable in the room.

Adriana was silently freaking out as she waited for Stanton to continue.

"Lucky for him, he had already made a plan. His room was on the third floor. It was a smaller, out-of-the-way hotel somewhere. He didn't tell me where. But there was a fire escape, and he immediately used it to get out of the building. Whoever was at the door obviously didn't put anyone outside the hotel on the ground because Nolan evaded them and ran."

"Fuck," Reid shouted, lifting one hand to reach for Adriana and draw her closer.

She hadn't realized how badly she'd been trembling until he tucked her into his side and literally held her upright with his arm around her waist.

"Where is he now?"

"On the run. He communicated all this to me as he grabbed a taxi. He wants you to pick him up."

Reid pushed off the table at that declaration and looked down at Adriana.

No way in hell was she going to be left behind. She could read the panic in his eyes as he considered both his horrible options. He would never leave her unattended. But he also didn't want to put her in harm's way. And there was no time to make alternative plans.

"I'm going to text you the address. He's going to have the taxi drop him off several blocks from his location."

"Getting in the SUV now." Reid released Adriana slowly, seeming to be unsure if she could stand on her own.

Maybe a moment or two ago he would have been right, but now her adrenaline had kicked into high gear. She raced across the room to grab their coats while Reid picked up the phone. She led the way down the stairs to the garage two steps at a time while Nolan continued to listen to Stanton.

The man's next words made Adriana stop dead at the bottom of the stairs with her hand on the doorknob. "Reid, there's something else."

"What?"

"Nolan believes a shifter is involved."

"Shit."

"Yes. He'll explain, but be careful."

"You know I will."

Adriana yanked the door open and rushed to the passenger side of the SUV while Reid climbed into the driver's seat. Seconds later they were on the street driving too fast while the GPS barked out instructions.

She put her seatbelt on as they rounded the first corner and held on to the handle above the door with a firm grip, her other hand braced against the dash.

The woman in the GPS indicated they were ten minutes away from their destination. Thank God. Adriana wasn't sure she could survive a long trip. Her nerves were shot as it was.

Friday night traffic in Calgary was dense. Every turn took too long. Every red light was excruciating.

"Where are we going?" Adriana asked. "This area doesn't look safe."

Reid nodded. "It's intentional. I know exactly where we're going."

"How?"

"I've been there before."

She shivered, not wanting to ask why. The answer would probably make her lose her dinner. She scanned the area closely as they approached, needing to see Nolan before she would truly believe he was safe. What if someone followed him?

Suddenly, Reid pulled over in front of an abandoned building with a large awning that protected a deep entry cove. He had barely come to a stop before disengaging the locks as Nolan rushed from the dark corner and yanked the back door open. In less than a heartbeat, he was in the car, and Reid was peeling away from the curb.

Adriana twisted in her seat to see him. This was only the second time they'd been in the same place in person. She drank him in. Other than the fact that his hair was a bit messy on top, from hand combing it most likely, he didn't look like a crazed man on the run. He wore a brown leather jacket, jeans, and loafers.

Shockingly, he appeared far calmer than she felt. He reached over the seat and grabbed her shoulder. "Take a breath, babe. I'm fine."

Adriana inhaled deeply. She hadn't realized she'd been holding her breath.

He smiled warmly and turned his attention toward Reid. "I figured you'd know exactly where I would be."

Adriana glanced at Reid. He had known. "How?"

Reid nodded, his eyes on the road as he drove nearly too fast to get away from the area. "I hid a client there once for several hours. Nolan and I joked that we'd remember the spot if either of us were ever in a bind."

There was nothing to joke about today, but she was certainly glad the two of them had had that conversation. It kept Nolan safe tonight.

"Is your grandpa's cabin still habitable?" Nolan asked Reid.

Reid took the next right turn, leading away from the city. "I haven't been there in a few weeks, but I assume it's fine. Water and electric are still on."

"At this point, water and electric would be a luxury. I'll settle for walls and a roof."

Reid chuckled. *Chuckled*. How could he find even a morsel of humor in this outing?

She turned to look at him, shaking. "I thought you were from Ottawa?"

He nodded again. "My parents moved there when I was a baby when my dad took a job there. Both of their parents were from this area of the country. None of my ancestors are living now, unfortunately, but my grandfather left me his cabin. I love having this little piece of him."

It was unusual for shifters to die so young. "You've lost all four grandparents?" Three of hers were still living north of here.

"Yeah. My parents were older when they had me after years of infertility. I was a surprise." He smiled. His memories were fond. She hoped she met his parents one day. She would if she bound herself to him. But if she didn't... She wrapped her arms around her middle, the chill back.

Nolan squeezed her shoulder again. "You're shaking. Come back here."

She glanced at the road, wondering if that was a wise choice with Reid driving so fast.

Reid pulled over to the side of the street, surprising her. "Go on. Be quick."

She unbuckled her seatbelt and climbed over the seat as ungracefully as humanly possible.

Nolan grabbed her waist to help her as she nearly fell into his lap. Apparently, that was his goal anyway because he angled her so that she indeed sat sideways across him and then nodded at Reid. "Keep driving."

He cupped her face. "I'm fine."

"You're not fine." Her voice was too high pitched. Shaky. "Men were after you. What if they'd broken into the room? What if you hadn't been able to go out a window?"

"But I was, and I'm okay now."

"Except people are still looking for you." She couldn't calm her voice. She leaned back a few inches to glance down at his body, half expecting to find him missing some parts.

He chuckled. "I didn't lose a limb, babe. I'm in one piece."

"For how long? This is too dangerous."

He sobered. "It's not ideal, and I hate that you're mixed up in it, but the less chivalrous side of me has never been so glad to see anyone in my life."

"You mean me, right?" Reid joked as he entered the highway heading west.

"Both of you."

"So what's the plan? You going to hide out at the cabin indefinitely?" Reid asked.

"No. But I'd like to let the authorities stew for a while before I contact them. I'd also like to know how the hell someone found me. I haven't left the hotel room in five days. I even cracked the window a few times thinking I might need some air to counteract the carbon dioxide build up," he teased, giving her a squeeze and a wink. "That's how I found the fire escape and knew the window wasn't painted shut. Thank God."

"Your dad said there was a shifter involved," Reid said.

Nolan sighed, leaning his head back against the headrest. "I'm sure of it. He wasn't one of the three men standing at my door, but a shifter has been hanging around for two days. I have scented him in the hallway several times even though he always continued to walk by without stopping and didn't seem to have a room on the same floor."

"Did you make contact with him?"

"Hell, no. I blocked that son of a bitch."

Adriana flinched at his outburst.

"Scenting an occasional shifter in downtown Calgary isn't super uncommon, but they don't usually stay in hotels for no good reason, and I'd bet my last dollar this one wasn't a guest of the hotel."

"You didn't recognize the scent I take it."

"Nope. Never smelled this man before."

"So what's the plan?" Reid asked.

"Hide out for a few days in the cabin and then use your phone to call the police and let them know I'm alive."

"You still willing to trust the cops?" Reid asked.

"You see another alternative?"

Adriana wrapped her hand around Nolan's and held on as if he were a life force while she let these two hash out the plan.

"We could stay at the cabin indefinitely until the trial gets closer. It's certainly safer than the city. No one's going to find you there. Hell, it's so remote even I have trouble locating it, and it's been in my family for fifty years. It's a bitch to locate in the dark."

Nolan rolled his eyes and winked at Adriana, making her stomach flutter. How could he be playful at a time like this? "Don't even try to convince me of that shit. You could get there on foot blindfolded. I've even been with you when we arrived in grizzly form."

"So we stay there," Reid declared as if it was settled.

Nolan shook his head, his gaze penetrating her so deeply she licked her lips. He tucked a lock of hair behind her ear. "Can't do that. Adriana has classes. You have a life."

"You might have noticed I don't have much of a life right now. It revolves around Adriana and now keeping your ass alive since it would seem the law enforcement in Calgary is incapable."

"Hey," Adriana quipped. "I resent that statement." She

leaned forward and reached with one hand to bop the side of Reid's head.

"I didn't say I wasn't enjoying every moment of your company. I just meant I have no other place to be right now."

"Awesome, but I have classes on Monday morning, and I need to get some homework done before then. I didn't exactly grab my backpack on the way out the door. So, my hands are tied. I'll need to return." She decided to taunt him with her next sentence. "Feel free to stay with Nolan in the cabin though. I'll be fine on my own. You two could probably use a bonding weekend."

Reid laughed. "She's so cute when she tries to be manipulative."

Ignoring him, Adriana gave a little push against Nolan's chest, needing to get off his lap and buckle into an actual seat. She tried to tell herself she was concerned about her safety, but the truth was, she was more concerned about her sanity if she remained sitting on Nolan's lap. He enveloped her. His scent, his heartbeat, his breath, his touch, the firmness of his chest and arms. The erection pressing into her thigh.

Besides, she was frustrated with her botched efforts to remain in a state of fear and unease that was slowly being replaced by arousal and desire in this most inopportune moment. Who got horny ten seconds after rescuing someone from imminent danger?

The worst part of all was there was no way for her, as a shifter, to hide her arousal from either man. And Reid was liable to drive off the road at the way her body was reacting to his best friend's presence.

"Sit still, Adriana," Nolan whispered, gripping her hips. Did he have any other tone in his repertoire besides authoritative? In this case, she was even more frustrated because when he made demands like that, her nipples jumped to attention. What the hell was wrong with her? She wasn't the sort of woman who liked to be bossed around. She'd made that perfectly clear on so many occasions. Except every time he made a demand, she reacted contrary to reason.

She even stopped moving when what she should have done was squirm even more until he agreed to release her into a seat of her own. But she liked being on his lap. She didn't want to like it. It was making her uncomfortable in front of the man who'd plastered her against the sliding door in his condo less than an hour ago and chased her brain cells from her head with the most potent kiss of her life.

Not that she had a giant list of kisses to compare it to.

"Your mind is racing," Nolan whispered in her ear, his lips so close he made her shiver.

"You make me unable to think," she retorted.

"And you're sure you could think better if I let you off my lap?"

She sighed. He was right. But her discomfort had more to do with the fact that Reid could see, hear, and smell every single detail. What kind of woman would let a man fondle her like this so soon after having her toes curled by another man? She'd lost her mind.

Other than a stiffness and slightly closed-off connection coming from Reid, he didn't seem angry. Frustrated maybe, but not angry. Insanity.

The testosterone inside the SUV was potent and making it hard to breathe. She was literally growing faint. Or maybe that was from the crash after her adrenaline rush. Either way, she relaxed into Nolan's grip and leaned her cheek against his shoulder. If he was going to insist on holding her all the way to the cabin, she didn't feel the need to make it easier on him.

Resting her lips close to the crook of his neck would serve as a constant reminder of his need to bind to her. Right in the sweet spot. And she knew she was hitting it with every breath because the table turned and Nolan was the one squirming now.

CHAPTER 12

"Adriana, wake up."

Someone was gently shaking her shoulders. Her neck was stiff. Where was she? She blinked her eyes open and remembered she was on Nolan's lap with Reid driving to some cabin. Except the SUV wasn't moving anymore.

"We're here."

She sat up straight, wincing at the tightness in her muscles. How long had she been asleep? "Where's here?"

"Cabin in the Canadian Rockies. Only about a half hour south of Silvertip. We'll be safe here."

For how long?

The passenger door opened and Reid leaned into the SUV to tuck his arms under her knees and back. She squealed when he lifted her out of the car and cradled her against his chest. "Put me down. Jeez. I can walk."

He continued to stride toward the small cabin she could barely see through the darkness. No wonder Reid had joked about having trouble finding it. It was extremely remote. Trees surrounded it. As her superior shifter vision adjusted to the night, she could see that the foliage

149

surrounding the cabin was overgrown. The road leading to it was more of a dirt path. And the structure itself was as unobtrusive with nature as it could get, built out of logs that came from the local evergreen trees. She realized as they got closer it was an A-frame.

She couldn't believe she'd slept through however long the last leg of the trip had taken on the dirt path up the mountain. She must have been totally out.

Nolan passed both of them to open the door, and Reid set his hand on the back of her head as he entered to ensure she didn't bang it on the frame. Did the two of them think they could win her over with points for chivalry? Maybe she needed two lists—one to account for all the times they ordered her around and another to keep track of the times they were gallant.

Instead of depositing her on her feet when they entered, he crossed the room and set her on a sofa.

She jerked her gaze around. The cabin was quaint. Cozy. It lacked a female touch. The entire inside was one room. Minimalistic. Small table and chairs. Worn older sofa, but not uncomfortable. Fireplace. The kitchen area in one corner was simple too. Oven, stove, refrigerator, sink. Nothing beyond the basics. This cabin was a blank slate. A decorator's nightmare...or dream.

Nolan headed back outside. Why?

Reid followed. A moment later they came back in with several grocery bags. "When did you go shopping?"

Nolan chuckled. "You *did* sleep hard in the car." He winked at her. "Reid ran into a store a ways back to grab a few supplies."

Impressive. She didn't usually sleep that soundly. Then again, she hadn't slept well in over a week. Between stressing about these two men and her classes, she was exhausted.

Reid headed straight for the fireplace and crouched down. "It's cold in here, but it's small. It'll heat up quickly."

She glanced around again. Where were they going to sleep? And then something caught her eye, and she lifted her gaze. There was a loft behind her. A ladder led to the platform above the kitchen. It looked like it extended about halfway across the main floor. There had to be a bed up there.

Reid turned to glance at her as soon as he had a flame lit under a carefully constructed pile of logs. "My grandfather built this over fifty years ago." He smiled warmly. "He liked to tease that he needed a place to get away from my grandmother's nagging. But we all knew he was full of shit. He adored my grandmother."

"That's so nice. I'm glad you have this piece of him. It's special," she said as she shrugged out of her coat.

He pushed to his feet as the fire caught and headed toward her. "I'll admit, it's rustic, and not many women come here, but it's shelter. Once the heat kicks on, we won't be cold at least."

"I think it's perfect. No way anyone will find us here either." She glanced at Nolan as he finished emptying the bags of groceries.

He tucked a few items into the small refrigerator and turned around. "I'm exhausted. I haven't slept well in a week. I could lie down on the floor and be out immediately."

Reid faced his friend. "You two take the bed in the loft. I'll sleep on the couch."

Adriana stiffened. Share a bed with Nolan? Was Reid crazy? "I'll take the couch," she declared.

Reid chuckled. "Not a chance. First of all, I'm not in the habit of sleeping with Nolan. And second of all, no way would we leave you down here alone."

She rolled her eyes. "This overprotective thing again? We're in the middle of nowhere. No one is going to find us here."

"True, but I never take chances." He pointed toward the corner of the room under the loft. "There's a bathroom there. It's small, but it has running water and heat."

Adriana pushed off the couch and headed that direction, though half of her wanted to tell him she didn't need the bathroom just to be defiant. It would have been a lie.

She had nothing with her. Not even a purse. So she couldn't do more than splash water on her face. There was a cup in the corner of the vanity with several unopened toothbrushes. Nice. It made all the difference. She felt slightly human after that small luxury.

Nolan followed after her and then he returned, set a hand on her back, and led her to the ladder.

Nerves set in that had calmed while she slept in the car. His face was too close to her butt as she climbed. Thank God she'd worn her favorite, most comfortable, stylish jeans at least. If she'd been wearing a skirt or dress, Nolan would be seeing far more than a denim-covered ass.

She inhaled. The cabin was filling with both men's pheromones to confuse her. And now she was going to sleep in the same bed with Nolan? Such a bad idea.

She wasn't sorry to get some time with him, however. She'd only spent a few hours in his presence one time. She'd spent a week with Reid. Flashes of some sort of dating game show flitted through her mind—one in which she was the prize, and she'd narrowed her male selection down to two men.

Except that was reality TV, and this was…reality. A very warped reality.

If Nature intended for her to choose, She was going to

have to make things a lot clearer because after a week, Adriana was only certain of one thing—she was still equally attracted to two men.

Reid spoke from down below as they stepped into the loft. "There're clean sheets folded on the bed. I usually bring clean and take the dirty to swap them out each time I'm up here."

The space was only large enough for the queen-sized bed, a dresser, and a bedside table. Luckily it had a railing, or she feared she might fall off in the middle of the night. The only spot where Nolan could stand upright was the center of the A-frame. Even Adriana had to duck as she got too close to the walls.

Nolan kicked off his loafers, pulled his long-sleeved navy shirt over his head, and surprised her by tugging her toward him as he sat heavily on the edge of the bed. But that wasn't all. He kept falling backward, drawing her with him until she landed on his chest. His bare chest. His muscular, sexy, bare chest.

She gasped but tried not to make a noise. Reid was only yards away without walls separating them. He would miss nothing. At the very least they needed to be quiet—so he could sleep.

Nolan slid her to his side, flattening her onto her back. He lifted onto an elbow and stared down at her face. His other hand reached to brush her hair off her forehead, and then he set his palm on her belly.

She stared at him, unsure what to do or think or feel except this surge of arousal that consumed her. Was it because he was so dominating? Because that annoyed her.

He smiled and opened a silent communication just between the two of them. *"You're so beautiful. I love it when you're flustered. When I catch you off balance."*

She swallowed. *"Well, you accomplished that goal."* She realized he always would—if she chose him.

His palm smoothed up her body, boldly pressing the space between her breasts until he reached her chin. He held it steady, staring into her eyes. *"I want to kiss you."*

"Okay." She was powerless. She craved his lips on hers more than she craved her next breath.

He lowered his mouth and tipped his head to one side to seal their lips.

The moment he made contact, she lost all ability to think. The world shrank to just Nolan and his soft lips, the way he licked the seam of hers, the way he held her chin between his fingers, the way he leaned closer until her breast was pressed against his pecs.

Her nipples pebbled. A restlessness climbed up her spine, making her squirm. She wanted to twist her body, so they more completely lined up. But he seemed to know that, and he stopped her with an elbow against her chest between her swollen breasts.

So controlling. She clenched her sex, knowing she was wet and he could smell her arousal through her jeans.

She could smell his too.

When he lifted his top leg and nestled it between hers, she gasped, unable to continue participating in the kiss. His penis was hard and thick and pressed against her thigh. He leaned into her more fully until his thigh rocked against the V of her legs.

A whimper escaped her lips, and her eyes flew open when Nolan covered her mouth with his hand. "Shhh," he mouthed, a twinkle in his eye.

She held his gaze while his leg moved between hers, parting them farther and applying more force against her sex. She'd been aroused a lot in the last week. Most of the time in the last seven days, but never as thoroughly as she was now. She grabbed his forearm with her free hand, the one that had been gripping the pile of sheets at her side.

They hadn't made the bed yet. They were lying on the comforter, but the sheets were next to her. She tried to concentrate on that fact and pictured herself putting them on the mattress—stretching the bottom one to tuck in the corners. Shaking out the top sheet…

His hand moved from her mouth to her breast, molding it through her shirt, mimicking Reid's actions from earlier in the evening. She loved the blouse she wore. It was a dark chocolate brown, and it hung loosely down her arms but fit snuggly across her chest. The material was incredibly delicate and thin, however, which for the second time that night provided her no protection against wandering hands.

Her eyes slid shut as her mouth fell open wide. Holy shit. She totally lost control of every limb and even her torso. Her body was his to control. And he was doing so brilliantly.

When his hand slid from her breast to her belly, his fingers touching the exposed skin between her shirt and her jeans, she nearly screamed. She clamped her mouth shut and shoved at his chest. *"You have to stop. I can't…"*

"Can't what?" he asked, his voice teasing in her head as he removed his hand and planted it on the bed next to her. His leg was still nestled against her sex, making it hard for her to speak even silently.

"Think."

As she blinked, he leaned forward and kissed her lips again, gently, without his tongue. And then he grabbed her hand, threaded their fingers together, and lifted it over her head to press into the mattress. *"Thinking is overrated."*

Her chest rose and fell with every deep breath.

"Damn, you're sexy." His gaze searched her face. *"I've barely touched you, and you're so close to orgasm I can smell it."*

"Barely touched me?" By her judgment, he'd touched every single inch of her at the same time.

He smiled. *"Your chin? An inch of skin across your stomach? Your lips?"*

He was right. In a way. But also not. *"Seriously? You think a little cotton and denim is keeping me from feeling your touch?"*

"Mmm." He kissed her nose next, and then her cheek. *"Five days. Five long days. I thought maybe I had imagined our connection."*

She hadn't been sure either. They'd spoken on the phone every night, but it wasn't the same. She knew the connection was there, but it was harder and harder to focus on while she lived day in and day out with another man she was equally attracted to. The very man who had kissed the sense out of her a few hours ago in his condo, making her head spin just as much as Nolan.

She shuddered. This was so wrong. Wasn't it? How could a woman be so totally attracted to two men at the same time—so enamored that she would stoop so low as to make out with one while the other was yards away?

"I need air. I can't breathe." She tugged her fingers free and pushed on his chest to get him to lean back. Scrambling out of his reach, she pushed herself to sit against the wall.

She was half surprised he permitted her to withdraw, perhaps even a little disappointed. What would it feel like to allow him to take things further?

She wrapped her arms around her body as she shivered. The thought of having sex with him—with either of them —shook her back to the present. She wasn't ready for that step and certainly not now while she was entertaining the concept of a relationship with both of them.

She wasn't the type of woman who would sleep with them first and then decide. It didn't work that way in her world. She hadn't saved herself for twenty-three years just to fuck two guys and then pick one.

Who was she kidding? She hadn't intentionally saved herself for any man. It had just happened that way. She'd never met anyone worthy of that piece of her. She wasn't some sort of prude who thought sex should be shared with only one person for her entire life. It just happened. Every time she dated someone, she tried to feel more… something…in their presence, but she never did. She'd kissed men, but the spark was never there.

Until now. Until the spark insisted on being there for two men. She couldn't keep this up. It wasn't fair to either of them. She needed to choose. Soon. Before she hurt them. And herself.

Nolan pulled himself up to sit next to her against the wall. He took her hand in his and lifted it to kiss her knuckles. *"You're thinking so hard."*

"Yeah. It's difficult not to with Reid downstairs. He isn't stupid."

"No. He's not. But he's had you for five days. I'm at a disadvantage. The scale is tipped in his direction by default. I'm sure that's why he graciously sent us up here tonight. I'm not sure I would have been man enough to turn you over to him if the roles were reversed."

She lifted her face to Nolan's. *"You've had more intimate contact with me than he has."*

His eyes widened, and his mouth fell open. *"Seriously? I thought… I mean, I assumed."*

"I'm not going to say it was easy. It was the hardest thing I've ever done. Him too I assume. But he's your friend, and I bet in the back of his mind he feels like it's unfair to take advantage of your isolation to home in on me."

Nolan cringed. *"Like I'm doing to him now."*

She reached across his body to touch his cheek with

two fingers. "I didn't mean to imply... That came out wrong," she whispered out loud. "I just didn't want you to think we'd spent the last week rolling around in bed. I've been in his guest room. He's been in his room. He didn't even kiss me until this evening." She hoped her voice was low enough not to carry to Reid's ears, but she wanted to be sure Nolan was super clear with no mistaking her tone or meaning.

He reached for her fingers and cupped her hand against his face. "I don't deserve you," he whispered.

She smiled. "I don't deserve to be in this position at all. But I am. And I have to deal with it."

"You're right. I'm sorry. I've spent all week feeling sorry for myself without considering how you felt."

"No need to apologize. I'll be the first to admit you have the worst end of this stick. It's enough to drive me insane, but I can't imagine being in your shoes. Helpless and isolated."

Nolan scooted back down the bed, pulling her alongside him. When he was flat on his back, he tucked her against his side and held her hand against his chest. "Sleep, Adriana."

She silently giggled at his high-handedness, as if she could possibly obey his command.

He tipped his head toward her and lifted a brow. Did he think that reprimand would bring her in line?

She smiled, still laughing in her mind as she settled her cheek against his bare chest and took deep breaths. It didn't seem possible that she would be able to fall asleep, but after several minutes, she lost the battle and slid into dreamland.

CHAPTER 13

Reid had one forearm thrown over his eyes where he lay on his back on the couch, trying desperately to ignore the two people in the bed above him. The sun was up, its rays stretching across the cabin through the window on one side of the little structure. He had spent half the night restlessly flopping around before finally getting a few hours' sleep.

Adriana had been the first to doze off in the loft. He'd felt her sliding until he knew she was unconscious. Nolan had lain awake for a long time after that, but Reid didn't communicate with him. He'd allowed the man his silence the same way he appreciated Nolan doing the same for him.

After a few minutes, Reid felt Nolan moving around and sat up as his friend climbed down the ladder. He knew Nolan's objective was to let Adriana sleep. And Reid knew better than Nolan how badly she needed it. He stood and pointed at the door.

Nolan nodded, and they slipped outside without

making a sound. Neither of them wore shoes, but they weren't going for a hike. They needed to talk.

Nolan sighed while he ran a hand through his hair. "You didn't make a play for her this week."

"No. I mean I tried not to, but I can't take all the credit. She enforced the distance between us better than I ever could have on my own."

"I'm torn. On the one hand, of course that makes me happy, but on the other hand, I don't want to come between you two if it's what's meant to be."

Reid glanced behind them at the cabin. "You just spent the night with her. Did you not feel the connection?" He knew he sounded sarcastic. It was intentional. Nolan was not going to martyr himself over Adriana.

Nolan sighed. "Of course. Strong as ever. And I hate that it seems she's so totally torn between us. What is the world telling us?"

"I have no idea. Your parents were telling me that wolf shifters sometimes meet more than one mate. They said Wyatt had been to Montana and knew a bit about their lifestyle. I haven't had a chance to get ahold of him. I should."

"I'm not sure what difference it makes. It changes nothing. No matter what weird customs the wolves have, Adriana still has to choose between us, and I have to believe it will happen when the time is right."

Reid inhaled slowly. "I wish that were sooner rather than later. This is tough. Maybe we're meant to get to know her better first. Maybe she plays a role in this crazy thing happening with you."

Nolan leaned against the side of the cabin. "I hope not because I could be in this for a long time. I'm starting to worry about my job. Hell, I'm worried about *your* job too."

"Lord, don't worry about me. I have employees. They're

handling things. I was due for a vacation anyway. And you know keeping Adriana safe is not altruistic. I care about her."

"A vacation?" Nolan chuckled. "Running from thugs in the middle of the night is not what I usually call a vacation."

Reid smiled. "You know what I mean."

Nolan's voice lowered. He sounded serious when he spoke again. "How's she doing?"

Reid stared at the ground. "Okay, I think. I mean she has a tendency to steer clear of me in the evenings and keep herself busy during the day with classes and homework."

"I swear if anyone finds out about her... If something happens to her..."

"It won't. Not on my watch," Reid assured him.

They both lifted their heads at the same time. And then Nolan pointed out the obvious. "She's up." He turned to grab the doorknob.

Reid followed him inside to find Adriana coming out of the bathroom. "You scared me for a moment when you weren't inside."

"Sorry."

She shrugged. "I scented you quickly. Everything okay?"

"Yes," Reid assured her. "Who wants coffee?" He headed for the kitchen area to pull things out of the cabinet before holding up a small box. "I bought tea too. Don't worry."

She came to his side and took the box from his hand. "Thank you," she whispered. There was a sheen of tears in her eyes.

He set the mugs down and turned toward her, grabbing her by the waist. "What's the matter?"

She wiped her eyes with the back of her hand and shook her head. "Nothing."

Nolan rushed over to flank her from behind. He set a hand on her shoulder. "Babe?"

More tears. She tried to laugh through them, but they kept falling until Reid had a ball of nerves in his throat. "Adriana?"

She leaned her forehead against his chest, heaving now while Nolan crowded closer, both of his hands on her biceps. They sandwiched her. Comforting her as best they could.

It hurt to see her in such emotional turmoil. All Reid could do was continue to hold her close and let her cry it out. After a few minutes, her sobs subsided and she hiccupped. Then she gave another nervous chuckle. "I'm getting your shirt wet."

"I don't care about my shirt, hon. I only care about you."

"I suppose I'm just tired. Mentally exhausted." She lifted her face to meet his gaze and then twisted her neck to meet Nolan's gaze behind her. "Thank you. Both of you. I can't decide if I'm cursed or doubly lucky."

Nolan leaned in and kissed her forehead. "For now, let's go with lucky. Neither of us wants you to feel stressed about binding. Don't try to force the issue in your mind. Let it go for now. Accept our mutual attraction and relax. No one's rushing you."

Oddly enough, it didn't bother Reid that Nolan had put his lips on Adriana or that he was the one comforting her at the moment. When he pondered his predicament thoroughly, he also realized he hadn't been upset last night either. Not angry that she was with Nolan in the bed. Just frustrated that he'd been left out. His own doing?

Maybe they were going about this all wrong. What if they stopped swapping her back and forth, making her dizzy, and openly cared for her at the same time? The stress of worrying about stepping on Nolan's toes or hurting Adriana's feelings by pressuring her was driving them all insane.

He decided to do an experiment. What harm was there in that? It wasn't as though things between them could be *more* uncomfortable.

Reid smoothed one hand up her body, intentionally grazing her breast along the way until he cupped her face.

She shuddered at the slight contact against her swollen chest, as he expected her to.

He closed the distance and gave her a chaste kiss. Chaste but unmistakable, and on the lips. "Deep breaths," he murmured against her mouth.

"Kiss her," he told Nolan privately. *"Now. Do it now."*

"What?" Nolan's brows lifted behind her.

"Kiss her," Reid insisted.

Thank fuck Nolan decided to follow his friend's instructions instead of arguing the point. They'd been friends forever. They trusted each other, and Reid wanted them to continue to trust each other.

Nolan gently turned her his direction and took her lips before she had any idea what he meant to do. He deepened the kiss a bit more than Reid, but only slightly. And then he released her and held her face in his hands. "Everything is going to be fine."

She panted.

Reid set his hands on her hips again, this time from behind. He stepped closer until he pressed his hard length against her lower back. He fought to avoid groaning.

Her breath hitched for a second, but when Reid lifted his gaze to Nolan, his friend understood his intent without any communication, and he too stepped closer, nestling his package against her belly.

Reid kissed her neck.

She moaned, her head lolling back against his shoulder.

Nolan kissed the exposed skin of her collarbone.

She grabbed his waist with one hand and reached back to clasp Reid's belt loop with the other.

Fuck yes. Why didn't he think of this before?

Nolan and Reid had never shared a woman, not on the same occasion nor at different times. But something about calming Adriana's nerves in this way felt right. Maybe if the two of them openly showed their intent to her in front of the other instead of pretending to hide and sneaking around, they would actually calm her.

She wouldn't have to hide anything from them or hold back stressful, unnecessary secrets. This could work. At least for the day. Tomorrow they needed to go back to Calgary. Reid didn't intend to keep her from her classes. They were the only thing she had that provided some semblance of normalcy. But for today, for the next twenty-four hours, he hoped to drop the façade and help lower her stress.

It wasn't a contest. It was simply them adapting to their reality. It was temporary. But if it gave her some relief... Could they even get her to relax enough to let them give her pleasure?

He wasn't thinking about having sex. Just making her feel good. If she weren't a virgin, maybe he would be able to take things further, but she was, and he wasn't going to take that from her. He knew Nolan would agree.

Nolan nibbled a path to her ear and must have licked or bit down with his teeth because she shuddered.

"*I like this plan,*" Nolan admitted to Reid.

"*Instinct. Seemed worth a try.*"

"*It's working. She's loosening up.*"

She broke the silent chat. "You're both discussing me.

Stop that. Say what you need to say out loud or add me to the conversation. It's unnerving knowing you're talking about me as if conspiring behind my back."

Reid winced. "Sorry. Won't happen again."

"Uh huh."

Nolan spoke next. "Nobody's conspiring. We're just worried about you."

That was true.

"You hungry?"

"You cooking?" she asked, her voice lighter.

"Yep."

"Starved then." She pushed on his chest with her hands and bucked her ass backward to dislodge Reid at the same time. "But you better not be lying." She grabbed a mug off the counter and reached for the faucet. "I guess I'm going to have to heat this in a pan."

There was no microwave in the cabin, and Reid made a mental note to rectify that soon.

Nolan ushered her to the table and took over the task of heating water and making a breakfast scramble.

Fifteen minutes later the three of them were seated at the table, stabbing into the combo of eggs, sausage, potatoes, and cheese.

"You *can* cook," Adriana said after swallowing a mouthful. "I'm impressed."

"I know Reid can't cook. I bet you've been hungry this week."

Reid shook his head. "Hell, no. I'm sorry to inform you I've been dining like a king. Adriana's being modest. She's a world-class chef."

Adriana rolled her eyes. "Hardly, but I like to cook. It's relaxing."

"I have an idea," Nolan said as they finished eating. "Let's shift and go for a run."

Adriana's smile lit up. "That would be wonderful. Reid took me for a run one night. It hadn't realized how much I miss the ability to do so at will any day of the week."

"I can imagine. It's hard to shift in the city. A huge drawback," Nolan added. "I've lived in Calgary most of my life. It has always been difficult, especially when the call to run presses against your skin like an unsatisfied itch."

Adriana smiled.

Reid would never tire of that smile.

She pushed from the table. "Let's do it."

Leaving the plates where they were, Reid stood at the same time as Nolan. They all three grabbed their shoes and met at the door.

Why was Reid's chest beating so fast at the promise of seeing his sweet mate in her bear form again? He needed to stop thinking of her as his mate. In the end, he would be a third wheel at best. Lost to both of them at worst.

Without saying another word, they stepped outside and moved a few yards from the cabin. The day was going to be beautiful. It was chilly out, but later it would warm up. Warmer than usual for this time of year. They were lucky the cabin wasn't surrounded by snow. That wouldn't have been unheard of either.

In silent agreement, they each took a step back and let the shift take over their bodies.

Reid had never before been this in tune with anyone shifting, but it felt as though they were in each other's heads as they dropped to all fours, shrugged off their human forms, and replaced their bodies with fur and claws. A half a minute later, they were transformed.

Reid lifted his snout to stare at Adriana. He'd seen Nolan many times, but he was salivating for a glimpse of her in the daylight.

She made his breath hitch. The same thick brown hair

he remembered from the other night shown in the sunshine. And her eyes... Damn. They were the same eyes she stared at him with in human form. He felt like he could see into her soul. She blinked and cocked her head to one side before turning toward Nolan.

Nolan also looked mesmerized, inching closer until he could nuzzle her with his snout. He communicated with both of them, opening up a connection, his eyes still locked on Adriana. *"Reid, we can run in any direction from here without detection, right?"*

"Yes."

"Then let's do it."

Reid turned around and led the way, loping toward the north and up the mountain. Although it was unseasonably warm, there were patches of snow on the ground from the last freeze. It was melting though, the shiny drips falling off branches and pine needles. The dewy moisture reminded him of spring. But Nature fooled no one. She would send several more feet of snow before she permitted spring to return to the Rockies.

The evergreen trees were thick in this area. Besides the fact that Reid knew his grandfather would have cut as few trees as possible to build his hideaway, it had been fifty years since the cabin was built. The foliage surrounding the A-frame had nearly consumed the structure, hiding it from anyone who wandered too close.

After giving his companions a chance to get their kinks worked out, Reid glanced back to find Adriana behind him and Nolan bringing up the rear. *"Ready to run?"* he asked them both.

"Waiting on you," Nolan teased into his and Adriana's heads.

Reid growled, more because he wanted to release pent-up frustration than anything else. And then he picked up speed and raced between the branches and brush. It didn't matter what he stepped on because he didn't let his feet spend more than half a second on the ground for each step.

He could feel Adriana behind him without looking, but he would rather be the one bringing up the rear. He would make sure to swap positions with Nolan on the way back.

"It's so gorgeous out here. Perhaps even more than in Silvertip," she communicated.

"I'm sure that's why my grandfather picked this spot to build. He loved it here."

They raced up the mountain so fast they were all three gasping for breath when they reached the spot Reid wanted to show Adriana. He shifted silently back to human form and waited while Adriana and Nolan did the same. And then he nodded at the horizon.

She gasped when she stepped into the clearing and saw the view, inching closer to the edge. "My God. It feels like we can see the entire country from here." She took a deep breath, her head tipping back to take in the clean air. "Love that smell."

"What smell is that?" Nolan asked.

"Purity. Life. It's invigorating."

"That it is." Reid wasn't looking at the scenery though. He was watching Adriana.

When he glanced at Nolan, he found him also staring at the woman who had taken both their hearts and twisted them in knots.

CHAPTER 14

"What do you mean you lost him?" Joe seethed.

The three imbeciles standing in front of Joe's desk in his downtown office were white as sheets and fidgeting like preteens, not grown men. A fourth man, Vinny, leaned casually against the wall to one side.

"Vinny insisted Osborn was in the hotel room. We went to a lot of trouble to get a fucking key from the cleaning lady on the hall, but the room was empty." The taller man shot a glare at Vinny.

Joe honestly couldn't blame the man. He didn't trust Vinny further than he could throw him either, but he still needed to figure out where the fuck Osborn was and take him out of the equation. Sooner rather than later.

The shortest man, a balding guy who rubbed his head constantly in a nervous habit, cleared his throat. "I think he knew we were in the hall and escaped through the window."

Joe's voice rose as he stood and leaned forward on his hands over the desk. "Through the window? What floor was he on?"

"The third, sir. There was a fire escape."

"And how the fuck did he know you were onto him? What did you do, knock?"

"No, sir." Mr. Baldheaded Moron winced. "Somehow he was alerted to our presence anyway. I'm sure of it."

"Unless you arrived banging drums or playing a trumpet down the hallway, I don't see why Osborn would have been watching for danger out the peephole. He can't stand at the door all day and all night." Joe was pissed. The boss wasn't going to like this. It was messy. And it got more complicated by the day. He needed to find Osborn and put an end to this latest threat to his boss.

Joe spun around to face his office window. He ran a hand through his short-cropped hair and sighed. Did he have to do everything himself? How the fuck were three men unable to sneak up on Osborn and bring him in?

Vinny pushed away from the wall where he'd been leaning and sauntered forward as if he were in charge. What did this asshole have that made Rimouski suck his dick? Joe would give his left nut to find out.

Right now his only concern was fixing this problem. Fast. He waved all four idiots out of his office. "Get out. I'll find someone else to do the job." *Fucking morons.*

"I got this one," Vinny suddenly stated. "Should have done it myself in the first place. I'm the one who located Osborn. I should have taken him out myself instead of waiting for the team to come in."

Stephen didn't issue any directives that indicated he wanted Vinny to do the dirty work. Joe was leery. He was also in over his head. Why not let this guy give it a try? "Okay. Find him. But keep me updated several times a day. I want to know what's going on and where you are. Got it?"

"Yep."

"If you fuck this up and make me regret this decision, I'll hold you personally responsible for the SNAFU."

Vinny nodded. "You won't be disappointed."

"Prove it." Joe lowered back down in his seat. "Now, I've got work to do. Get out of here."

It was late morning when Nolan returned to the cabin with Reid and Adriana. Nolan shifted first and opened the door for the others. When they were safely ensconced back in their tiny haven, he headed for the fireplace. This wasn't his first visit to the cabin. He'd even come there alone a few times over the years when he needed peace and quiet.

It was rustic, no denying that, but he loved it for its simplicity.

"I think I'll take a shower," Adriana announced.

Nolan gritted his teeth. The idea of her getting naked in that tiny bathroom only yards from where he stood made his libido shoot back to full force. A glance at Reid told him his friend was experiencing the same discomfort.

They held their breath until the water was running and they were certain she was out of earshot.

Nolan spoke first, plopping down on the couch. "This isn't long enough for your frame. How did you sleep here last night?"

"Mostly I didn't." Reid dropped himself next to Nolan.

"So what are you thinking is the plan for the day?"

"I'm thinking my experiment earlier was a success. She hates feeling like she's sneaking around behind our backs when she's with one of us. We eliminate the sneaking, and she's calmer."

"I agree." Nolan picked on a loose thread on his jeans. "It's weird though. Both of us touching her at once. Kissing her." He shuddered. "I never imagined sharing a woman with you."

"Well, it's not like we're going to have sex. I'm only suggesting we not avoid contact just because the other one is in the room."

Nolan nodded as he glanced at his best friend. Did Reid know she was a virgin?

Reid either read his mind or guessed his line of thinking. "She told me."

Nolan swallowed. This alternate universe he'd stepped into kept getting weirder.

Reid leaned forward, elbows on his knees. "I would never take her virginity, you know. It wouldn't be fair. Only one of us will get that piece of her. In the end, I mean."

Nolan stared at his friend. Damn, he was lucky. How did he deserve having Reid of all people for a best friend? Any other man would have run off with Adriana and never looked back. That humbled Nolan. It was also tough to swallow, and he had to remind himself to return the favor. "Do not forget your promise."

Reid rolled his eyes. "How could I? You remind me every day."

"Rope."

"Rope. Got it. Stop harping. It won't come to that."

"It might."

"It won't."

Nolan glanced across the room. His mind wandered to the scene next to the sink earlier. His dick had kicked into overdrive as he pressed his length against her belly and kissed her. It didn't even bother him that Reid had been watching, also holding her by the waist. Guiding her. It was hot.

It was crazy, but it was still hot. Sure, there were men

who shared women in the world. He simply didn't know any of them. And he certainly hadn't ever done so himself. Why hadn't it been awkward? He should have felt guilt or at least some discomfort touching Adriana so intimately in front of Reid. Or fuck, watching Reid do so. But none of those feelings had surfaced. He'd felt nothing but... consuming arousal, and once again, heat.

He shook the thought from his mind. It was only for today. One day. He just prayed his friendship would still be intact when this was over.

Except who was he kidding? There was no way their friendship could survive this woman. Only one of them would win. The other would spend their life without her. The world wasn't perfect enough for whoever got left behind to hang around like a third wheel. No matter how strong the binding was, Nolan for one knew for certain he would never forget how he felt about Adriana if she chose Reid. It was insane to think it could be erased.

"When are you going to call the police? They must be crazy wondering where you are," Reid pointed out.

Nolan chuckled. "My dad called them last night. Told them they could take a chill pill for a few days since they failed to keep me safe. He was a bit livid. Wouldn't even hint at where I might be, although I didn't tell him. I doubt they care very much. Every day I'm hiding on my own is one more day they don't have to foot the bill."

"So we get this entire day before we have to return to reality."

"What do you think we should do with our time?" Nolan wiggled his brows.

"I can think of a few things. Let's make her forget this cabin exists."

Nolan's cock jumped to attention. The idea of what

Reid was suggesting should have given him pause. But it didn't. It made his arousal spike. He could do this.

The bathroom door opened, making both of them twist around to find Adriana standing behind them wrapped in nothing but a towel. "So, the worst part is not having clean clothes."

Nolan opened his mouth to tell her Reid always kept spare clothing in the cabin and that the drawers upstairs were filled with various items she could go through, even things Nolan's sisters had left on occasion.

For some reason, Reid interrupted Nolan before he could point this out. "Clothes are so overrated."

Adriana rolled her eyes. She held her folded pile of clothing from the day before under her arm. "It was too warm in that tiny room to put yesterday's clothes back on. I'll go to the loft and do it."

"Or not?" Nolan offered, feeling out what her level of playfulness might be.

"Sure," she stated sarcastically. "That's a great idea."

"I'm not opposed to you wearing a towel," Reid added. "Are you, Nolan?"

"Nope." His dick was standing fully at attention now, but he wasn't in disagreement. Not a bit.

"I mean it's a bit too warm in the cabin now that you mention it. The fire is too high." Reid stood and rounded the couch, sauntering toward her.

Nolan had no idea how his friend managed to get his legs to move, but he watched, wondering what Reid's plan was.

A glance at Adriana told him she wasn't buying this. She gripped the towel tighter and held out a hand. "Don't even think of getting close to me."

"What?" Reid asked in a mock-innocent voice. "I was

just going to help you maneuver the ladder. Your hands are full. I should carry something for you."

Like the towel, Nolan thought as he somehow managed to push to standing also.

She took another step back.

Reid was sharp though. He turned things around in a hurry. "Just kidding. There are some spare clothes upstairs. I'll grab you something clean to wear."

"Damn. I was hoping we wouldn't have to tell her that," Nolan communicated to Reid.

"Never underestimate me," Reid returned as he climbed the ladder. Fifteen seconds later he was back, and he had a men's T-shirt in his hand.

Nolan wanted to pump his fist. Instead, he watched Reid hand it to Adriana. "It's huge. It will cover you."

She eyed him suspiciously before turning her gaze on Nolan next. "Why do I get the impression you're conspiring against me?"

Reid pasted on a ridiculous innocent look, his brows raised, his mouth open. "Us? No. Just being a gentleman."

"By handing me almost nothing to wear," she deadpanned.

He shrugged. "Suit yourself. Just providing options."

Adriana yanked the T-shirt from Reid dramatically. "I hate putting on dirty clothes."

Nolan wondered how deep Reid had dug in the drawer to come up with a white one. Again, he reminded himself not to grin.

Adriana's gaze was narrowed as she turned back around and reentered the bathroom.

Neither man moved. Nolan wasn't breathing.

Two minutes later, Adriana resurfaced, flinching when she found them in the same spots. "You two are acting suspicious. Stop it."

She stepped around Reid and then gave a wide circumference to Nolan as well before lowering her sweet body onto the corner of the couch and tucking her legs under her. "Do you have anything to read in this cabin? I can't even use my phone for fear it will die."

CHAPTER 15

Adriana was completely out of her element. What was she thinking agreeing to put on this flimsy T-shirt? She'd lost her mind.

Reid and Nolan were now so tongue-tied they hadn't moved from where they'd been standing since suggesting the idea and then handing her the almost nonexistent piece of clothing.

It didn't matter that it covered her ass. It left nothing to the imagination since it was nearly see-through and she was wearing nothing underneath. *Nothing.*

She hadn't been overly excited about putting the clothes she'd been wearing for over twenty-four hours back on, but the real truth was that she was feeling flirtatious. She shouldn't be doing this. It was a horrible idea. There were two men in the cabin. *Two.*

She didn't habitually flirt with one man, let alone two. But ever since this morning when they'd sandwiched her and taken turns kissing her, all four hands on her body, she'd been living in a different dimension. She was glad they'd shifted and gone for a run. For one thing, she needed the exercise and fresh air. For another thing, she needed the release.

The problem was she'd come back to the cabin more invigorated than before they left. More aroused. More in tune with her men. Both of them.

She rubbed her temples with both hands, trying to gather her wits, but no matter what she did, the pheromones that were controlling her didn't go away. They grew stronger and more potent by the second. Even in the bathroom, they had made it difficult for her to concentrate. She wasn't sure if she washed her hair twice or three times. She kept getting distracted. She had also shaved, shocked that she didn't cut herself.

Why all the fanfare?

Shit. She was totally baiting them. Both of them. She wanted to feel what she'd felt this morning. She wanted to feel even more. Would it ruin things between them? Make everything more awkward than it already was?

The problem was she was past the ability to make good decisions or even care. She just wanted to *feel*.

She gripped her hands into fists on her thighs and watched, waiting. It was someone else's turn to make the next move. She didn't think she could have put herself out there any further than she had, and she certainly couldn't have made her position any clearer.

Nolan and Reid stood like statues for long moments. She knew she'd gotten to them. Their breathing was heavy, and the scent of their combined arousal filled the small space. If they hadn't wanted to tempt her like this, they shouldn't have brought her to such a remote tiny cabin in the woods. What did they expect?

They were communicating with each other again. She could see the shared blank look a shifter often got while they spoke remotely to someone. They were facing each other, too. Neither of them was currently looking at her. And then Nolan nodded and turned toward the bathroom. He shut the door with a *snick* two seconds before the water came on.

She didn't even care if they had a private side conversation as long as they were plotting how to stoke the flames burning inside her. Closing her eyes, she took deep breaths. She needed more clothing. Her breasts were heavy, her nipples aching to be touched. The brush of the T-shirt over the tips was stimulating her as if someone was stroking them with their fingers. Or two someones.

Moisture pooled between her legs, and she was cognizant of the fact that she couldn't hide her plight. Would that help or hurt her cause?

The water shut off. She didn't need to open her eyes to know Nolan was back in the room. In seconds Reid replaced him.

Adriana didn't open her eyes, afraid of what she might see. What was Nolan wearing? She shivered, not willing to find out yet.

He said nothing. She could feel his presence and even sense him moving across the room. She heard the refrigerator open and the distinct sound of the cap coming off a water bottle. He chugged it. She followed him around the room in her mind until the bathroom door opened again and Reid joined the hormone-fest.

They were closing in on her. Her heart rate picked up as they approached, and she finally lifted her face and opened her eyes. She couldn't speak. Two male chests— one light skinned and broad, the other darker toned and slightly narrower. They both wore nothing but low-hung jeans. Any woman would swoon to be with either man.

Was she lucky to have both of them? Or was she playing with fire? Probably a little of both.

Nolan's blond hair was sun-kissed, and the sprinkle of it on his chest matched. His blue eyes were piercing, nailing her to the couch.

Reid's hair was so dark it was almost black, his eyes the green shade of the ocean at twilight.

They were so very different and so very similar at the same time. Mostly because they were both eyeing her with the brooding look she'd come to expect from them when they placed a demand on her or didn't like where her thoughts were going—usually concerning her safety.

Nolan leaned over her, his hands landing on the back of the couch, only inches separating them. "Trust us?"

Did she? Hell, she didn't even trust herself right now. And she wasn't sure she cared. She was so turned on she would gladly have sex with either of them while the other one watched. Or both. Or one at a time. She didn't care as long as someone did something to push her off this cliff she'd been hanging on for hours. Days. No, a week. Tiptoeing around both of them. Tiptoeing around her life. Putting them off for fear of hurting either man's feelings.

Today they were all in the same room. It didn't seem to matter to either Nolan or Reid that she was attracted to both of them. Was this a contest for her affection? A trial of sorts to see who she responded to with more vehemence? Because she had news for them, her reaction to them was not the same but equal.

A tight ball had formed in her stomach the moment she put the T-shirt on. It smelled like both of them. How was that reasonable?

Reid circled the couch to come up behind her. He reached between Nolan's hands and set his palms on her shoulders. Her heart raced, but her body was somehow soothed by his touch. He spread his fingers and slid them down her arms until he reached her hands and threaded their fingers together in her lap. And then he held her tight and lifted her arms above her head.

She gasped as she realized his intentions. Her elbows rested by her ears, her hands now clasped in one of his behind the sofa.

Nolan lifted his hands from outside her arms to gently trail his fingers down toward her torso.

She shivered as goosebumps rose all over her body.

"I can smell your arousal," Nolan stated out loud. "You like the idea of having both of us touching you."

She didn't answer. She couldn't. All of her attention was focused on the way her nipples were puckered against the thin T-shirt.

Nolan's fingers landed on the top swells of her breasts and danced lightly, teasing them until they felt heavier. He traced around to the bottoms, avoiding her nipples.

She couldn't keep from arching toward him.

"Uncurl your legs, Adriana." Nolan's voice was soft, that way he had of saying her name rolling off his tongue and calling to her like a siren.

Her feet were tucked under her, but at his command, she unfolded them and set them on the floor.

"That's it." He inhaled deeply, his eyelids lowering as if the scent of something delicious had reached his nose. Perhaps it had.

Reid leaned in closer, his lips on her ear. "Trust us."

She did. She had no idea why, and perhaps it was a bad idea, but she did. Or maybe she didn't care. She knew they wouldn't hurt her, and beyond that, she didn't care what they did. It no longer mattered that she was a virgin. She hadn't saved herself for some altruistic reason. She'd saved herself because no man had ever elicited a feeling in her that caused her to want to give him that gift.

These two men did. Would it hurt their relationship later if she slept with both of them?

At least it would never be a secret. She knew deep in her soul today was a once-in-a-lifetime gift she hadn't expected or asked for. She would follow through with it primarily because she couldn't stop herself.

And she would have no regrets.

There was no way to know what the Universe had in store for her in the coming weeks and months, but for now, two amazing sexy men seemed intent on pleasuring her in ways she couldn't imagine.

Nolan continued to tease the sensitive skin of her breasts until he finally circled her nipples and then flicked his thumbs over them.

She writhed, thrusting her chest forward. She might have squirmed completely out of his reach to escape the sensory overload, but Reid had a firm grip on her hands.

Nolan lowered onto his knees in front of her and eased his hands down to her thighs. When he pressed them apart in order to situate his torso between her legs, she bit her lip. Holy shit. Her sex was wide open, embarrassingly wet, and exposed.

Exposed to Nolan. All he had to do was lift the T-shirt out of the way, and he would be able to see every secret she had. With Reid leaning over the couch from behind, he too would not miss a beat.

Nolan set his hands on her bare thighs and rubbed them up and down. "Look at me, Adriana."

Her vision was blurry. It was difficult to focus on anything, as if all her brain cells were focused on her exposure and unavailable to command her eyes. She blinked to clear the cloudiness.

He smiled. His hands slid closer to her sex, his thumbs noticeably reaching the apex.

She sucked in a sharp breath as he slowly pulled on her inner thighs, forcing her sex to open. Cool air hit her wetness and made her bite down hard on her lip. A moan escaped anyway.

"So responsive."

What did that mean? How else was she supposed to react to the way they were both staring at her like she was the finest piece of dessert on a buffet table? She knew the answer though. She'd never reacted like this to another man, shifter or human. So, yes. She was responding to them in a foreign way. But was it the same for them?

Had neither of them been able to elicit this level of arousal from previous partners?

Reid spoke too close to her ear again. "I can smell your arousal. It's intoxicating. I need to taste it."

Her eyes opened wide. Was she ready for that? She wasn't a prude. Okay, maybe she was a prude, but again, not by design. It had just happened. But she was knowledgeable. She understood logistically how people ordinarily had sex. She knew it would likely eventually involve tasting by both parties. But now? Already? She didn't think she was mentally prepared to handle that sort of overload.

And there are two of them, she reminded herself. If they ganged up on her, which they already had, she would be putty in their hands—which again, she already was.

"My fingers would be soaked if I touched your pussy, wouldn't they, Adriana?" Nolan asked.

His crude word and the fact that he'd not only said something that carnal out loud—let alone spoke it in the form of a question—made her face heat.

"Adriana?"

She jerked her gaze to meet Nolan's, half pissed that his voice alone commanded so much authority. At the same time, she had no choice but to admit to herself his demands turned her on. Every time.

He smiled. "You're so fucking sexy when you're aroused. Makes my cock so hard, the thickness of it is threatening revolt in my jeans."

Cock... Shit. She was in over her head.

"I'm going to make you come, babe. Take the edge off so you can focus. And then we're going to do it again. Slower. Take you places you've only dreamed of."

Her face flushed hotter. She had no doubt he could do exactly as he said, especially since she was on the edge of an orgasm from his words alone.

Reid's free hand trailed down her neck and between her breasts until he fisted the T-shirt between his fingers and tugged it up her body.

She held her breath, her nudity making her self-conscious as he revealed every inch of her to Nolan.

Nolan's gaze was on her sex, and then it trailed up to her breasts as they too were exposed.

Her nipples were so hard and tight they looked unnaturally large to her. She had to look away. Her own body was sexually appealing. No wonder Nolan was licking his lips.

Reid pulled the cotton over her head and left it tangled behind her neck, trapping her arms more fully than his hand on her wrists. He cupped her cheek, angled her head back, and leaned over to take her lips.

The position was erotic. Her neck was elongated and exposed. Either of them could easily bind her to them in a second. A simple bite right in the sweet spot where her neck and shoulders met was all it would take. Well, that and the release of the binding serum from one mate to the other, ensuring it flowed into their bloodstream.

Visions of either of them sinking his teeth into her

made her arousal spike higher. It didn't have to be her neck. Nolan could bite her thigh too. A part of her didn't care who did it or where as long as someone bound her to them.

She also wasn't at their mercy. She could complete the binding herself if she desired. Not without permission, of course. That was strictly forbidden, but was there any chance in hell either of them would turn her down?

Reid's lips were still teasing hers, soft but demanding. He entered her with his tongue from this upside-down position and stroked the inside of her mouth.

For a moment she kissed him back, but then Nolan's thumbs found her sex and stroked over her lower lips. "So soft," he whispered. When his fingertips made contact with her moisture, she lifted her hips off the couch, pleading silently for more. She didn't even care how wanton she was as long as he made good on his promise to let her come soon.

She wasn't sure about his next promise to do it again, but one thing at a time. She was on edge. More aroused than she'd been in her life. She'd been living in a state of constant need for the past week with no way to abate it. There was no way she would risk masturbating in Reid's condo. For one thing, she was afraid she would end up screaming and cause him to come running into her room. For another thing, he would have smelled her increased pheromones from anywhere in the house. Apparently, he had masturbated in the shower often, but she hadn't trusted herself to do the same with him always nearby. She would have fallen if she attempted such a thing in the shower.

She was so focused on Nolan's sweet torture of her pussy that she didn't notice Reid's hand smoothing down from her face to her breast. When he cupped her swollen flesh and then pinched her tight nipple, she groaned into his mouth. *"Please,"* she silently begged the room at large, blocking no one.

Reid released her nipple but only to switch his attention to the other one.

Nolan spread her wetness from between her lips to her clit. The second he made contact with the little nub, she almost screamed. Only Reid's mouth stopped her. She had long since ceased kissing him back, but her lips were parted, and he continued to nibble around the seam.

Her eyes were closed. And that was a mistake because she hadn't noticed Nolan lowering his face until his lips were wrapped around her clit and his tongue was flicking over the sensitive tip rapidly.

Reid released her mouth to speak against it. "Come for us, hon. I want to watch you explode."

She didn't have a choice. Nolan's mouth was far better than any vibrator. He switched from tonguing her to sucking her clit into his mouth. And that was all it took. She tipped over the edge of a cliff she'd been dangling from for a week. Falling. Falling. Falling. Her pussy pulsed, as unamused as she was that nothing had penetrated her.

The waves of pleasure continued for so long she was afraid the orgasm would never end. At that point, it felt so damn good, she wouldn't have been sorry. Slowly it subsided though, and she blinked her eyes open to find Reid staring down at her.

He smiled. "So fucking gorgeous."

CHAPTER 16

Reid could have died right then and been a happy man without regrets. Damn, she was amazing. He wasn't sure who got the better end of the deal—Nolan who was afforded permission to taste her, or Reid who had the pleasure of watching her come undone.

It was a tossup. And it didn't matter because before the sun went down, he intended for both of them to have ravished her so thoroughly there were no longer any tally marks for who'd gotten the bigger piece.

This was not a contest. This was his mate. Or Nolan's mate. Whatever. For now, she belonged to both of them. And he intended to make the most of it while the opportunity existed.

There were no guarantees for tomorrow. He would take this gift and guard it close to his heart for the rest of his life. He didn't want regrets. He wanted a full day of worshiping the woman he knew in his heart was his. If it turned out later she belonged to Nolan instead of him, at least Reid would have this memory. He would not squander it.

He kissed her with renewed reverence. She had no idea how affected he was by her. Humbled. She would never know. He would guard that detail. Keep it to himself. If he didn't, the vulnerability would eat him alive.

As he released her lips, he met her gaze. Her eyes were dilated and intense. She was still breathing heavily. Fuck, she was beautiful. She licked her lips. "Need you," she whispered.

He still held her arms above her head and against his chest.

Nolan was kneeling between her legs, though his hands had smoothed up to her waist. Her thighs were parted wide. Inviting. Even though she'd just come against Nolan's mouth, Reid could smell renewed arousal leaking from her sweet pussy. He needed to switch places with Nolan or get creative.

He opted for creative. Holding her gaze, he tugged the T-shirt free and lowered her arms to her sides. *"Hold her hands for me,"* he communicated to Nolan.

Nolan wrapped his fingers around her wrists and pressed them into the sofa.

Reid cupped Adriana's chin, forcing her head to lean back again for another kiss. He dipped his tongue in deep, tasting her again, memorizing her flavor while his cock begged him to add the taste of her pussy to the repertoire.

He released her lips again as his hands inched down to cup her full breasts. Her head lolled back against the couch as he thumbed her nipples and then pinched them between his thumbs and fingers. A slight tug forced her back to arch deliciously at the same time she moaned.

In his peripheral vision, he saw her give a tug to her hands, but Nolan held her firmly. When she tried to draw her legs together, Nolan pressed his torso against the sofa, forcing her wider instead.

Reid didn't need to communicate his intentions to his friend. It was understood he would get her off this second time in his way. He smoothed his hands down her belly as it dipped. Her eyes fluttered shut, and she bit her lower lip against the soft moan.

Reid let his gaze roam down her body to take in her swollen nipples and the fullness of her breasts before trailing lower to stare at the soft dark curls cupping her pussy. He flattened his palms on her thighs, his thumbs pulling her lower lips apart as she gasped.

Even though she'd come moments ago, she was so aroused there was no hiding it.

Reid lifted one hand, cupped her pussy, and then dragged two fingers through the opening of her warmth.

She arched farther, squirming but unable to stop him. Nolan had a firm grip on her wrists and was trapping her thighs open.

Reid had difficultly withholding a moan of his own as he watched her return to fully aroused, so damn sexy he thought his cock would bust out of his jeans in protest. He ignored the little head though. No one was going to fuck her today. All Reid wanted was to taste her and watch her unravel for him as she'd done for Nolan.

When he flicked a finger across her clit, she let out a sharp squeal and flinched in an attempt to lift her bottom off the couch.

Nolan set his elbows on her thighs and held her steady.

A glance at her face showed pure bliss. Her lips were parted and her eyes shut. Skin flushed a gorgeous pink. Tongue flicking out to moisten her bottom lip.

Sexy as hell.

Mine.

My God this woman is mine.

He shook that certainty from his head. She was no

more his than she was Nolan's. And there was no indication which way this thing would go in the end.

Reid lowered his fingers back down to her opening, pressed his palm against her clit, and slowly eased his middle finger into her channel. *"Fuck, she's tight,"* he muttered into Nolan's head.

"Felt her with my tongue. You aren't kidding. My dick is hard just watching you."

Reid semi-chuckled into his friend's mind. *"As if your dick wasn't hard already."* He then put all his attention on Adriana's pussy.

She panted as he stroked in and out of her tight heat. Her head fell forward. "Oh, God. Reid... Nolan..." Her words were pleading.

He bent his finger at the knuckles and dragged it over her G-spot.

Adriana stiffened, her breath catching, her entire body tight and so fucking sexy. Her tits rose and fell with every breath, and her breaths were short and quick. She was close.

When he removed his finger, teasing her outer lips, she groaned. "Reid..."

He knew what she needed, but he wanted to draw out the moment, make her wait for it, add to the tension. He wanted her to remember this for a long time. Always. This moment when he provided what he would bet was her first G-spot orgasm. The first of many, if her responsiveness was anything to go by.

No woman had been this hot beneath his touch before. Of course, no woman had been his mate either. There was a driving bond between them that made his cock harder than ever and her sexy body more alert than she would be with another man. Except Nolan.

She'd blossomed under Nolan's touch. She was opening

up like a rose now. "Please," she begged. Her thighs shook. Her tits jiggled. Her stiff little nipples were a shade darker than earlier, swollen, tight, thrusting outward.

He cupped one breasts lightly, thrumming one finger across the tip while he lifted his other hand to his mouth and sucked his finger to taste her juices. Honey. Sweetness like nothing else he'd ever tasted. He was instantly addicted.

And she was watching him, eyes wide. Her heart beat faster under his palm.

Damn. *Fuck me.* She was aroused further by his actions. He was a lucky man.

Finally, he removed his finger from his mouth with a soft *pop* and eased it back into her pussy.

She arched her chest again, tipping her head back.

He glanced at her face to find her staring up at him, eyes wide, pleading. When her tongue reached out to lick her lips, he couldn't deny her any longer. He lowered his lips to hers and gave her a gentle kiss before returning his gaze to her pussy. She was going to explode for him. And he was going to watch.

Nolan's attention was also focused on her pussy. His elbows strained to hold her thighs wider. Hopefully he was cognizant enough of his grip on her wrists that he wasn't hurting her. A quick glance proved Nolan was in control. His fingers circled her tiny wrists, and he was pressing them against the couch, but he wasn't cutting off circulation to her hands. In fact, her fingers were curled into the cushion, nails digging as deep as they could.

Adriana moaned louder. "Reid," she begged again. "Please. Oh, God, please."

He added a second finger to the first and started fucking her tight pussy faster, dragging the bent fingers over her sensitive spot again and again.

He moved his gaze back and forth between her face and her sweet pussy, unsure which he wanted to watch as she came. But the decision was made for him easily when her mouth opened wider and a gasp escaped her lips. Her pussy tightened around his fingers, gripping them, pulsing around them, but he kept his gaze on her fantastic features.

Damn, she was gorgeous when she came. Even better the second time. Her head fell back as if she'd lost the ability to hold it up, her lips still parted, her cheeks slack, her breath stopping.

He would never forget this moment as long as he lived.

"Fuck...me..." Nolan murmured out loud. Apparently Reid wasn't the only person affected by this beautiful experience.

Adriana had never been more sated and relaxed in her life. Even ten hours later, she was still blissfully happy, snuggled in the loft bed between both men. It would have been better if Reid and Nolan had actually had sex with her. She'd pleaded with them for a while, but they had emphatically denied her the pleasure.

In her opinion, they'd gotten nothing out of her afternoon of heaven. Neither man had taken off his jeans. She had easily seen the strain of both their erections against the denim, but they still turned her down. They insisted watching her come had been beyond their dreams, and they were the ones who benefitted most from the experience.

They were both obviously mental.

So many firsts. She'd never been naked with a man. She'd never had an orgasm at someone else's hand. She'd never had anyone go down on her or thrust their fingers into her or hold her down or kiss the life out of her or stare at her with such devotion.

And she'd given all those things to not one but two men. Still she found herself equally attracted to them both. If she allowed herself to think too hard about that problem, she would lose her sanity. So, she pushed it to the back of her mind—mostly at their insistence—and ignored the looming problem for the day.

What she had not gotten was penetration, at least not from anyone's cock. Her body craved the completion, but both men had insisted she should save that piece of herself. Unspoken was the second half of that sentence—*for the one she eventually chose.*

At some point during the day, she had discovered they had duped her. There were plenty of female clothes in the A-frame. Paige and Ryann had left them there on several occasions. Nolan and Reid simply hadn't wanted Adriana to be dressed.

She smiled again, for the millionth time.

Tucking herself against Nolan's hard body, she set a hand on his chest. Reid was behind her on his side, his pec against her back, one leg tossed over hers, his hand on her hip. His thumb had been stroking her skin maddeningly for several minutes. She inhaled their combined scents slowly and let out a breath on a sigh.

Reid kissed her neck. "You're still awake," he whispered against her skin. "Apparently we didn't work hard enough to wear you out," he teased.

She giggled, her body vibrating against Nolan's.

Nolan had one arm under her head and the other hand on top of hers over his chest. He squeezed her fingers. "That sound... Baby..." His voice was deep, sexy, aroused. Because she had laughed.

Her face heated. Again.

Perhaps in the real world, the fact that she was currently snuggled in between two men would be ludicrous, but for today, she was not living in the real world. She was in the middle of a fantasy. A beautiful one she never wanted to end.

She had homework she should be doing. Laundry awaited her. She hadn't called her parents in days. And there was a hit man intent on killing Nolan—and possibly even her and Reid—out there somewhere. But she had pushed all that to the back of her mind about twenty-four hours ago and left it there. Tomorrow she would deal. Tonight, she would sleep between these two amazing men.

"Thank you for today," she told Nolan's chest.

He squeezed her hand again. "Baby, our pleasure."

Reid kissed her neck again, his lips lingering there to bring chills to her shoulders as his words vibrated against her skin. "The perfect day. I'll never forget it."

She wore nothing but the T-shirt they'd given her earlier. Though they had insisted she should sleep naked between them, she had declined. After all, her body was seemingly permanently on fire for both men. There would be no sleeping if she let her naked skin rest against either man.

There wasn't likely to be much sleeping anyway, no matter how many times they told her to relax and close her eyes.

It wasn't as if *they* were asleep either. And she couldn't imagine how they could be. Surely they were close to self-combusting after fondling her all day without any relief themselves.

"You're worrying too much," Nolan said. His hand smoothed up her arm to cup her cheek. He tipped his head toward her to kiss her lips.

It should have been weird, kissing one man in front of

another. It should have made her uncomfortable. But it didn't. It felt…natural. How was she ever going to choose between them? And why was it her responsibility? It was super clear the ball was in her court. The ball had always been in her court. Both men were waiting for her to choose. It was unfair to them and was making her insane.

"Stop it, baby," Reid stated, again breathing the words against her neck. "You've been relaxed with us all day. Don't let your mind take over now."

He read her well. She sighed. "If only it were that easy."

Reid's hand trailed over her hip and gripped her thigh. "We could wear you out some more as incentive."

She lifted her hand from Nolan's chest and grabbed Reid's, precariously close to her pussy. "Don't you dare. I gave you an ultimatum earlier, and it still stands." She had. She wasn't kidding. But how long could she hold out under pressure?

Reid chuckled. Damn, his breath on her neck. Her pussy clenched every time. "Baby, surely you realize we've been humoring you."

She tugged his fingers, trying to get them away from her sex. Too close. Way too close. Inches separated his hand from her wetness. "You're not playing fair."

Nolan chuckled next, his chest vibrating against her. "Hon, we never agreed to your demands, nor did we say we would play fair."

She let go of Reid's hand to swat at Nolan's chest. Huge mistake. Reid let his hand slide between her legs, the tips of his fingers now so close to her opening. She shouldn't have set one leg over Nolan's. The position opened her pussy, and she wasn't wearing panties.

"Reid," she warned, grabbing at his hand.

"You're so fucking sexy when you come. I want to see it again."

Her belly dropped. They hadn't touched her pussy or her breasts since the two orgasms they'd given her that afternoon. Once she'd realized they had no intention of having sex with her, she'd insisted they not tempt her again.

They had teased her mercilessly all day, insisting she wear nothing but the T-shirt and touching her everywhere but those two spots every time they got the chance. But neither of them had pushed her since earlier. Not that she hadn't spent the day in a state of arousal to rival most shifters and all humans, but at least she had half her brain cells functioning. Half was more than none.

"I mean it," she stated, trying to sound serious. "If you aren't willing to have sex with me, stop playing with me." She really, really wanted either of them or both of them or one of them inside her. Her body had craved being filled from the moment she'd had her first orgasm against Nolan's mouth.

They'd denied her. She'd made this ultimatum, mostly in the hopes they would give in. She hadn't been successful, and right about now she could tell she was losing every inch of ground fast.

Suddenly, in a whirlwind of movement, she found herself flat on her back between them, her shirt yanked over her head, her hands held high with the removal, and her legs spread open.

She gasped, trying to figure out what the hell had happened and how she'd missed the signs. Obviously, they'd been plotting silently. They flanked her, leaning on their sides, each of them trapping her closest thigh with their respective top legs.

Before she had her head wrapped around the new plan she hadn't been privy to, both men had a hand on her inner thighs, inching toward her pussy.

She tugged on her arms to no avail. "Guys. Oh God. What the…?" Her body lit up, going from the steady seven out of ten she'd been at all day to an eleven out of ten now. Her breasts swelled, her nipples puckered, and moisture increased between her legs.

She licked her lips, forgetting how to speak when two heads dipped to suck her nipples at the same time two sets of fingers spread her lower lips. Her head was spinning. All she knew was sensation, amazing, wonderful warmth. All of her blood rushed to her nipples and her clit.

Two seconds later, one finger worked her swollen nub while another thrust into her. She bucked, but they held her down. A second finger joined the first inside her, stroking every inch of her sensitive channel.

Nolan released her nipple with a pop and set his forehead against hers. "Let it go, baby," he whispered against her mouth before nibbling on her lower lip.

Just like that, she came undone, shattering against whoever had their fingers inside her. She had no idea which one. The other set of fingers pinched her clit the moment she crested, forcing one orgasm to morph into two or maybe three. It went on for so long she had no idea how many times she came. Lips teased her mouth. Lips teased her breast. So many fingers worked her pussy she couldn't focus. Her vision swam, and she couldn't inhale her next breath.

Reid must have nudged Nolan out of the way because as she floated back to earth, his lips replaced Nolan's on her mouth, kissing her, his tongue dipping inside to dance with hers.

She was overcome with emotion. Overwhelmed with arousal and desire. A carnal need to have one of them inside her bubbled to the surface as it had earlier. As if

Nature intended for a man and a woman to join in that fashion, she felt the urge climbing up her spine.

But no one moved to do anything about it.

Even though she'd just had the most fantastic orgasms of her life, following two amazing ones earlier in the day, a tear escaped her eye to trail down her cheek toward her ear. The impulse to fuck was heady and insistent. The urge to bind was right on its heels. And yet, she was going to be left frustrated.

Reid lifted his face, his brow furrowed as he stared down at her. "Adriana?"

She shook her head, trying to swallow back her emotional overload.

"Baby?" Nolan's voice followed Reid's. Both men set a hand on her belly and released her wrists above her head. Nolan's face was filled with the same concern she read on Reid's. He licked his lips. "Did we hurt you?"

She shook her head again, trying to find words. She closed her eyes, bit her lip, and wrapped her arms around their necks. Finally, she spoke. "I need more."

Her eyes fluttered open to find Nolan's face transforming as a smile replaced the concerned frown. "I know."

"It hurts," she whispered. It did. A tight knot in her stomach was causing actual physical pain. It demanded release.

Reid stroked her skin, cupping her breast and casually thumbing her nipple. "So sorry. We hoped this would help."

"It didn't. It's worse." She released her grip on them and wiggled free between them to sit up and crawl from the bed. Without looking at either of them, she found her T-shirt, tugged it from under half of Nolan's thigh, and pulled it over her head. She then climbed down the ladder. They didn't stop her. They didn't even speak. She was grateful. She needed some space. Time. To breathe. To think. To process.

She cleaned up in the tiny bathroom and returned to the living area, heavy, shaking. Scared. What the hell was going to happen to the three of them?

Both men had descended the steps and were leaning casually against the back of the sofa, waiting for her, side by side. They didn't move. Perhaps they were afraid to.

She took a deep breath and headed toward them. When she stepped into their space, she let them wrap her into their embrace, tucking her arms around two torsos. She spoke against their chests. "I'm falling in love with you," she whispered. She hoped they realized she meant both of them. It hurt. Today had been amazing and fun, but reality was sinking in. She couldn't have two men. It didn't work that way. How was this nightmare ever going to end except in heartbreak? For all three of them. No matter what choice she made, they would all hurt.

She let them lead her back up the ladder and settled once again between them on the bed. And amazingly, she fell asleep. Warm. Loved. Cherished.

CHAPTER 17

Vinny held the phone to his ear while he waited for his contact to pick up. He was standing outside a gas station, freezing his ass off, and pissed. If he didn't find Osborn soon, Stringer was going to get pissed.

Finally, the call connected. An exasperated man's voice rang loud and clear. "Don't have anything for you, Vinny. If I did, I would have contacted you."

"Dude, it's been two days. How the fuck did you lose him for two goddamn days?"

"I'm working on it."

"You're working on it?" Vinny's voice rose. "That's not good enough."

"Don't you dare threaten me. It's your fault Osborn ran in the first place. Who did you send to pick him off? Elmo, Snuffleupagus, and the Cookie Monster?"

Vinny growled. He was pissed at himself for letting those three morons sweep in to pick up Osborn from the hotel. He didn't need the reminder. What this asshole didn't know was that there was no way for Vinny to sneak up on Osborn himself. Nolan would scent him from a mile away and be tipped off.

The only option had been to send humans. Not that Osborn couldn't also scent a human, but they were far less suspicious. Although somehow Nolan had been tipped off anyway and fled the scene. No known person had had contact with him since then. Friday night. This was Sunday morning.

Vinny was growing impatient. He needed to find Osborn ASAP. If he didn't, there was no telling what Joe Stringer might do to him while the boss was behind bars. Rimouski would never fire Vinny, but the problem was Rimouski was the only person who knew what Vinny's real capabilities were. Joe did not. Joe was leery and hesitant. And the clock was ticking.

Vinny schooled his voice to be as menacing as possible. "For all I know, you're the one who tipped off Nolan Osborn. Don't fuck with me."

The man inhaled sharply. "Fuck you."

"No thanks. I don't swing that way." It was juvenile. Vinny knew it. But he was exasperated. "Just find him. And call me." He hung up without waiting for a response.

The truth was, half the reason Vinny was so on edge was because he didn't know who his contact was. He'd never met the guy and didn't have a name. The important thing was the guy knew stuff. He provided information in exchange for money. Lots of money. Money Vinny was going to run out of if his boss didn't get out on bond soon.

Vinny had a pile of problems, and they weighed on him heavily. His boss was in jail. His boss's right-hand man didn't trust Vinny. Vinny was running out of discretionary income. And he would never tell Stringer he was a shifter. He didn't trust Stringer any more than Stringer trusted him. For one thing, the guy was human. For another thing, Joe thought his shit didn't stink.

Vinny's only goal was to get his boss released, get paid heftily for the job, and blow out of town without leaving a forwarding address. He didn't need this shit or this headache.

He needed cash. Lots of it.

Nolan held the phone to his ear, his ass leaning against the small kitchen table, his ankles crossed, his free arm also crossed over his chest. "Why the hell would I do that?" he asked Detective Schaefer. "I'm telling you I'm safe here. No one will find me."

Schaefer cleared his throat. "And I'm telling you we don't operate this way. We need to keep you safe until the trial. We don't leave it up to our witnesses to provide their own safety. You need to come out of hiding and let us protect you."

Nolan chuckled sardonically. "Like you protected me Friday night?"

He listened to Carl sigh. "That was an error on our part. Won't happen again."

"Right. How could you possibly guarantee that? It happened once. It could happen again." Why was Stringer even arguing this point? Nolan had been much safer from the moment Reid picked him up than the prior week. The hotel had made him anxious. Rightfully so.

Carl took a deep breath. "Please. Humor me. Meet me somewhere."

"I'm with friends. It's not like I drove here. I didn't have a car. I had to rely on my friends to pick me up and keep me safe. They've done a splendid job for two days."

"Yeah. Yeah. I know. Your father filled me in. He did not, however, tell me where to find you or who these friends are. He's a stubborn man."

"He's my father, not yours. Who do you think he's going to be loyal to? You're lucky I asked him to call you at all and let you know I was alive. See how courteous I am? Besides, I'm not stupid. He doesn't have the first clue where I am." That last part was only half true. Although Nolan hadn't told his dad where he was, the man was not stupid. He could easily figure out where Nolan and Adriana might have gone with Reid. Carl didn't need to know that.

"So, you're planning on hiding with two other people until the trial? Don't your friends have lives to live?"

Was Carl being an asshole on purpose?

He was right, however. Reid and Adriana needed to get back home. Adriana had school the next day and homework to do. Nolan did think the best plan would be for them to leave him at the cabin.

The only problem with that idea was Nolan wouldn't have a vehicle. He could shift and run on foot, but he didn't like being cornered with few options. Nolan was still uneasy this morning. "Fine," he consented. At least in police protection, he had access to information. Out here in the middle of nowhere, he could hide for weeks without sufficient contact with Schaefer. Cell service sucked, and his battery was going to die soon. It wasn't as if he'd stopped to grab a charger when he fled down the fire escape. A coat, yes. A charger, no. He was lucky he'd been wearing shoes.

Schaefer blew out a relieved breath. "I'll text you a spot to meet up."

"Not this time. I'll text *you* the location. Meet me in two hours." He ended the call before Carl could protest and lowered the phone to send the text. He was certain the detective was having a coronary at his total lack of control, but Nolan didn't want the man to think he was completely in charge anymore. He'd fucked up. Nolan's faith in his abilities was waning.

When he lifted his gaze, he found both Reid and Adriana standing several feet away at the bottom of the ladder. They hadn't been up yet when he slid from the bed to come downstairs, but he'd known they were awake. And they would have heard everything.

"Guess we're leaving," Reid stated.

Nolan sighed. "I'm not fond of this plan. I've lost faith in the police. But you two need to return, and I'm a sitting duck if I stay here without a car."

"You could come back here, I guess," Reid pointed out.

Nolan tipped his head back and spoke to the ceiling. "I considered that option, but if I went to your condo, there would be a good chance I would be found out and then followed. As it is I hate that you're even with me. That's why we're going to meet Schaefer on the side of the highway. I'll text him a mile marker. I don't want either of you to be exposed to anyone anywhere."

Adriana inched forward until she was right in front of him. "You think it's that bad?" she asked as she set her hands on his chest and leaned into him.

He lowered his face, wrapped his arms around her, and held her close. "I'm not taking any chances."

"Okay," she whispered. "Guess we better get going." She lifted onto her tiptoes and kissed his lips.

He returned the kiss, angling his head to one side to deepen it, if only for a moment. It literally caused him pain, leaving her like this. But he had no choice. She needed to have a normal life while he waited for this trial. It would be selfish of him to ask her to drop her classes to hang with him in a remote cabin in the woods. Not to mention Reid.

She set her face against his neck and inhaled. "Love your scent."

He held her closer, his nose in her thick hair. "Mmm," he agreed. Her scent was like a drug. The thought of not smelling her again for a while made his heart race.

God, he hated this.

Reid had approached and now stood behind Adriana, his hands on her shoulders.

They'd been living in another dimension for over twenty-four hours. A strange world where it seemed natural that Nolan had shared a woman with his best friend. At no point had it even felt awkward. As if everyone in the universe had two mates. Insane.

He swallowed, fighting back the realization that the earth didn't spin this direction normally, and eventually they would need to alter the course. Or rather, Adriana needed to choose.

It didn't seem fair. Why did she have to make this decision? Several times yesterday, even though no one said a word out loud or even silently, he'd caught her brow furrowed in concentration, her gaze glancing back and forth between them. She was troubled. Rightfully so. He truly understood and believed she felt the same pull toward both of them.

"Fuck," he muttered before he could stop himself.

Both Adriana and Reid flinched, but neither said a word. They all knew what he was referring to. Reid leaned in closer, pinning Adriana between them. He lifted one hand off her shoulder and reached the extra few inches to set it on Nolan's shoulder instead and gave a squeeze.

Nolan moved one hand from Adriana's waist to Reid's. The connection was intense.

No one moved for long moments. If anything, they held each other tighter, closer, firmer. A bond buzzed between them in the air as if they were one. What did it mean?

For the first time since Nolan met Adriana and then found out she also felt connected to Reid, he considered the possibility that they all three were meant to be together.

Was it possible?

He shook the idea from his mind. Of course not. How would they explain such a connection to…well, anyone? Shifters didn't have two mates. At least bear shifters didn't. He remembered his dad had pointed out something about the wolves in Montana. Nolan assumed his dad meant that wolves sometimes met more than one mate and had to choose. Maybe that wasn't it at all. Did the wolves bind in threes?

He really needed to call Wyatt Arthur and get some details.

He swallowed. What was he thinking? It didn't matter what the wolves did. Bears did not bind in threes. Society wouldn't accept such a union. Not shifters or humans. Especially not humans. They would be ostracized. They wouldn't fit in anywhere. Nature wouldn't do that to them. Would She?

Adriana squirmed. "Hate to break up this bonding moment, but I can't breathe."

Reid chuckled and eased back, releasing his grip on Nolan's shoulder.

Nolan let go of Reid's waist at the same time. He lifted his head and locked his gaze with his friend. Something passed between them. Something unspoken and profound. Had Reid been having the same thoughts? It was certainly possible.

Nolan continued to stare at his friend. He replayed the

weekend in his mind like a film reel. Everything had been so natural between them. So fluid. So perfect. But the most important element of a normal sexual relationship had been taken off the table. It was one thing for the two of them to worship Adriana's body and make her boil for them both. It would have been another thing entirely for the two of them to have removed their jeans. That would be taking things too far.

Maybe Nolan could kiss a woman and pass her to Reid... No. Shit. Just thinking about that was weirder than fuck. They had shared Adriana. Passed her back and forth. Kissed her entire sexy naked body at the same time without so much as flinching. How had that not been weird?

He swallowed. Okay. Fine. They made her hum. They made her scream. It was hot as hell. But cocks? No. No no no no no.

It wasn't as though Nolan and Reid had never been naked in the same room. They were dudes. It happened. They'd seen each other's junk. But not in front of a woman. They couldn't take off their jeans and seal the deal with her at the same time.

No.

Of course not.

How could they do that without rubbing against each other?

Nolan shuddered and jerked his gaze from Reid's, feeling a flush crawl up his cheeks. He wasn't one to normally get embarrassed, but his thoughts had led him in the craziest direction.

"Guys?" Adriana set one hand on Reid's chest, her other still on Nolan's. She turned her body so she was sideways between them, glancing back and forth. "You're in like a trance."

Nolan forced himself to look at her, but not before glancing again at Reid to find the man's cheeks just as flushed.

"What were you two discussing?" she asked, her brow furrowing.

"Nothing," they both stated at once.

She lifted a brow at that. "Really?" The one word was laced with sarcasm. "Why am I not buying that?"

Reid set his hand on top of hers and lifted their combined fingers to his lips. He kissed her knuckles before he spoke. "It's true. I'm not going to deny we might have been thinking the same thing, but we were both in our own world, not sharing."

She nodded slowly. "Okay."

"We should go." It was the last thing Nolan wanted to do, but he needed to figure out a mile marker and text Schaefer soon. He lifted Adriana's other hand and pressed her palm to his cheek, closing his eyes and inhaling her scent deeply.

She leaned into his side.

He didn't look, but he felt Reid moving away, and then he heard the door to the cabin quietly open and close. Reid was giving them a moment. Bless him.

With a deep breath, Nolan wrapped his arms around Adriana and pulled her around to fully face him. He eased his hands to her jaw and cupped her face, meeting her gaze. "Adriana…"

She smiled.

What was she thinking? "What?"

"I love the way you say my name."

"Do I say it differently from anyone else?" He furrowed his brow.

"Yes. It rolls off your tongue like a caress. Even the first time you said it I got wet."

At that, he grinned widely. "Really now."

She smiled broader. "Yes." And then she lifted onto her tiptoes and kissed his lips briefly.

"Well, I love your name. It's mysterious and sexy."

"Only when you say it."

He'd take that. He threaded his fingers through her hair and held her face, staring deep into her gorgeous brown eyes. *I love you.* He didn't say the words out loud or even communicate them into her mind, but he wanted to. It seemed too soon. They'd known each other a week and spent only two days together.

Part of him knew without a doubt that if it weren't for her connection to Reid, Nolan would have bound her to him already. But that wasn't an option. It might not ever be. It was possible he would never have another moment like this with her again. So he soaked it in, grateful to Reid for the opportunity.

The three of them had been together constantly for over thirty hours, never separated except to use the bathroom. But these precious seconds were for Nolan. He glanced down at her clothes, smiling. "If you make a habit of coming here, you might want to stock the place with some things that fit you better."

She groaned. "If I ever come back here again, I'm bringing a trunk of stuff, not just clothes. I'm completely out of my element without my usual supplies."

He lifted a lock of her hair. "What do you need? You look gorgeous."

She giggled. "Seriously? I can't remember a time when I went two full days without makeup, hair products, my blow dryer. There isn't even any proper shampoo or conditioner in this cabin."

He laughed. He didn't care that she was wearing a T-shirt that was too large and a pair of yoga pants that belonged to Paige. Maybe it was unusual for her to go without all the extras she normally enjoyed, but ironically, both times he'd had the pleasure of her company, she'd been her natural self.

"Except for a few minutes in the dark in the car Friday night, you've never seen me once put together. I swear this is not me. I own clothes that fit and I clean up nice," she joked.

He dropped the lock of hair he held, tucked it behind her ear, and stared at her face, memorizing it. "You don't need any of that stuff. You're stunning without."

She rolled her eyes. "Men."

He smiled. "I've seen your posts on social media. I know you have an amazing sense of fashion, and your hair and makeup usually look like they were done by a professional for a movie shoot. But I'm always going to be partial to the woman who walked into my hotel room last week without enough warning to apply all that extra stuff. She's smokin' hot."

She leaned into him closer. "You have to say that. Your perception is warped by pheromones."

He laughed again. "That may be, but it also means you don't have to do a damn thing to impress me." He was serious. She was the sexiest woman on earth. Everything about her. Her eyes were mesmerizing and bright. Her body could not be hidden even under loose-fitting clothes. He loved the way her hair hung in long waves down her back. Natural. Loose.

God, she was amazing. If he had stood in a crowded stadium full of women and been given the opportunity to pick one out of thousands, he would have chosen her.

And yet...

He didn't want to think about tomorrow. He needed to get through today. Once they left, he couldn't have some long, drawn-out goodbye with Adriana on the side of the road where they met up with Schaefer. As far as the officer was concerned, Adriana would be Reid's girlfriend.

In Nolan's crazy, messed-up world, he had told the police he didn't have anyone special in his life last Saturday morning. He didn't have a significant other. He couldn't very well have turned around later that day and told Carl he had a fiancée in his parents' home. So, he'd been stuck. He had no choice but to stick to the story as it had begun.

She broke the stare to set her forehead against his chest and gripped his shirt in her fists at his back. *"I don't know what to say,"* she communicated into his mind.

"I know, baby. It's okay. Just want to hold you a minute." He took in several long breaths, stalling, feeling her heartbeat against his chest, wanting more. More time. More of her. More.

But they had to go.

He kissed the top of her head and grabbed her hand to lead her from the cabin.

CHAPTER 18

Reid exited the highway and pulled the SUV to the side of the ramp at the agreed-upon mile marker. A nondescript, tan four-door already sat on the shoulder, and Reid slowed down to ease up behind it.

Nolan sat in the passenger seat. He twisted around to face Adriana in the back as they stopped, grabbing her hand and kissing her palm. "Please, baby. Be safe. Be careful. Do what Reid asks. Please. Now isn't the time to assert your independence."

She nodded. "Okay."

Reid wondered if she could follow that instruction. She was feisty and didn't like anyone telling her what to do, where to go, when to leave. She was out of her element having a man, let alone two, bossing her around, even if it was with every good intention—to keep her safe.

Nolan released her and opened his door. "Wait in the car, Adriana."

Reid watched her flinch in the rearview mirror, but she made no move to disconnect her seatbelt. He climbed out of the driver's side and rounded the hood at the same time as Nolan.

The officer approached the two of them from the rear of his car. He held out a hand toward Reid. "Carl Schaefer."

"Reid Terrance," Reid responded.

"I'm impressed. You managed to go totally off the grid. I'd love to know your secret."

Reid nodded but didn't answer.

Nolan spoke, stepping casually in front of the officer who was now peering into the SUV. "We should get going. I don't want my friends involved in this any more than necessary."

"Of course." Carl's gaze was still on Reid's vehicle.

Reid stepped closer to Nolan under the pretense of slapping his friend on the shoulder as a departure gesture. "Take care." He also managed to get Schaefer to stop staring at Adriana.

"Well then," Carl stated. "Let's go." He rocked forward on his feet and then turned back toward the car.

Nolan shot Reid a look as he rounded to the passenger side. *"Keep her safe."*

"You know I will."

Before he ducked into the car, he met Reid's gaze again. *"Rope."*

"Rope." Reid nodded. He couldn't imagine a scenario in which he'd need to execute that last-resort plan, but then again, he also couldn't have imagined Nolan needing to escape through a third-floor window and climb down a fire escape either. The stakes were high. The game was serious.

As the unmarked patrol car pulled away, Reid spun around and bee-lined for the SUV. By the time he was inside, Adriana had climbed over the seat and was buckling into the front passenger side. "That guy gave me the chills."

"You and me both." Reid started the engine and pulled back onto the highway. It was crazy occupying the same space as Adriana without touching her—or mauling her—but in this new weird upside-down world, he was practically growing accustomed to sharing oxygen with her without flattening her to the nearest surface and ripping her clothes off.

They'd done it for an entire week until they picked up Nolan. They'd shockingly survived. In fact, if Reid was honest with himself, he'd been more drawn to her while they were with Nolan than without him. Was that even a thing? Was it the competition that made her more appealing?

Now that Nolan had separated from them, the urgency tamped down marginally. He still felt a powerful magnetic pull to her, but not as strong somehow. It made no sense.

"You're not crazy. I feel it too," she stated softly, shaking him out of his pondering as she reached across the center console and wrapped her fingers over the top of his hand.

He hadn't blocked her. That was so unlike him. He flipped his hand and threaded their fingers together over the console.

"What do you think it means?"

"I don't know, baby. I don't know." His voice was husky. Emotion welled up inside. He feared it meant that she belonged to Nolan. He hated the idea while at the same time knew it was for the best. Nolan met her first. Nolan knew she was his fourteen hours before Reid stepped into Stanton and Oleta's home last Sunday. Maybe the Universe had put Reid in her path and made him think she was his in order to keep her safe. If so, She was a cruel bitch. But it was possible.

They drove in silence. Not uncomfortable. But quiet.

When they got to his condo, he pulled into the garage

and shut it before opening his car door. He'd surveyed the surrounding area closely on approach and found nothing out of the ordinary. With a hand on Adriana's lower back, he led her to the door, reset the alarm, and then followed her up the stairs.

"I need a real shower and some better-fitting clothes," she announced.

He nodded. "You go on upstairs. I'm going to check my email and then figure out what we can eat for lunch." He made eye contact with her briefly and watched as she headed up the stairs.

God, she was gorgeous. Every single move made his cock hard. He stared at the spot where she'd disappeared from his view for a long time, gripping the edge of the granite countertop on his island. He'd never been more confused in his life, and he didn't like it one bit.

While she showered, he forced himself to ignore the sound of running water, knowing she was naked and remembering every inch of her delicious body. He was unsteady as he padded to the kitchen table and opened his laptop where he'd left it Friday night. He was shaking as he eased into the chair.

Life was a bitch. A very unfair bitch. He wanted to scream. He didn't. Instead, he opened his email, scrolled through it, deleted the trash, and decided nothing looked urgent. He couldn't concentrate anyway.

The water shut off, making him flinch. She would be wrapped in a towel now. Was she standing at the mirror combing her hair? He wanted to run his hands through the long thick locks. He wanted to gently comb it out for her. He wanted to pat her sweet body dry with the towel. He wanted to lure her to his bed and hold her naked body against his own.

He wanted so many unattainable things.

With an abrupt push, he shoved from the table and headed for the fridge to grab a beer. A pilsner from Glacial Brewing Company, one of her family's competition. Did she care that he stocked beer from both breweries? She'd never said a word.

Hell, she wasn't the type. She would never complain about something like that. She might joke about it one day, but it wouldn't piss her off that he drank from the competition.

His cell phone rang in his pocket as he took a long drag. He pulled it out to find Stanton's name across the top. "Hey," he answered.

"You get back okay?"

"Yes."

"I've communicated with Nolan a few times since he left with the officer. They moved him to another hotel."

"Thanks for updating us." Reid sighed.

"You sound tired."

"I am. This is stressful."

"I can't even imagine. Listen, I don't know if it will help or not, but I got Wyatt Arthur's number for you. Maybe he can shed some light on how wolf shifters choose their mates when they find themselves in a similar situation as yours. I'll text you the number. Use it. Don't use it. It's up to you. I just thought it might be helpful."

"Thank you. Appreciate it." It had to be strange for Stanton. His own son had scented his mate only to have her slip through his fingers before he set eyes on her.

Stanton took a breath and changed the subject. "I also spoke to Laurence and Charles from the Arcadian Council earlier. They came by the house."

"Shit. I didn't think to contact them when we fled."

"No worries. They wanted to make sure you were all

okay. If they had needed to physically find you, they would have."

"No doubt." Reid shuddered. The council members were powerful. They had abilities far more advanced than the average shifter.

Stanton sighed. "Oleta's worried about you. All three of you." He paused. "Not going to lie, I am too. Nolan sounded about as despondent as you do now."

That didn't surprise Reid. "We're fine. It's hard. It's crazy. It's wacked. But we're doing the best we can."

"I'm sure you are. Anything we can do to help?"

"No. I appreciate the offer though." There was no way the two of them could even visit Stanton and Oleta. It would put them in jeopardy. All of them.

"Well, keep in touch."

"We will. Thank you. It means a lot to know you're supporting us."

"Always. You know that, Reid. No matter what happens, you will always be a member of our family."

Reid nodded though Stanton couldn't see him. How could Stanton be so sure? What if Reid bound himself to Adriana and left Nolan without a mate? How would the Osborns feel then?

"I'll let you go, son. Be safe."

"Will do." He ended the call and put the phone back in his pocket. He didn't want to miss a call from Nolan. There was no way to know when he might check in, but Reid didn't intend to leave his cell unattended even for a moment. Adriana wouldn't want to miss a call either.

Reid lifted his gaze to the staircase again. Adriana hadn't come back. He didn't sense she was moving around anymore either, which meant she was resting or hiding in his guest room.

He couldn't blame her. He hated it, but he still understood.

He took another drink of his beer, shoved off the counter, and headed for the stairs. He too needed a shower.

~

Adriana lay curled on her side in a fetal position on the bed. She wore nothing but her silk robe. After showering and brushing out her hair, she'd felt an overwhelming sense of exhaustion.

And a profound sadness.

The stress was getting to her. She couldn't take this much longer. She needed answers. She was living in limbo. The weekend had been amazing, beyond her wildest dreams. Two men had pampered her so thoroughly that by morning it had seemed perfectly natural to be doted on by two of them.

And then they'd returned to reality. She couldn't help thinking the intense feelings they'd experienced over the weekend had been more imagined than real. Sort of like vacation mode. She'd gone on lots of vacations in her life, and every time she'd felt this sense of disassociation from the real world. She could be a different person when out of town. Wear clothes she didn't ordinarily wear. Get dressed up. Put on more makeup. Curl her hair. Laugh and eat and dance and enjoy herself.

Maybe the trip to the cabin had been similar. Surreal. Like a vacation. She'd been someone else for almost two days. A wonton wild woman who would let two men bring her to orgasm over and over again. It seemed more like a dream than reality. She might read a novel about something like that, but no one actually did such a thing.

Two men. What the hell had she been thinking?

And even weirder, she had yet to see inside either man's pants. They'd stripped her naked and kept her that way for hours. They'd rocked her world time and again, pushing her over the edge until she couldn't think about anything except when she might get her next orgasm.

Her emotions were all over the place now. She was embarrassed, for one thing. Who did that?

The moment they'd dropped Nolan off, she'd slipped back into her regular dimension, so to speak. Nothing in her life was "normal" at the moment, but at least she was back in the condo where her sketches needed attention, and no one was holding her down and fucking the sense out of her with their fingers.

She stiffened almost painfully at the thought. Drawing her knees up closer to her chest, she clenched her thighs together. Her pussy was once again swollen and wet at the memory. She gripped her hands together between her breasts, feeling the soft brush of silk as it teased her nipples mercilessly.

This couldn't go on. She would lose her mind soon.

She was so tired.

A tear slid from her eye. She tried to stop the emotional overload, but it was too late. Another tear joined the first, and then the dam let loose. She bit her lip to keep from making a sound as she silently sobbed.

Her eyes were puffy and swollen in moments as she succumbed to the release.

She had been aware of Reid entering his room across the hall and turning on the shower, but she hadn't noticed when he finished. She must have been pretty upset and wrapped up in her pity party because suddenly Reid was climbing onto the bed.

She swallowed, but couldn't form words.

He crawled up behind her, tucked his front against her back, and draped his arm across her body to hold her tight. His large hand wrapped around both of hers between her breasts. His other arm wiggled under her head to pillow her cheek against his biceps. He kissed her shoulder right at the base of her neck, the edge of the robe having fallen open a few inches.

She cried. So many tears. They got worse when he came in all perfect and quiet and understanding. For the longest time, he never said a word, but he stroked her hands with his fingers and her neck with his other hand.

His lips remained on her sweet spot, making her far too aware of how easy it would be for him to bite her and put an end to the charade. He could do it. He could bind her to him and cut Nolan out of the equation in less time than he could snap his fingers.

He wouldn't though. And that fact made her love him even more.

Love him?

Did she love him?

If she was honest, she loved both of them. And she was fairly certain Nolan had thought the words right before they'd left the cabin. He had been blocking her, but his emotions spilled out anyway. Her knees had nearly buckled when his mind whispered *I love you*. She didn't think she'd imagined it.

Had he realized she'd been thinking the same thing? Did Reid know it just as strongly?

The tears kept falling, silently but steadily. Unrelenting. She didn't bother to try to stop them. Reid didn't seem to mind. He never stopped stroking her skin while his lips grazed her neck and shoulder over and over. So lightly she might have imagined it. Willed it even.

It seemed like hours went by. In reality, only minutes had passed. Eventually, her eyelids grew heavy, and she let them flutter closed one last time, grateful as sleep sucked her under.

CHAPTER 19

After waiting all day on pins and needles, pacing, Vinny finally got the call he'd been waiting for. He headed across town by car and then walked the last few blocks to the exchange point he'd been using for weeks with his contact.

The jogging path was an ideal place to swap information and money. It was well-used, but easy enough to approach without notice. Vinny sauntered casually toward the tree he used for the trade, bent down as if tying his shoe, and brushed a pile of leaves to one side. He easily grabbed the envelope tucked in the dip under the tree and left a matching one.

He didn't breathe easy until the leaves were once again covering his drop location and he was walking back toward the car. *His* envelope was filled with cash. The one he picked up had better contain information he desperately needed.

There was no need to worry about a random jogger stumbling upon the money. Vinny was beyond certain someone in the distance was watching his every move, and they would move in as soon as he was gone.

He didn't open the new envelope until he was back in his car.

Bingo.

Not only did he have the latest location where Nolan Osborn had been taken, but a bonus tip—Nolan had two people helping him for the last few days.

What fucking good luck.

Reid Terrance and an unknown woman.

If those three were so thick that Reid had helped Nolan get away from the hotel room Friday night, there was a chance he could be used as leverage to lure Nolan out.

Perfect.

Vinny had a slower heart rate than he'd had in days as he pulled back onto the road and headed home.

Plotting. Always plotting his next move. Was Reid Terrance a shifter? What about the woman? Mostly likely.

He beat his thumbs against the steering wheel as he drove, his mind wandering to all the possibilities. He needed to act fast. There was no telling how long Osborn would be kept at the new location.

Vinny needed help. He needed manpower to pull off the plan developing in his mind.

It could work.

It had to work.

It was dark when Adriana opened her eyes. She wasn't confused about her location for even a moment though. Reid was still exactly where he'd been when she fell asleep, curled around her, holding her. He wasn't asleep. Had he ever been? Or had he watched her sleep?

"You okay, baby?" he whispered, his fingers stroking her cheek.

"I'm not sure I ever will be again," she answered truthfully.

He didn't negate the statement. He understood.

But he did ease back and then rolled her onto her back. "My arm's asleep," he told her as he pulled it free and smiled. He shook out his undoubtedly tingling appendage while he watched her face.

What did he see?

She wasn't thinking of her tearstained swollen eyes and cheeks. She was wondering what he could see in her eyes, the portals to her soul.

Finally, he leaned on one elbow, tossed a leg over hers, and reached with his free hand to tuck a lock of hair gently behind her ear. "You sleep so peacefully, and then the moment you wake up your mind rushes back to its agitated state. I hate that for you."

She forced a smile. "Me too."

Reid continued to stroke her cheek with his thumb after he corralled the stray hairs. He was deep in thought, his brow slightly furrowed. His voice was controlled when he spoke. "What's going through your head, baby?"

She swallowed. "It's like a hurricane in there."

He smiled, meeting her gaze. "I can imagine. Can I help?"

"I don't think so. I have to figure this out on my own." It wasn't as though he couldn't imagine what was weighing on her, although it was possible he didn't realize the specifics. The disconnect she felt with him from the moment Nolan folded into the cop car hadn't abated.

She couldn't explain it, not even to herself. It wasn't that she felt less for him. The pull was still strong. She knew he was her mate. She knew it like she knew the sky was blue and the sun would rise. But something was off. Different.

She wanted him. She wanted to be close to him. Have him hold her like he was. Enjoy the intense way he looked at her. She wanted more. Everything.

But there was a hesitation too. What did it mean? Was it Fate's way of guiding her more toward Nolan than Reid? She wondered if she would feel the same exact level of magnetism toward Nolan if the men were reversed. What if Reid was the one in hiding and Nolan was leaning over her?

She licked her lips and pulled them between her teeth, fighting the renewed need to cry. She had no idea why she was so emotional. Overloaded. Between her classes, her homework, living with a man she wanted to fuck and wasn't sleeping with, and carrying on a long-distance relationship with a man in hiding… Shit.

"You need someone to talk to. Someone who isn't me to work out all the storms in your brain. Have you reached out to your mom lately?"

"Not since the other day." It wasn't a bad idea. She could share her turmoil with her mom. They'd always been close. The only problem was her mom had no idea what Adriana was going through. No one did. It was causing a sense of isolation.

As far as she knew, not one person alive could relate to her strange predicament. Who the hell could give her advice? Or worse, who could listen to her plight without judging her or gasping?

She shuddered. There was no one. But at least her mother wouldn't make her feel like a freak. She might not be able to understand, but she would listen and give advice without judgment.

"You need to eat something. How about I go cook, and you call your mom and talk to her? It might help."

She nodded. How did he know exactly what to say?

After lowering his face to gently kiss her lips, he shoved off the bed and padded from the room, shutting the door behind him.

Adriana reached for her cell on the bedside table and dialed her mom.

"Hey, honey. How are you?"

"I'm…" Emotions flooded her. Even though she'd spoken to her mom earlier in the week, Adriana felt a renewed sense of pressure and stress tonight.

She also missed Nolan desperately. From the moment he'd gotten out of the SUV, she'd felt the loss. It had only been a few hours, but she wanted him with her. It wasn't natural for mates to go on and on like this without binding.

In a way, it seemed as though the looming trial and the need to keep Nolan in witness protection was the culprit, but the reality was Adriana didn't believe that had any influence or effect on her situation. The bottom line was she felt the pull toward two men. Equally. Criminal bad guys on the loose or not, she still had the same problem.

"Sweetie?" Beth's voice was gentle. Sad. Filled with worry for her daughter.

Adriana realized she was crying again, not silently. She wiped the tears from her cheeks and rolled onto her side to once again curl into herself. "I don't know what's happening to me or what to do, Mom."

"I'm so sorry. I can't even imagine. Tell me what's going on."

Adriana took a deep breath and then let the events of the last few days tumble rapidly from her lips. Facts. Not emotions. She left out all the parts she had no intention of sharing with her mother. Finally, she ended with, "Nolan went back into witness protection this afternoon. Reid and I are back at his condo." Those words revealed nothing.

"How was the weekend? Did it help being with both of them? Or was it stressful and awkward?"

"I don't know. It wasn't awkward, but I can't say it was helpful. If anything I'm more conflicted than I was before." She sighed. "No. That's not true either. I've never been conflicted, Mom. That's just it. I know in my heart I want them both equally. Not to say they're the same. They're very different. But I'm attracted to both. I'm surely clinically insane."

Her mom chuckled softly. "I don't think that's true."

"I can't choose, Mom. I'm not any closer to choosing than I was a week ago. I don't see how I'll ever be able to."

"I think you need to take a step back and stop trying to force it. Whatever is meant to happen will undoubtedly happen at the right time. Maybe you're meant to feel exactly as you do for some reason we can't fathom yet. Maybe your bond to Nolan is keeping him alert somehow, and your bond to Reid is helping him keep you safe."

"Yeah, but whatever the future holds scares the hell out of me. Someone's going to get hurt, and the more days that go by, the more pain will be inflicted. And the worst part is I'm the one who will be causing the pain. I can't stand the idea of hurting either of them. It's not fair."

"I know, hon. It certainly does seem like a cruel twist of fate. But I have to believe there's a plan for you, and you need to have the patience to wait and see what it is. There's no rush, right? I mean you're waiting for a trial. It could be a while. In the meantime, focus on other things. Let Nature figure Herself out on Her terms."

"You're right." It made sense. Adriana had spent a lot of time forcing something that clearly wasn't in the cards yet. She squeezed her eyes closed and pictured both men hovering over her, suckling her nipples, fingering her pussy simultaneously, working in tandem to make her come.

When she tried to shake the image and replace it with a vision of her with just one of the men, nothing came to her. Was it because she hadn't had many experiences with either of them separately? Why would that stop her from visualizing them individually?

Once again she allowed herself to ponder the wisdom of the two of them refusing to have sex with her. So many times she'd been on edge, needing to be filled and not caring which man did it as long as someone did.

But every time, they denied her. Why? The level of willpower they exhibited made her think they didn't experience the same magnetic pull toward her as she did to them. She didn't have that willpower. There had been too many moments to count when she would have begged them to make love to her. She had done so a few times yesterday.

Perhaps this entire thing was all her and neither man truly felt the lure she felt. Maybe she wasn't meant to be with either of them, and she would find someone else she had an even more powerful connection to someday.

That idea made her physically shudder. If there was a man out there—shifter or otherwise—who could cause even more powerful emotions than the ones she'd been feeling for the past week, she would have to be hospitalized in the psych ward.

"Honey," her mother's soothing voice began again, interrupting her random thoughts, "you're putting too much stress on yourself. I'm worried about you."

She was not wrong. But how was Adriana supposed to stop the bombardment of concerns plaguing her night and day?

When Adriana hung up with her mom, she was at least feeling slightly more human. She forced herself to get off the bed, put on some clothes, and join Reid in the kitchen. The saint had made dinner while she spoke to her mom, and Adriana found herself starving.

After they ate and cleaned up, she went back to her room and buried herself in schoolwork, making a huge dent in what needed to be done for the week. Luckily it was a light week. She didn't have any presentations or exams looming.

It was midnight when she closed her sketch pad and headed to the bathroom. With her face washed, teeth brushed, and sleepwear on, she turned around and walked straight into the wall of Reid's chest. The only thing stopping her from stumbling backward was him grabbing her elbows to steady her. How had she not felt his presence so close to her?

"Whoa…" he said as he gripped her arms and hauled her toward him. "Sorry. Didn't mean to sneak up on you."

She took several quick short breaths. "I must have been in another world."

One side of his mouth lifted. "That happens a lot."

"Only lately. I was never this distracted until the two of you stepped into my life," she pointed out.

"I believe you." He slid his palms down her arms until he had their fingers threaded together. "Listen, I want you to sleep in my room."

She licked her lips. Her heart pounded at the idea. What was he insinuating?

"Don't panic. We aren't going to do anything but sleep."

"I can sleep fine in my own room." She shook her head. She wouldn't be able to sleep a single moment in his bed.

"I'll sleep better with you closer to me." He gave her hands a tug.

She followed him, but she wasn't done arguing. "I don't think it's a good idea, Reid."

He led her around the corner and into his room. She had been in there a few times earlier in the week but had avoided it more as the week wore on. For one thing, it felt too personal. For another thing, the scent of him was stronger in his bedroom than any other part of the house. Luring her in.

And sure enough, the moment she found herself several feet inside, her knees grew weak and her stomach dipped. "Reid…"

He let go of one hand and tugged the other closer to the bed before pulling back the comforter. He hadn't bothered turning on the lights. In fact, he clearly intended for them to get into his bed right that second. He wore nothing but low-hanging, navy sleep pants. She was used to seeing him like that. He did it often. His chest had become a distraction she couldn't avoid. Most of the time she forced herself to keep her gaze on his face or look away when they were alone in the house and he wasn't wearing a shirt.

Right now, she couldn't avoid it. He was too close to her, and his muscles were flexing with the effort to tug her closer. "We're just going to sleep. You slept like a rock with me last night and this afternoon."

He was correct. She'd slept hard when the two of them had finally stopped touching her last night and her heart rate had returned to normal. Now, her pulse was pounding again.

He sat on the edge of the bed and reached for her other hand again to pull her into the V of his legs. The position put them at eye level, and he searched her face for something she didn't know how to describe.

He was so calm. Not forcing her to do as he requested but clearly not willing to relent either. His hands slid to her waist, and she set hers on his shoulders.

It might have been a mistake. His warm, smooth skin made her flatten her palms with the urge to explore the rest of his chest and abs. She didn't.

She realized she needed to say something. Her mind had wandered again. "It's not the same."

He would know what she meant without elaborating.

"I know, baby." He pulled her closer and kissed her forehead before leaning back again and meeting her gaze. "But I slept better last night too. When you're across the hallway, I toss and turn. I thought it was better. I wanted to heed your wishes all week. I understand your hesitation. Really I do. But it's torture having you so close and so far at the same time. After last night, I realized my bed was huge and empty without you in it."

It was tempting. But was it wise? His voice alone was making her melt. And the look in his eyes was more than she could bear. He sometimes radiated an intensity that consumed her. In truth, Nolan did too. It was difficult to tell either of them *no*.

She didn't want to. She wanted this man to hold her throughout the night. She wanted his warm, firm body wrapped around her, his leg over hers tucking her close. She wanted his lips on her neck, his breath in her space, his heart beating against her. She wanted to feel every inch of him pressing her into the mattress.

Standing in the circle of his arms, she grew weak.

Reid slid one hand up her side and then cupped her neck. She shivered at his touch. It would help if she were wearing more than a thin white tank top and pink sleep shorts. She didn't have on enough clothing to protect herself against his advances. Her nipples were hard peaks he would not miss if he glanced down.

What did it matter? He'd seen every inch of her naked. A war was battling, one she would not win because she didn't even know which side she was on. She both wanted him to let her go back to her room, and she wanted to stay. In her room, at least half her brain could function without being under his spell. In his room, she could relax in the safety of his embrace and sleep more soundly. He was right about that.

It wasn't logical. In his presence, she often couldn't relax at all. Even now—especially now—she wanted more.

His thumb brushed against her cheek. "I can see your mind battling, but there's no need. I'm not going to have sex with you. I just want you with me. It's that simple. No ulterior motives."

"That's half of what worries me, Reid," she blurted out.

His brow furrowed. She could see it easily in the dim light coming from nothing but the moon. "What do you mean?"

She shook her head. "Never mind." No way did she want to get into her crazy confusion with him at this hour. It was late. She had class in the morning.

He gripped her jaw tighter. "Adriana, hon, talk to me."

"It's nothing. Forget I said anything."

"I'll never ignore or forget anything you say. Talk to me," he repeated...demanded. "What's going on in that head of yours? It bothers you that I don't have ulterior motives?"

She swallowed, not committing to the truth.

He must have taken that as confirmation because he stiffened. "I'm trying to understand, baby."

She sighed. She wasn't going to get out of this conversation. "Both of you. You're so...calm. You're not...

Neither of you is..." She couldn't manage to get the words out.

He looked confused, searching her eyes and obviously coming up blank. "Not what?"

"Reid..." She tried to pull away. How had she gotten into this with him? She didn't want to discuss her insecurities. The entire thing was embarrassing.

His hand at her waist slid around to the small of her back, his fingers splaying wider and holding her closer. His other palm pressed against her neck. "You're not going to get out of this, hon. Spit it out. I don't have enough information to read your mind, and you're blocking me with walls so thick and high I can't see over them."

Jesus. Even now in his room after midnight in the dark with so many problems looming between them...Even now he was both sweet and demanding. He deserved her openness. "I don't think I belong to either of you." That wasn't exactly what she meant to say, but it came out anyway.

He flinched, his body jerking, but he didn't release her. "What? Why?"

She licked her lips. "Because neither of you is as into me as I'm into you."

He nearly jumped at her statement. His voice rose. "What the hell, Adriana? Where did you get that idea?"

She stayed surprisingly strong. "From your willpower. Your ability to deny me. The fact that you can so calmly hold me all night without touching me intimately." This conversation was making her so vulnerable, but she was in it now. "When I'm in your arms or even in your space—the same room or house or building—I'm consumed by your pheromones. I can't think properly or breathe. My body is not under my control. My sex clenches. My breasts swell. I turn into someone I've never met, like I'm some kind of sex addict who will never get enough."

His jaw dropped. "And you don't think the feeling is mutual?"

"I can see it isn't. You wouldn't be able to keep your jeans on if you felt half of what I feel. It's confusing, and I've been trying to figure it out all weekend. Finally, it dawned on me. Neither of you feels as strongly as I do. I don't know what that means in the long run, but it has to mean something."

Silence stretched for several heartbeats while Reid stared at her, not blinking. His mouth was open, but she didn't think he was breathing.

Finally, he took a long deep breath and drew her closer, if that were possible. His fingers gripped her neck with so much vehemence. "You couldn't be more wrong."

She flinched. That was not the response she expected.

"Adriana, after the past few days, I'm confident I can easily speak for both Nolan and myself when I say you're mistaken. You've misread us."

She didn't see how that was possible.

"I have never in my life felt this strongly about anyone. Neither has Nolan."

"That doesn't mean it's enough, Reid. I'm not denying you care about me. I'm simply pointing out you aren't as drawn to me as I am to you."

His face tensed. "And I'm pointing out you're wrong. You're misinterpreting our actions. You're my world, Adriana. Nolan's too. My entire world. Neither of us is capable of grasping how we will go on after this is over and you have chosen."

She flinched again at the reminder that the entire thing came down to her choice. She alone would be to blame for whatever the outcome was. In fact, maybe she was lying to herself and made up the entire belief that they weren't interested in her with the same force she felt to avoid having to choose. At least if she chose neither of them, they would both be equally hurt and could remain friends. Any other outcome in her mind ended with a rift between them that could never be repaired.

He gave her another squeeze to get her attention. "I didn't mean to put more pressure on you. That didn't come out right. I'm sorry." He paused. Took a breath. "What I'm trying to say is that everything you feel is mirrored in me, baby."

She didn't move.

His voice dipped and softened. "I've spent the entire week with a stiff cock. My heart races in your presence. I sometimes find myself speechless while I watch you move around a room. Mesmerized by the way you tuck your hair behind your ear or cut your food or sip a glass of wine or concentrate on your designs. My chest seizes, and I can't breathe.

"I've taken my cock in my hand every single time I've been in the shower since I met you. It's the only way I can dampen the lust consuming me. And it doesn't even work. If you think the fact that Nolan and I can keep our pants on in front of you is an indication that we aren't interested, you're dead wrong. We don't have a choice here."

She drew back the centimeter he permitted.

He gave her neck a little shake. "Baby, we made a commitment not to take your virginity. Maybe it would have been different if you'd had other partners, but you haven't, and we take that seriously. You deserve to belong completely to one man and one man only. I wouldn't be able to live with myself if I took that from you. And neither would Nolan. So we haven't. And I don't have the self-control to let you see and touch me and then not slide into your warmth." His voice cracked.

She'd never seen him this emotional.

"So no. You don't have a monopoly on how intense you feel. It's mutual. I speak for both of us when I say I know for a fact Nolan would state these same things if he were in the room. Does it suck? Hell, yes. I've been in unimaginable turmoil for a week and fourteen hours. So has Nolan. It makes my heart hurt to know I not only can't control the outcome but that you're hurting so badly, agonizing over the decision only you can make. I hate that for you. More than I hate to see what the outcome looks like."

Her mouth was dry. Her heart pounded. She'd been wrong.

He set his forehead against hers. "I will not make things worse for you. Ever. I can and will control my carnal urge to flip you onto your back and claim your body. I don't have the right. You would never forgive me. I wouldn't do that to you or to Nolan or to myself. I would hate myself later if I took what doesn't belong to me from you. Something so precious it deserves to be cherished.

"Maybe we made a mistake this weekend by showing you how good we could make you feel. I'm not sure it was the right choice. We simply didn't want you to walk on eggshells around us worrying about treating us equally and keeping us at arm's length when we were all in the same confined space.

"Was it weird? At first, yes. But we got over it fast. All we cared about was making you feel good and giving you a taste of what's in store for you for life. No matter who you end up with, I can assure you either of us will do everything in our power to make your body come alive in a way you've only seen the fringe of. You'll be cherished and worshiped and loved until you die, baby. I promise you."

A tear slid down her cheek. She hadn't realized her eyes were clouded with moisture.

Reid brushed his thumb up to swipe it away. "Please don't retreat from us. I don't want you to feel like you have to bottle up your thoughts and feelings to avoid hurting either of us or keep a confrontation at bay. If you're hurting, share. Okay?"

"I have been hurting for over seven days, Reid. I can't possibly share that any more thoroughly."

He nodded. "I know. And I'm so sorry." He released her neck finally and wrapped both arms around her to close the few inches between them.

When her chest pressed against his, her nipples tightened further. She wanted his hands on her, cupping her breasts, pinching the tips, making her feel. Taking away the edge of need and pain. But he wouldn't do it while Nolan wasn't in the room.

Something had shifted between them. A change. Before the weekend spent in their arms, she'd had fleeting limited contact with both of them on separate occasions. A kiss, some groping. Nothing beyond that. But somehow she knew it wouldn't happen again. The stakes were too high. Reid was too much of a gentleman to put her in any position that would leave her uncomfortable and force her to keep things from Nolan.

Yep. She'd been wrong. It wasn't that Nolan and Reid didn't feel as strongly about her as she did them. Not at all. If anything, they felt even more intensely. They also found a deep strength that allowed them to cherish her in a way most men would never do.

She was falling in love. With two men. It wasn't getting easier. It was getting worse.

With this knowledge, she let Reid pull her onto his lap and then roll her onto the bed beside him. She allowed him to spoon her against his chest and wrap his arm around her middle. She relaxed as he lifted one leg over both of hers to cocoon her completely.

And she found peace in the way he kissed her neck gently at the very spot where one of them would one day claim her.

She didn't freak out or fight him. Instead, she fell into a deep sleep.

CHAPTER 20

"You're sure this is going to work?" Joe Stringer looked skeptically at Vinny, his eyes narrowed to mere slits.

"Positive. Trust me."

The man didn't waver, but he did lift a hand to run it through his short, thick hair. He was only about thirty-five, but his black hair was graying at the temple. "I've said this before, and I'll say it again, I don't know what sort of arrangement you have with Rimouski, but I do know if you fuck this up, your ass will be toast. I've put a lot of manpower and financial backing behind your scheme."

"It'll work." Vinny was as confident as he could be. Joe was right. He had no idea what Rimouski knew about Vinny. And he never would. Hopefully, when this was over, and Vinny had proven himself to be a respected, loyal team player, Joe would stop treating him like pond scum.

"You have everyone in place?"

"Yes. Eight men are positioned to move in on Reid Terrance's condo when I give the word." Human men. Human men with guns. So far they were awaiting word several blocks away.

Vinny wasn't about to risk alerting Reid to the scent of unknown people around his home until the last second. Several of the men had approached the condo close enough in the last few hours to get a lay of the land and then retreated. They didn't understand the need to pull back so far, but at least they'd followed Vinny's instructions.

"And Osborn?"

"I'm handling Osborn myself." Vinny turned toward the window and stared out at the twinkling lights of Calgary down below. He would be heading closer to Nolan's location in a few minutes. Four men were waiting to go with him. Also human. No one besides Vinny was a shifter in this entire operation.

"You aren't planning to approach him are you?"

When Vinny turned around, he found Joe's gaze roaming up and down his body.

Vinny fought the urge to snarl. No, he wasn't the largest man alive, but what Joe didn't know was Vinny could end Joe's life in two seconds flat if he wanted to. Nevertheless, he had no intention of taking Nolan out of the picture himself. The men with him had guns. Vinny didn't need any blood on his hands. Especially not shifter blood. If the Arcadian Council ever found out he'd been involved in the murder of a shifter, his life would be toast.

He was lucky the council hadn't bothered to hunt him down the last time he'd been involved in a borderline illegal scheme. If he killed a man, the council would hunt him to the ends of the earth and never let him get away.

Nope. He'd leave that messy task to the humans. But damn, he couldn't wait to watch.

"Vinny?" Joe prompted.

He realized he hadn't answered the question. "No. Of

course not. Just gonna supervise." He shoved away from the window. "Gotta go. I'll text you when it's done."

Nolan was in bed, but he wasn't asleep. He'd been tossing around for over an hour when the hair on his arms suddenly stood on end. There was no explanation for the intense feeling of unease except intuition. Sure, several humans were nearby. It was a hotel. People were staying on both sides of him and occasionally wandering the hallway.

But something was off. He swung his legs around, grabbed his jeans, and shrugged into them. As he was zipping them up, a loud knock sounded on his door. Four quick raps that made him race forward. They ended just as quickly, and although he sensed the presence of a human in the hallway, he didn't know the scent, and it was moving away so fast he couldn't get to the door to open it before it was gone.

And he didn't need to. Whoever it was had slid something under the door. A piece of paper folded in half.

Nolan wouldn't have opened the door anyway. Too risky.

He flipped on the light and bent to pick up the paper. When he read the words, he froze. "Fuck."

If you ever want to see your friends alive again, you'll do as instructed. Be at the park two blocks south of your hotel in fifteen minutes. The orange slide. If you fail to show, they're both dead. If you call for help, they're both dead.

Under those words was a URL.

"Fuck," He muttered as he lowered into the chair at the

small desk in his hotel room and powered up his laptop. He had no doubt he was not going to like whatever the fuck he was about to see. "Please God. Please." He tapped his fingers on the table as he waited for the computer to boot up. It seemed to take a decade.

Visions of Reid and Adriana held hostage somewhere raced through his mind. Where would these fuckers take them? He worried whoever had them would kill them anyway even if Nolan gave himself up. While the computer powered up, Nolan shoved from the table to grab his cell phone from the bedside table. He palmed it and then set it on the desk next to his mouse as he resumed his seat.

Finally, the screen came into view. He entered his password and opened the internet. It took another thirty seconds to type in the URL with shaky hands and wait. He was shocked by what he saw. Not Reid and Adriana somewhere unknown, but the two of them asleep in Reid's bed. Neither was moving. Reid was curled around their woman, holding her tight.

It took him a moment to realize it was a still shot. The picture was blurry. Whoever took the photo did so from a distance through the bedroom window. And then the photo disappeared and left him watching live video from outside Reid's condo. The camera panned around the area to show several men dressed in black inching toward the home. They had guns. He wasn't sure yet how many there were before he grabbed his phone.

All Nolan could do was pray no one noticed Reid reaching out for his phone. Although in truth, whoever wanted Nolan dead had to realize there wasn't a chance in hell Nolan wouldn't warn his friends. There apparently wasn't a video camera positioned on the bedroom— neither inside or outside—just the long-distance blurry shot taken from south of the window.

How the hell had someone found him? And more importantly, how had they made a connection to Reid and Adriana?

Nolan had no choice but to alert his friends. It was time to put an end to the charade. In a few minutes, Adriana would be lost to him forever.

～

The sound of an incoming text drew Reid from his sleep. He was aware he had only recently managed to doze off, so he was alert enough to know an incoming text at this hour was not a good sign. He lifted the hand holding Adriana to his chest and snaked it out to snag the phone from the bedside table.

His heart raced as he saw the message from Nolan.

Don't move. You're being watched. Rope.

Reid yanked the phone under the covers, hoping to avoid anyone detecting the glare of the screen while assuming it was probably too late. The last word made him stop breathing. If Nolan was using their agreed-upon code word, something serious had happened.

The moment he pulled it out of sight, with his body fully alert, it rang. Nolan.

He clicked the screen beneath the covers and pulled it to his ear. Before he could answer, Nolan was speaking. "Camera is on you from outside, aimed through the shutters. Not a video. Still shots. But don't take any chances. I have no idea how fast that camera is clicking."

"Fuck."

"Yeah."

At his expletive, Adriana stirred. "Reid?" she whispered, attempting to twist in his arms.

He held her tight. "Stay still, baby."

"Give me a sec to reach out to my dad," Nolan stated.

Adriana stiffened. "Is everything okay?"

"No, hon. It's not. Don't move." He waited for Nolan to come back on the line.

"Okay. I'm back. My dad will get the Arcadian Council moving. He's also calling the police."

"Talk to me," Reid gripped the phone.

"Got a note under my door. They want me to meet them. I get to choose—me or you two."

"Don't you fucking meet them."

"Oh, believe me, I'm clear on that. But they obviously know where I am and you too. It's time, Reid. Do it."

Reid's hands were shaking so badly he had trouble holding the phone.

Adriana's adrenaline was racing also. She didn't try to move away from him—thankfully obeying his demand—but that also meant she could hear Nolan clear as day with her head so close to Reid's.

"Do what?" she asked tentatively.

Reid squeezed his eyes shut and held her so tight it had to hurt. He didn't want to do it. It wasn't fair. "Nolan..."

"You promised."

"Only to placate you," Reid retorted, frustration building.

"Don't you fucking renege on me, Reid. Not tonight. Her life is at stake. So is yours." Nolan's voice was louder.

Adriana's voice shook when she spoke again. "Reid? What did you promise?"

Reid leaned his head toward her and nuzzled her neck. "Dammit."

She jerked in his arms.

He drew her so close he could feel every inch of her sweet body tensing. "How do you know it's not just a cameraman?" He closed his eyes and inhaled long and slow, cursing under his breath at the exhale.

"There's a live video feed I'm watching. Men are surrounding you. Black clothes. Guns at their sides. I can't identify them. Can you scent them?"

"Yes." He inhaled again. So did Adriana. Reid continued to speak. "There are a lot of people in the vicinity. It's hard to say which ones don't belong, but I'm going to guess about eight. Human."

"Not a single shifter?" Nolan asked.

"Not that I can detect."

"The man who left the note was human also. Let's hope no shifter is involved. That will give us leverage."

"Marginally," Reid responded, not feeling all that hopeful. Eight humans with guns could do a fuck lot of damage if they wanted. Even shifters couldn't live through fatal gunshot wounds.

"Please tell me you have a weapon."

"Of course I do." It wasn't legal, but Reid had one. He was a bodyguard. Granted, he was a legit bodyguard who didn't carry a weapon as far as his clients were concerned. But he wasn't stupid.

There was a moment of silence. "Reid…" Nolan's voice was calmer, but the urgency was there.

"I know."

"They aren't there to kill anyone."

"I know," he repeated. Those men wanted hostages. Leverage.

"You can't leave her unprotected."

"I know that, too." Reid blew out a breath.

Adriana gasped, squirming in his arms. "No," she stated

245

emphatically the instant she must have realized what Nolan and Reid had agreed upon.

"Baby…" Reid grasped her wrist with his free hand and held it between her breasts. "Calm down."

"No. We can't." She sobbed.

"Let me talk to her," Nolan stated calmly.

Reid pulled the phone from his ear and held it to hers. He could hear every word Nolan said just as she obviously had.

"Adriana," Nolan began. "Listen to me."

"No. Not this time. Maybe you can order me to move in with a bodyguard and let him drive me around everywhere, but you can't order me to bind to him. That's crazy, Nolan."

Reid stiffened as she referred to him so flippantly as if he were nothing but a hired man. He knew it wasn't true, but it still hurt.

"Baby, there's no other choice. Do this for me."

"No." Her voice cracked. She was near hysteria. "It's not right, Nolan. I won't."

"Adriana. It's not about right or wrong. It's about keeping you alive. I've seen you with Reid. I know you feel the same thing for him you feel for me. Maybe this is Fate's way of stepping in and making the choice easier for you."

"No." She shook her head, making it hard for Reid to hold the phone and keep her from squirming away from him.

He was having trouble keeping his own emotions in check. He needed to get his shit together and think about her.

Nolan's voice dipped lower, soothing. "It's done, baby. You're surrounded. You can't take a chance of being kidnapped and vulnerable. You need the connection. It's the only way to keep you safe. And Reid too."

That last part was true. Neither of them had stopped to consider what would happen if Reid were taken hostage. They'd only ever thought about protecting Adriana. After all, originally Reid hadn't been a factor in this equation at all. But things had changed.

How much did Stephen Rimouski know about the three of them?

Reid shuddered.

Adriana breathed heavily, probably pondering Nolan's last words. She also cried, silent tears running down her face. "I'm in love with you," she whispered.

"I know, baby. It's okay. Everything will be fine."

"You would give me up to keep me safe?"

"I would do anything in the world for you, Adriana. So, yes. I'm going to do this. I'd rather know you were alive and leading a happy, full life than never see you again because I was too selfish to make the tough decision to let you go."

She sobbed out loud again, her body shaking in Reid's arms.

Reid tucked his lips between his teeth and bit down to keep his own emotions from tumbling out. It was time. He pulled the phone back to his ear. "I love you, man."

"I love you too. Keep her safe."

"You know I will."

"I'm a sitting duck here."

"I know. Wait for help. Don't try to leave."

"I've never felt so helpless in my life," Nolan stated.

"Nor have I. I'll wait as long as I can before I do it."

"*No.*" The urgency in that word was intense. "Do it now. I'm watching the live feed. They're inching closer, Reid. You don't have much time. Moments. I don't care what kind of gun you have, you can't fight them. There are too many."

Reid knew Nolan was right. He could scent the approaching danger. They were closing in on the house. They weren't in a hurry because they thought he was sleeping. He needed to stay as still as possible until the last second to buy them some time. Any movement on his part or Adriana's might be caught on camera, and then the unknown enemy would rush in.

"Later, man."

"Later." Nolan ended the call. If there were any other options... They couldn't even shift. Not in the middle of a populated neighborhood surrounded by humans. Too risky. It was forbidden anyway. Shifting was never a choice, not even as a last resort if there was even a chance humans would discover them. With at least eight humans closing in, Reid and Adriana needed to remain smart. Alert.

And bound.

Reid dropped the phone to the pillow behind him and held a sniffling Adriana closer. He tucked her free wrist in with the first to hold them between her breasts. It wasn't that he was trying to restrain her, but that he wanted her to feel secure. Loved. Cherished.

With his free hand, he brushed her hair from her neck and kissed the spot where her neck met her shoulder. "Adriana?"

He needed her consent. Binding a woman without consent was strictly forbidden.

She shuddered, panting.

"You know I love you, right?" he stated.

"Yes."

"Adriana?" He still needed verbal consent. Someone was literally on his front porch. Another two men were on the back deck. He knew it. She did too. They were probably waiting for a command that would come when Nolan didn't show up at the planned location.

"I love you too."

"I know, baby. It's going to be okay." He wasn't sure of his own words at all. How was this ever going to be okay? But he had to trust that Fate knew what She was doing. They were out of time. There were no other options.

"Do it," she whispered.

Reid didn't hesitate. He licked the spot he intended to bite and immediately sank his teeth into her. A second later he let the serum that would bind them together for life flow into her bloodstream.

She flinched at the initial bite, but then she slowly relaxed against him. Her heart rate picked up, as did her arousal. She moaned.

Reid's cock jumped to attention. It wasn't surprising. That's how a binding worked. They would be thrust into a new level of lust neither of them could imagine. After living with her for the past week, he couldn't fathom craving her more than he already did, but he'd heard the stories from everyone he'd ever met who was bound to another. Intellectually, he knew. In real life, it was still shocking.

Her breath came heavily as he released her neck and licked the puncture wounds with his tongue. A war raged inside him. Half of his body insisted he flip her onto her back and fuck her until she couldn't see straight and didn't have the ability to form words. The other half was fully aware there was a threat to their lives looming outside.

He had no choice but to deal with the second problem first. Later they would consummate this union. Not now.

"Reid…" Her voice was nothing but a thready breath of intense need.

"Pull it together, baby." He gripped her wrists tighter and spoke into her ear.

She started shivering and then flat out shaking. "Oh God."

"I know," he whispered, his lips on her sweet lobe. "Ignore it. We have to neutralize this situation before anything else."

"Right." She panted, her ass thrusting back against his cock. And then she moaned. "My God. Reid…"

Damn, this was hard. He hadn't considered how fucking difficult it would be to fight the hard battle right after binding to his mate. A near impossibility.

"They aren't moving."

"I know." He tipped his head back, partly to draw in a deep breath that wasn't laced with pure Adriana and partly to assess the situation. No one was moving. He still counted eight men. All close. All stationary. They had no idea the people they were hunting were aware of their arrival and far more than human.

"What do we do now?" she panted out.

"Wait. I want them to think we're still asleep and unaware."

"They will come inside though, right? I mean soon? Because they'll have to show Nolan they meant business."

"Yes." Seconds ticked by. The longest ones of his life. He alternated between concentrating on the imminent threat and fighting back the lust he felt for the woman in his arms.

"Need you," she murmured, tipping her head to kiss his knuckles between her breasts.

"Hold it at bay, baby. You have to."

"I know." She kissed him again, her tongue darting out to taste his skin.

He moaned, reaching for her jaw with the hand he had

on her shoulder and gripping it to keep her from touching her lips to his hand again. "Adriana, help me out here."

She sucked in a breath. Or a sob. "My skin is crawling."

"I know."

"I'm too hot."

That was also true. He wished he could fling back the covers to give them space and air, but he couldn't. They needed to remain as still as possible for as long as they could. He concentrated on her breaths, shallow, slow, in and out. In and out. In and out. She was breathing through her mouth. He couldn't blame her. It wouldn't completely keep her from scenting him, but it would cut down on the powerful nature of the binding.

He did the same, parting his lips but realizing the difference was subtle. He could taste her on his tongue with every breath as if her pheromones were a palpable solid in the air. Hardly different from breathing her scent in through his nose.

No one outside moved. How long had it been? Would they give Nolan extra time? Maybe they were negotiating with him again.

"Terrance." Hearing his last name spoken into his head so abruptly startled him. He didn't recognize the voice.

"Yes?"

"Laurence here. From the Arcadian Council."

"Thank God."

"Can you hear me too, Adriana?"

"Yes," she communicated. Her body relaxed marginally in his arms.

"We're watching your condo. Charles and I. Waiting for backup. There are only two of us. Eight of them. They have no idea we're behind them."

Thank Fuck.

"Nolan Osborn. You need to get someone to him. He's—"

"Already on it. Henry and George are at his hotel."

Reid blew out a long breath.

Adriana started to move.

He held her tighter. "Don't move, baby. They still don't know we're onto them."

"Right," she muttered.

"Hang tight. I wasn't sure at first that you two were aware of the danger."

"Yes. Nolan called."

"There's a man with a camera aimed at your room and another with a video scanning the area."

If Nolan was still watching, he had to be freaking out.

"We know. That's why we haven't moved an inch since Nolan called."

Did Laurence chuckle into their minds? *"It seems like you moved at least an inch. Smart decision, by the way. I was wondering if it was a coincidence or you had inside info."*

Right. Of course. Laurence could scent the fact that they had completed the binding.

Adriana twisted her hands in Reid's grip and threaded her fingers with some of his.

"Last resort," Reid replied, flinching the second the words left his mind. That didn't come out right.

Laurence definitely chuckled this time. *"In my experience, a woman doesn't usually appreciate it if her man refers to their binding as a last resort."*

Was Adriana giggling? Her body shook. Yes. She was. Thank fuck. *"It wasn't romantic. That's for sure,"* she added.

"I bet. But no less powerful," Laurence added, his voice serious once again.

"True," she added softly.

Suddenly Laurence was in only Reid's mind, the subtle difference obvious to him. *"Don't mean to sound crass or make light of things, son. I'm just trying to keep your mate's mind off the threat."*

"Appreciated."

And then Laurence was back in both their heads. *"When this is over, you might want to swat him upside the head a few times, miss."*

Reid wasn't sure he liked this particular advice even if it was an intentional tactic to occupy his mate's mind.

She giggled again, her sweet behind rubbing against his cock as her body shook. Her nipples were rock hard peaks against his forearms.

How she could so easily be distracted was beyond him, but the council members had powers no one could ever understand. No doubt Laurence was controlling her mind enough to calm her. Luckily he left Reid alone, enabling him to pay close attention to their surroundings.

It was also possible that Laurence was manipulating Reid too. Perhaps helping tamp down the arousal to keep him focused. Reid wasn't sure how he felt about that either, but he assumed, in the end, he would be grateful. Keeping his head in the game could be the difference between life and death.

"I need to make contact with my parents," Adriana communicated.

"We already have," Laurence responded. *"They're fully informed. You concentrate on keeping safe."*

She nodded against Reid, her fingers tightening in his.

CHAPTER 21

Nolan was pacing in front of his computer while he watched the insanity unfold in front of him. There was nothing else he could do for the time being. His hands were tied. He wouldn't interrupt Reid and Adriana again. For one thing, they deserved a private moment without him interfering in their binding. For another thing, they needed to concentrate on the danger without adding anything else to their plate.

It hurt. The pain was deep and powerful. Nolan closed his eyes several times. It was a wonder he didn't go insane from helplessness and worry and the deep, profound loss of his mate. He assumed eventually he wouldn't feel the connection to her anymore, but he had no idea when that would occur. Would he sense the break from her immediately?

He hoped not because if that were to be the case, it would mean they didn't bind when he hung up. Because so far he felt no change. He still held her close to his heart.

What if he always did and he had to watch his best

friend live his life with the woman Nolan needed more than his next breath?

It was overwhelming. He shook the thoughts from his head and watched the screen again as the men surrounding Reid's house crept closer. When would they be given the go-ahead to break into the house?

Thank God whoever was surrounding them was human. It made all the difference in the world. They had no idea the occupants were onto them.

Nolan nearly jumped out of his skin when a voice sounded in his head. *"Nolan."* He didn't recognize the tone, but he thought the speaker was older. *"George here. I'm outside your hotel."*

Thank God.

"Your dad contacted us, but Henry and I were already watching. I'm just outside your range." He meant scent range, and indeed after a long inhale, Nolan realized he couldn't scent George nearby.

"You were already outside? How long have you been there?"

"About an hour. We've been following your stalker."

"For how long?"

"Two days."

Shit. *"Why didn't anyone tell me?"* He hated to sound accusatory, but if the council had filled him in earlier, maybe... He shook the thought from his head. The Arcadian Council was very powerful. They had their reasons.

"When we found him, we weren't sure there was a connection to you yet. The man trying to lure you outside was already on our radar for other offenses. He doesn't know we're watching."

"Shit. Other offenses?" That meant whoever was after Nolan was undoubtedly a shifter. Perhaps the man who'd been hanging around the hotel.

"Yes. From last year. Don't worry about that now. Let's get you safe."

"Reid and Adriana. They—"

"Laurence and Charles are watching them."

That was a relief. "What's happening?"

"Eight men have your friends surrounded. But they must be waiting for the all clear to break into the house. If they have an ounce of sense, which I highly doubt, they would know Reid is a private bodyguard and realize he isn't stupid enough to not have his house overly protected with the finest alarm system."

"Do you suppose whoever is trying to kill me is that stupid?"

"Let's hope."

Nolan couldn't scent any shifters inside the hotel or even nearby, which meant whoever was after him was either human or smart enough to keep his distance. If it was the same man he'd scented several times in the last hotel he'd hidden in, at least Nolan would recognize that smell as soon as it grew closer again. But what good would that do?

"Are Reid and Adriana safe?" What were the council members waiting on?

"So far. We're monitoring the situation while we wait on additional manpower. If we have to move in, we will. For now, it's better to keep tabs. The man we need to pick off is your stalker. The kingpin. We think he's in charge of all the others. If we can grab him, we might be able to keep him from issuing further orders."

"It's been thirteen minutes since he slid his demand under my door. He's going to be expecting me in two."

"Henry's at the park now, watching from a short distance."

Nolan took a breath. The council members could easily sneak up on whoever was waiting for Nolan since they had the power to block any shifter from scenting their approach.

"I don't think the man will be there to meet me himself. He wouldn't take that risk."

"You're right. He's actually in the car that just pulled up. Showtime. I'll get back to you as soon as I can."

Nolan couldn't catch his breath when George cut the connection. For several moments, he stood rooted to his spot, unable to move or make a decision. And then he jumped into action. If the council had two representatives at the meeting point, he wanted to be there too.

Maybe it wasn't the brightest decision he'd ever made, but sitting in his hotel room waiting for the all clear sucked as an option too. So, he grabbed his jacket and raced from the room.

Vinny sat in his car a safe enough distance from the park, intending to watch Nolan arrive through his long-distance lens but still keep his identity a secret. Nolan didn't need to know a shifter worked for Stephen Rimouski. Besides, Nolan would be dead before too long and then it wouldn't matter.

Still, Vinny preferred to keep his hands clean and let the humans take the rap and go down if things went south.

Vinny's only job here was to confirm Osborn was dead and call off the men surrounding his friends. There was a small gamble. Vinny had to hope Osborn gave enough fucks about his friends to trade his life for theirs. He was counting on it. After all, whoever Reid Terrance and his girlfriend were, they cared enough to pick Nolan up Friday night when he was on the run.

Vinny knew Reid was a shifter. He'd looked him up. He had no idea if the woman was also a shifter or if she was even a permanent part of Reid's life. She could simply be someone he was currently fucking. Judging from the pictures Vinny had seen of the two of them wrapped around each other in Reid's condo, he had to assume they were at least fucking. Perhaps they were also bound together. Didn't matter. He had never approached close enough to find out in order to avoid detection, and Vinny's informant wouldn't have a clue. The man was human.

The man hired to pick off Osborn arrived, setting up about a block from the meeting place exactly where Vinny had instructed him to go for the best aim. All he needed was a good shot with a silencer, and Nolan's life would officially be over. Without their key witness, the cops wouldn't have enough intel to put Rimouski on trial.

Vinny assumed Osborn must have alerted the police to something that didn't add up in Rimouski's books. In fact, in the last few days, Vinny had scoured every ledger Rimouski had with a variety of accountants under multiple aliases. Each ledger had inconsistencies, which meant Stephen had never been careful enough with his books. The accounting Osborn was in charge of had been a bit too far off. Apparently, Nolan was sharp and decided to call the police instead of questioning his client.

Eliminating Osborn was paramount. As soon as he was out of the picture, Vinny would find a way to easily explain away the inconsistencies in the ledger. Typos. Errors. There would likely be other messes to clean up. It had only been a week. The police were probably looking for other accountants to question, but the job would be difficult since Rimouski used so many different aliases.

Nevertheless, Vinny could only handle one problem at a time. Osborn today. Someone else tomorrow.

Vinny glanced at his watch. Nolan was late. It had been sixteen minutes. *Fuck*. Vinny had a lot riding on this play.

He was counting on Osborn caring more about keeping his friends alive than his own life.

"Get out of the car, Vinson."

Vinny jerked his gaze to the driver's side window, shocked to realize a member of the Arcadian Council was standing by his door. He knew the council members could block themselves thoroughly enough to sneak up on people, but he'd never experienced it firsthand.

Another older man who was also on the council stood at the hood of the car, both men casually staring down at Vinny.

Fuck. How the hell did Osborn manage to contact these guys and mobilize them in just a few minutes? The cops he had counted on at any moment and frankly didn't care about. His hired hit man was good. The presence of police wouldn't thwart him. But the Arcadians? He hadn't thought that possible. *Fuck.*

He considered hitting the gas and either running over the man in front of him or backing up at a high rate of speed and peeling away. But that would draw too much attention to the situation and ruin his chances of picking off Nolan. Osborn was his top priority. He was better off pretending to cooperate with these council members and shaking them later than preventing his hit man from finishing the job.

With a fake sigh, Vinny let his shoulders fall, turned off his engine, and opened the car door. "How did you find me?" he asked as he stepped outside.

"Been tracking you for a while, Tarben. You're not very smart. After you took off from the brewery incident earlier this year, we figured you were long gone. I was guessing Asia."

Vinny recognized this man as George. "I didn't do anything illegal last year."

"Nope," George agreed. "That's why we didn't search too hard for you. But you're sloppy and stupid. Why the hell would you stay so close to home?"

Vinny leaned against the car door as he shut it behind him, still aiming for casual. He shrugged. "Didn't think it mattered. There's no law that says a man can't share pictures of beer with his girlfriend or leave town whenever he wants."

That was essentially what he'd done several months ago when he fled Silvertip after helping his family's brewery beat the competition at the creation of a new product. The weird bitch from the Arthur pack who happily and ignorantly fed him information had proven invaluable. But that didn't mean Vinny intended to bind to her. Just remembering the time he'd spent pretending to care about her gave him the chills.

Vinny decided to play stupid. "What can I do for you fellows tonight?"

George lifted a brow. "Sharing company secrets and getting yourself banished from your pack isn't a crime, but hiring a hit man to pick off the key witness to your boss's crimes is certainly punishable."

"I have no idea what you're talking about. I was simply enjoying the evening."

George chuckled sardonically. "It's about two in the morning, and I wasn't born yesterday."

"You have no proof."

"You're stupid *and* funny. Let me suggest you come with us willingly or suffer the consequences."

Vinny had no choice but to continue to go along and hope nothing these guys had on him would stick later. Or better yet, he could possibly get away from them without much fuss in no time if they thought he was cooperating.

So he quietly followed them toward their SUV parked only a block away.

It wasn't ideal, and it meant he had no way to call off the men guarding Reid and his bitch, but who cared? The two of them might end up casualties in this war. Vinny didn't give a single fuck at this point.

George opened the rear passenger door to the black, nondescript SUV and swept a hand to indicate Vinny should get inside.

He did, surveying his surroundings. For now, there was nothing he could do. He couldn't contact the man stationed to take out Nolan, and he had no way to reach the men surrounding Reid. As long as everyone did their job, they didn't need contact from him anyway.

Surprising Vinny, George leaned in to speak as the other man got in the driver's seat. "I'll leave you in Henry's hands. Don't fuck with me, Vinson. You'll regret it."

"Why would I do that?" Vinny asked.

George didn't respond. He simply shut the door and nodded at Henry, who pulled the SUV away from the curb.

The park was too quiet. As Nolan approached, adrenaline pumping through his veins, a chill raced down his spine. Where was the man he was supposed to meet? And where were the council members? Hell, the police should have arrived too.

He didn't head for the slide as instructed. Instead, he found a large tree a safe distance away and hid behind it, scanning the area. There were human scents. Where were George and Henry? And what about the shifter who hired someone to kill him?

"You have a death wish, Osborn?"

Nolan spun around to find George standing behind him. Of course. He wouldn't have scented George. The man was blocking. "I couldn't just stand in that hotel room and wait."

"So you thought it would be a good idea to come out here and get shot when we have things under control?" George hissed. He wasn't pleased.

"*Do* you?"

George nodded. "Picked up your stalker already. If you don't fuck this up by getting yourself killed, the police are going to have your hired hit man in custody any second."

Thank God.

George tipped his head back and closed his eyes.

Nolan watched him, knowing he could sense things far more powerfully than regular shifters. The forty council members had amazing abilities.

Loud voices across the park drew Nolan's attention.

"Hands in the air, asshole. *Now.*"

Someone screamed. A shot rang out.

Nolan flinched.

George took him by the arm and led him silently between the trees to a row of bushes that created a barrier on one side of the playground. He bent a few inches to peek through an opening and then stood back and motioned for Nolan to do the same.

Three officers surrounded a man who lay face down on the ground, not moving. One of the officers nudged the prone guy with his foot. He checked his pulse next. Nothing.

"Looks like your hit man tried to shoot at the police. Won't be wasting any taxpayer dollars to prosecute him."

Nolan's eyes were wide. Holy shit. It was over. At least this part.

"What about Reid and Adriana?"

"They're safe."

For the first time in hours or perhaps days, Nolan blew out a breath. It was over. It was truly over.

He had no idea how he was going to pick up the pieces of his life and move forward, but at least he wouldn't be doing so any more from a confined space. If he never saw the inside of a hotel room again, it would be too soon.

He silently followed George across the street, heading away from the commotion. "Do you have a car?"

"Yes. A few blocks away."

He considered asking George to take him to Reid's condo but swallowed the words. Reid and Adriana would need to be alone tonight. It hurt more than he would ever be able to process. When would he stop feeling the bond? Shouldn't it have severed by now? He could ask George a few questions to see what insight the man might have in this strange circumstance, but he didn't think he could bring it up without losing his man card along the way, so he pursed his lips and followed George down a side street.

George said nothing as he fished around in his pocket, pulled out a key ring that had a ridiculous number of keys on it, and opened the doors to the small compact car along the street. "Good. Wasn't sure I had the keys to this one."

Nolan slid inside as George climbed behind the wheel. "This one?" Nolan asked.

George shot him a small grin as he started the engine. "I like to keep several vehicles near any possible crime scene, just in case. Henry has custody of your stalker in my SUV."

"I see." Nolan shuddered. Fucking weird.

George drove Nolan back to the hotel in silence. When they pulled up, he turned to face Nolan. "I don't scent your officer inside, but you should return to your room and contact him." His look was serious.

Nolan stated the obvious as a light bulb went off in his head. "They don't know about my stalker."

"Right."

"They need to believe it was the dead guy in the park."

"Right."

"Got it. And the men who were surrounding Reid and Adriana?"

"They were all human. They've been neutralized. Your stalker hired them just like he hired your hit man."

"I assume he's a shifter?"

"Yes," George agreed but said nothing else. Apparently, he wasn't going to divulge who yet.

What was that about? Was it someone Nolan knew? "So everyone's in custody," he said to change the subject. "I'm free to return to my regularly scheduled life."

George stared at him and shook his head. "Not even close."

"Why?" Nolan gasped.

George paused as if he were patiently waiting for Nolan to regain his senses.

Finally, he did, groaning. "I'm still alive."

"Exactly."

"Rimouski can just hire someone else to take me out."

"Yes." George's voice was low. "I'm sorry."

Son of a bitch.

"It will take Rimouski time to regroup. He lost a lot of men tonight, but don't let your guard down. He still needs to pick you off. I need to handle this situation with your current stalker, and I'll be back as soon as I can."

Nolan nodded. Without another word, mostly because he wanted to punch something and fought to keep that urge under control in front of George, he climbed from the car and shut the door.

His life was a fucking disaster. Not only was he still

facing months of hiding, but he'd lost the only woman he would ever love to his best friend. And on top of everything else, he still felt a connection to her that worried him more than anything.

The window rolled down behind him, and George leaned over to speak. "Nolan."

Nolan spun around to face the council member.

"Don't give up. Things might not be as bleak as they seem. Have faith."

Before Nolan could process George's words or respond, the man pulled away from the curb. What was he referring to? The fucking court case? Did he know something about Rimouski that would put an end to this shitstorm sooner rather than later?

Anything was possible.

He was Arcadian Council after all.

CHAPTER 22

Half an hour earlier...

Adriana thought she might lose her mind soon if something didn't happen and fast. She couldn't compartmentalize the two things happening to her at once. On the one hand, Reid had just bound them together for life. Her body was reacting accordingly. If she thought she'd been horny for the last week since she met first Nolan and then Reid, she was sadly mistaken.

This new level of arousal made the past week look like a teenage crush. Concern over the realization that their actions had cut Nolan off forever made her want to cry. She couldn't even face that fact at the moment.

Because holy mother of god, eight men had Reid's condo surrounded with the intent to either kill both of them or take them hostage, probably the latter.

"What do we do? We can't lie here forever," she pointed out. Her fingers hurt from gripping Reid's so tightly.

"Hang on, baby. We need to wait."

She knew he was suffering from the same exact issues she was, partly because his cock was pressing into her lower back to remind her how badly he wanted her and partly because Nolan was his best friend and he had to be worried and hurting about cutting him out of the equation at least as much as she was. Probably more.

The scent of newcomers reached her nose. She stiffened. "There are more people out there."

"Let's hope they're cops."

Long exhale. He was right. Laurence would have called the police. If the Arcadian Council could avoid getting involved, they would, especially in a human matter. There were no shifters outside.

Adriana had no doubt at least one shifter was involved in the big picture, but whoever that was, he wasn't at Reid's condo. He was undoubtedly tracking Nolan.

She considered reaching out to her parents but decided against it. She had too many things going on in her mind as it was. She needed to remain as alert as possible.

Laurence reached into their minds again. *"Police have the place surrounded now. I'd get yourselves somewhere safe in case shots are fired."*

Before Laurence could even finish communicating this thought, Adriana found herself yanked backward and off the bed. She gasped as Reid, still holding her around the waist, pulled her to the floor and hovered over her. He shoved her halfway under the bed. "Stay down. Don't move." And then he released her and crouched low, crawling across the room toward the bedroom door. He would have the advantage over anyone who breached the home in the dark because grizzly shifters could see better in the dark than humans.

Two shots rang out. Adriana screamed, unable to stop the guttural reaction. She covered her head with both hands as if the ceiling were in danger of falling. A glance at the doorway proved Reid was gone. He'd left the room.

Another shot. Shouting. It was outside, but she could hear it clearly. She didn't want to cower under the bed, so she crawled on her hands and knees toward the bedroom door and peered out into the hallway.

Reid's scent was not close enough to be on the second floor. He was downstairs. He would kill her if she left the bedroom. So she waited, straining to hear what was happening.

Someone else screamed, and then she could hear loud voices shouting orders. The police. "Get down... Hands in the air... Drop your weapon..."

Her heart raced when the front door opened. She'd been living here a week. She knew that distinct sound. The alarm started blaring. Was Reid still inside? Or had he stepped out?

Something crashed. No. Glass shattered. She pinpointed the sound over the waves of the alarm.

Shit. Adriana pulled back, flattening herself against the wall inside the bedroom. She didn't have a weapon, nor did she know how to fire one. But she knew Reid did.

More noise. Reid's voice rang clear from downstairs. "Face to the ground, you fucker." Another crash. A chair? The table? "I said to stay the fuck *down*," Reid screamed. The alarm stopped blaring. He must have shut it off.

More voices. The scent of several people entering the condo. She prayed they were police. People were talking over each other. Some still yelling. So many people were in the house. She thought she could scent ten of them. Most were new. Only one of the scents belonged to one of the eight men who had surrounded the condo before the police arrived.

When she heard heavy footsteps taking the stairs two at

a time in rapid succession, she panicked, scrambling away from the door in a crab crawl. It wasn't until Reid was rounding the doorway that she realized it was him coming into the room. It happened so fast, and she was so frightened that she hadn't had a chance to process Reid's approach.

His gaze darted around before settling on her, and then he rushed the last few feet and crouched down to wrap his arms around her and pull her into his chest. He stood, taking her to her feet with him. "It's okay. You're okay."

Her heart beat fast, not getting the message. She planted her palms on his chest and lifted her gaze to his. "You're sure?"

"Yes. The police have everyone in custody now."

"Someone broke into the house," she pointed out.

"Yes. He rushed at me from the bushes when I opened the front door. Plowed past me so fast I couldn't stop him. Stupid fool. He's going to have a hell of a headache." Reid grinned.

Adriana licked her lips. "It's over."

"Yes. Will you be okay a few more minutes while I speak to the officers out front?"

She nodded. She wasn't sure she was telling the truth, but she couldn't very well tell him *no*.

Reid led her back to the bed and sat her on the edge. He tipped her chin back and kissed her nose. "I'll be quick."

She nodded again and watched his back as he left her sitting on the mattress, her arms going around her to hug her torso. As the voices calmed and people left the house, she started to relax. When the last person was gone, the only scent in the condo was Reid's. She rose on shaky legs, grabbed one of Reid's sweatshirts where it lay tossed across the back of a chair, and shrugged it over her head. With a deep breath, she headed downstairs.

Reid was standing in the kitchen, still wearing nothing but his sleep pants, a broom in one hand, a dustpan in the other. He lifted his face when she padded into the room. "Stay on that side of the island, baby, until I can get this swept up."

"What was it?"

"Just a glass. It was sitting on the island when I slammed that asshole's head against the corner." He winked at her and resumed sweeping.

She flinched, trying to avoid the visual. "Just a glass? Sounded like the entire back wall of windows from upstairs."

He chuckled. "Nope."

"I heard gunshots."

"Luckily those were outside, and no one was injured. The police fired warning shots into the air."

She swallowed. He was so calm. All she could do was watch as he emptied the dustpan into the trash and then came to her. He wrapped his hands around her biceps and stared into her eyes, all humor gone. His expression was guarded and serious. "You okay?"

She shook her head, biting her lip. She was still scared, adrenaline coursing through her body. But when he pulled her closer, tucking her head under his chin, she started to relax. His heart wasn't beating as ferociously as hers, and her body began to align with his, her pulse slowing, her breathing evening out. All that from nothing more than his touch.

He threaded a hand in her hair at the nape of her neck.

She spoke against his chest. "You think it's over?"

He sighed. "No."

She jerked, lifting her face. "Why?"

"Because Nolan isn't dead."

She gasped, a weird noise escaping her lips.

"I don't know how to put it more bluntly, but that's the reality."

"But all these men were arrested. How... What happened at the hotel?" Obviously, Reid knew more than she was aware of. He'd either communicated with Nolan, or the police had filled him in, or perhaps Laurence had shared.

"Nolan's fine. The man sent to take him out of the equation is dead. Whoever orchestrated this charade is also in custody. Henry left with him a while ago, so I'm betting he's a shifter. I hope he enjoys his nice jaunt to the Northwest Territories. He's going to be there a while."

She flinched. "You think it's the shifter Nolan scented in the hotel?"

"No idea, but it makes me nervous."

"Me too. Why would a shifter be after us? Why would a shifter's loyalty be with a human criminal instead of our own kind?" It made no sense. And how did he find out about Reid and Adriana?

Reid squeezed the back of her neck. "We don't have all the answers yet."

That was for sure. "Where's Nolan now?"

"Back at the hotel."

"What do you mean, *back*? Where did he go?"

"He's stubborn. Unwilling to wait in his room while shit was going down. He went to the meeting point."

She leaned back several inches. "That's crazy."

"He apparently remained on the fringe, hiding, watching. The police took out the hit man."

"Have you spoken to him?" When would he have had time to do that?

Reid shook his head. "No, hon. Laurence filled me in." He licked his lips as he cupped her face with his free hand.

They stared at each other for a long time.

Her heart rate, which had finally subsided, picked back up.

When Reid's lips slowly lowered to hers, she parted her mouth.

He closed the distance between their bodies by flattening one palm between her shoulder blades and hauling her chest against his.

Her breasts jumped to attention, her nipples hardening against his pecs. Suddenly the sweatshirt was too much clothing. Her hands landed on his hips, and she fisted the soft material of his sleep pants.

Their tongues dueled. She needed this. Needed to taste him. It was life-affirming. Maybe it was crazy to feel so much arousal so soon after the end of their ordeal, but she was a shifter, and her blood ran hot for this man who'd bound her to him less than an hour ago.

All the energy she'd exerted worrying about the threat to their lives switched to a new focus. Getting Reid out of these pants and consummating this binding.

It wasn't imperative to the binding. The binding would be solid for the rest of their lives even if they never had sex, but that same connection brought their arousal to the surface with a force that could not be denied. It was as Nature intended.

For as long as grizzly shifters had been in existence, the draw to bind to another and then seal that bond through sex had been predominant. It was a part of life. Like breathing and eating. Grizzly shifters bound together for life. And they completed that attachment immediately after the binding with a bite and didn't usually come up for air for days.

The process had been put on hold for the last hour. The urge to have Reid become totally hers bubbled under the surface. It clawed at her skin from the inside. She slid her hands around to his back, her fingers digging into his warm skin as he angled the kiss to one side and devoured her.

His tongue danced around as if he needed to taste every inch of her mouth and then do so again. Meanwhile, Reid found the hem of her sweatshirt and dragged it up her body. He broke the kiss only long enough to whip it over her head.

Their mouths slammed back together moments later.

She needed to feel his skin against hers. She was still wearing her tank top and shorts.

When his hands found her breasts and molded them in his palms, she moaned into his mouth. She couldn't breathe. Not enough oxygen was getting into her. She almost didn't care.

She was aware of him backing her up but didn't know where they were until her ass hit the wall. Flattened against the cool surface, she reached higher up his back, clawing at him. She needed him inside her. Now. Yesterday.

He pinched her nipples.

She moaned into his mouth.

He released her breasts abruptly, and his hands trailed down to her ass, wiggling between her cheeks and the wall to cup her globes and pull her tighter against him.

His cock was flattened to her belly, thick and hard beneath his sleep pants. Instinctively, she dragged her hands from his back around to the front and cupped his hard length for the first time, reveling in the feel of him beneath her palm. It was warm even under the pants. He groaned.

She needed more. She needed him inside her. She didn't care that ten minutes ago they had been dealing with an intruder and eight people who wanted to take them hostage. Now was another time. Separated. Like before and after.

He slid a hand around from her ass to her pussy and cupped her through the cotton of her shorts. He broke the kiss, panting as he met her gaze. "My God, you're so wet." He slid his hand into her shorts and dragged two fingers through her wetness.

She rose onto her tiptoes, biting her lip.

His lips slammed back down on hers as if he could only stand those brief moments to catch their breath and then needed to taste her again.

She agreed. And then he slid a finger into her tight channel. Deep. It felt amazing. So fucking sensitive. She gripped his cock, wrapping her fingers around the length. She still hadn't seen him naked.

Her concentration returned to her sex where his finger pulled out and then thrust back inside. So good…

Right?

Her mind flashed to visions of Nolan and Reid both bringing her to orgasm that first time on the couch in the cabin. They'd made her come twice. Flashes of Nolan's mouth between her legs seeped into her consciousness. It amped up her arousal even now.

She closed her eyes, picturing Nolan's mouth on her while Reid fucked her pussy with that finger. She squeezed her eyes tighter. This was wrong. Something was off. She shouldn't be picturing Nolan while Reid fucked her.

From one second to the next she went from totally aroused and anxious to have sex to confused and more than a little freaked out.

Reid's finger slowed. He pulled it out, stroking it across her clit. She gritted her teeth even though his lips were still on hers.

He yanked his face back, his hand coming out of her

shorts. He searched her eyes as he grabbed her hips. His brow was furrowed. For a heartbeat, she thought he had read her mind and was angry. Why was she thinking about another man when she'd just bound herself to Reid?

But then he spoke. "Adriana..." His hand came up to cup her face. His brow was knit together, but his word was soft. Not angry.

Her breath came out in sharp pants. She released his cock to grab his hips too. "Reid." She didn't know what to say or think or do. Worry and pain leaked into her chest, a pressure making her fear she would stop breathing.

"It's not right," he stated. He shook his head. "Fuck." He licked his lips. "Oh, my God. Baby, it's not right."

She agreed. But what? What was this? What did it mean? They should be fucking now. He should be buried deep inside her, her mind consumed with nothing but Reid. Tears welled up in her eyes. Why was this happening?

Grizzlies didn't bind and then not have sex. Ever. What was Fate trying to tell her? Had she made the wrong choice?

The worry on Reid's face slid away, and he smiled. What was he smiling about?

A tear escaped to run down her cheek. "Reid?"

He shook her by the hips. "Baby, don't you see?"

No. She most certainly didn't see anything.

He chuckled. "We've had it all wrong all this time."

Obviously. But why was this making him happy? "Reid?"

"It's not about choosing. It never was. You belong to both of us."

What?

Reid released her hips and grabbed her hand. He yanked almost too hard to get her to follow him as he glanced around and then raced up the stairs, nearly dragging her with him.

She was confused and so worried, but she followed. She had no other options.

When they reached the master bedroom, Reid swiped his phone from the bed and used the one free hand to both hold it and touch the screen.

She set her other hand on his chest and stepped into his space. "Who are you calling?" she asked. They had questions. Yes. But did he think someone had answers?

His grin grew wider. Suddenly he spoke. "Nolan. Thank God."

It all clicked into place. She understood. Holy shit, she understood. Her smile was slow, but she finally joined him.

CHAPTER 23

Nolan pulled his phone out of his pocket and glanced at the screen. Reid? Why would he be calling? He should have been fucking the daylight out of Adriana by now. Making her his in every way after the delay.

He considered ignoring the call. After all, he needed to be packing the rest of his shit so he could move to another safe house. An officer was picking him up in five minutes. Not only did he not have time to talk to Reid, but it would be too painful.

Maybe someday the pressure on his chest would lessen, but it wasn't going to happen as abruptly as he'd expected.

It almost seemed cruel for them to call him. Like they were rubbing it in. They probably wanted to make sure he was okay. A friendly call. But tonight wasn't a good time.

Something told him to answer the call though. His next thought was that they were still in danger. So he connected. "Reid?"

"Nolan. Thank God."

"What are you calling me for?" He didn't mean to sound angry, but it came out that way anyway.

"Get over here. Like now."

"Where?" What was Reid talking about?

"My condo. Call a cab or get a ride or something. Just get here."

"Why?" That seemed like a horrible idea. And yet, his chest tightened further, and the thought of seeing Adriana made his cock stiffen too. No. It was a very bad idea. The worst. "I can't, Reid. I'm waiting for the police to pick me up, and then I'm heading to another location. I'm so tired." *In so many ways.*

"Not tonight. Shake the cop. Get your ass here."

"Reid? What the hell?"

"It's not what we thought," he continued.

"What isn't?"

"The binding. We had it all wrong."

He had no idea what Reid was rambling about, but he also didn't want to discuss it with him at that moment. The pain was raw and growing.

Reid continued. "Nolan, listen to me. She belongs to both of us."

"What?" Nolan's voice rose to a pitch he hadn't ever reached before. His hand shook, making him fear he might drop the phone.

"Adriana. She's as much yours as mine."

Nolan lowered himself to the chair, hope rising inside him. "What are you saying?" Did he dare understand this correctly? "Didn't you bind to her?"

"Yes. But that's it. All I did was bite her. The binding is complete between us, but it's...not right."

"You aren't making sense." Nolan gripped the arm of the chair with his free hand.

"Actually this is the first time anything has made sense in a week. Adriana Tarben belongs to both of us," he repeated. "Get your ass here and bind to her before the two of us self-combust waiting."

Nolan tried to breathe. He couldn't make sense of what Reid was saying.

"Nolan?"

He swallowed. "Yeah, I'm here."

"Cab. Downstairs. Now."

He nodded, his chest loosening. Jumping to his feet, he spun around and stuffed the last of his belongings into his suitcase. Everything he'd had at the previous hotel had been moved to this one, courtesy of Carl Schaefer or someone he'd hired to do so.

He needed both hands. "Be there in ten." He stuffed the phone in his pocket, finished packing in record time, and raced out of the room and down the hall. One minute after ending the call, he was in a cab, shouting the address to the driver.

Nolan couldn't stop tapping his fingers on his thighs as the cab driver made his way across Calgary. It was the middle of the night. There wasn't much traffic. But the city didn't sleep. Lights were everywhere, buildings loomed, cars filled the streets. It wasn't far, but it seemed like a hundred miles. When they finally pulled up outside Reid's condo, Nolan tossed some bills at the driver and grabbed his stuff. He rushed toward the front door, which opened before he could get there.

Reid stepped outside, his face beaming. He grabbed Nolan's bags and hauled them inside.

Adriana, wearing nothing but a tiny white tank top and soft pink sleep shorts stood two feet inside the door. She was chewing on her lower lip, her face a mixture of excitement and concern. Curiosity.

Nolan dropped the computer case he'd worn over his shoulder and rushed toward her. His only thought was touching her. Holding her. Finding out if this insanity was true.

The second he cupped her face, he knew in his soul Reid was right. He searched her eyes.

She sighed, her shoulders lowering. "He's right," she whispered.

"You're sure?"

"Never been more certain of anything in my life. I need you to bind to me too."

Nolan glanced at Reid who had shut the front door and dropped Nolan's suitcase. He stepped up beside them and set a hand on Nolan's shoulder. His other hand wrapped around Adriana's neck. "She belongs to both of us."

"I see that." Nolan let himself believe it as he smiled and turned his gaze back to Adriana. He leaned forward and set his forehead against hers. "I love you. Do you know that?"

She smiled back. "Yes. I love you too." She lifted onto her tiptoes and grabbed the front of his jacket to pull herself up to his lips.

The moment her mouth touched his, he melted, wrapping his arms around her and flattening her body to his. He couldn't get enough of her taste.

Her hands went to the zipper on his jacket and pulled it down.

Reid was behind him, pulling the sleeves off. "Before you two get completely carried away, let's go upstairs. We can fuck on every surface of the house all night if you want, but let's start with my bed."

"Mmm." Nolan agreed, though he was reluctant to break the kiss. He did it anyway and then reached down to sweep Adriana into his arms.

She squealed, grabbing his neck.

Nolan took the stairs two at a time, sensing Reid on his heels. When he hit the master bedroom, he could smell the two of them, potent on the sheets. Had they already had sex? Not that he could blame them. He was simply curious.

"Nolan." Adriana's voice was soft. She cupped his face. "Set me down. Take off your damn clothes."

"So bossy." He dropped her on the bed a few inches higher than necessary, making her bounce.

She rose onto her knees.

Reid climbed up behind her, straddled her shins with his legs, and wrapped one arm around her body under her breasts. He brushed the hair off her shoulder with one hand and kissed her neck.

Nolan whipped his shirt over his head and kicked off his shoes. He spotted the location where Reid had bitten her and salivated. He considered removing his jeans and then opted to bind to her first.

Closing the gap, he reached for her face. His gaze slid to her full breasts resting against Reid's forearm. The tank top needed to go. "Take off her shirt," he ordered.

"He *is* bossy," Reid teased as he dragged the cotton over her head and then resumed holding her around the waist, tucking her body against his.

She squirmed.

Reid held her still.

"It makes me so horny when you hold me like that." Her voice was dreamy now. Arousal evident in every syllable.

Nolan lowered his face to kiss her lips briefly. Damn, she was gorgeous. Her nipples were so rosy and tight. He couldn't take his eyes off them. He considered dipping his mouth to the upper swell of her breast and sinking his teeth into the delicate skin there. Would it hurt?

"You're taking too long," she muttered.

He smiled.

She narrowed her gaze, looking mischievous. And then she shocked the shit out of him by wrapping one hand around the back of his neck and tugging him closer. She kissed the corner of his lips and then nibbled a path toward his ear. When her tongue hit the edge of the lobe, he groaned and grabbed her waist. "You took too long," she whispered.

What was that supposed to mean?

He found out two seconds later when she licked a path down from his ear to his neck and lower. She kissed him reverently in that perfect spot where his neck met his shoulder, and then she bit into his skin.

The tiny puncture wounds sent a sharp, quick pain racing down his body, but it was immediately replaced by nirvana when her serum flowed from her teeth to his bloodstream.

He swayed toward her, instantly lost in all that was Adriana. Visions of her flashed through his mind like photographs. When he first spotted her in the hallway at the hotel last Sunday. The way she moaned when he first kissed her so sweetly on the couch that same afternoon. Her brown eyes rolling back when he flicked his tongue over her clit Saturday morning. The slow smile she shot him minutes ago as he entered the condo.

A rush of awareness flooded his system, his cock coming completely alive. All the pent-up need he'd experienced for the last several days doubled and continued to rise exponentially.

He blinked his eyes open as she sealed the nick in his skin and his gaze met the slow smile on Reid's face. "How the hell did you two manage to wait for me?" He knew they hadn't consummated this binding yet. The scent of their combined pheromones was potent in the air.

Adriana's hands trailed down to the button on Nolan's jeans. When her fingers touched the tip of his cock pressing at the opening, he nearly choked. Her hands were shaking, but she popped the button, lowering the zipper next. Her voice was deep and rough when she spoke. "It's like there was a barrier. We tried to have sex, but we couldn't. We didn't even get this far."

"She's right," Reid added. "Craziest thing I've ever experienced. She had her hand on my cock over my pants, but that was as far as she got, as if the Universe froze us in that state."

Nolan's smile grew. He released her hips to tug the denim over his ass and shrug out of the jeans.

Adriana's gaze was on his erection as she reached with a tentative hand and stroked one finger from tip to base. She continued telling their story. "Reid was touching me, but all I could think about was you. Scared me to death thinking I had royally fucked things up."

Nolan couldn't respond. He caught Reid shrugging out of his loose pants out of the corner of his eye, but his attention was on Adriana's chest. Her pert nipples called to him.

Reid divested her of her shorts, sliding them down her thighs and then tapping her knees one at a time to get her free of them.

A moment in time froze. The first time they were totally naked together. It should have been weird seeing Reid erect and horny for the same woman Nolan wanted more than his next breath, but it wasn't. They were not going to be able to avoid brushing against one another to make love to her.

Nolan didn't care. It no longer mattered.

He had no understanding of how this crazy ménage was going to play out over the course of a lifetime, but he did know with complete confidence that it would. Everything would fall into place and be perfect.

First, they needed to fully claim her.

She wrapped her hand around his cock and gently stroked up and down.

He tolerated that for about two seconds and then gripped her wrist and pulled her hand away. "I don't want to come for the first time against your thigh, baby. If you do that…" His voice trailed off.

She reached up on her knees and kissed his lips briefly before trailing her hand down his chest. Her gaze switched to Reid at her side.

He had one hand at the base of her neck and the other reaching for her breast.

She wiggled around to touch his cock in the same way she'd so reverently treated Nolan's.

He also humored her for about two seconds before halting her with a grip on her wrist. "Later. We need to be inside you now, baby. You can explore later."

Her face was flushed when she lifted her gaze. "Do it." She glanced back and forth. "Whatever it is, do it. I can't wait any longer."

Nolan chuckled. He glanced at Reid. "I think now's a good time to show our bossy little mate who's in charge."

She lifted a brow. "Under the circumstances, since it's two against one, I think I should be in charge. Always." She gave a fake pout, cocking her head to one side and narrowing her gaze.

Reid moved first. He also moved fast, tackling her around the waist and flattening her on the bed on her back.

Before she could even gasp, he had her hands above her head and was climbing between her legs, forcing them wide enough to accommodate his body. He hovered over her, staring down into her eyes. "Let's get something straight," he half teased.

She giggled, tugging on her wrists to no avail.

Nolan crawled to her side and cupped her breast. As he slowly pinched a nipple between two fingers, he spoke for both men, "We haven't ever shared a woman before. This is going to be awkward at first, and I'm sure we're going to struggle to find positions that are comfortable and satisfying to everyone, but..." He let the word hang in the air for a moment until he was sure he had her attention. "Reid and I have been friends for a long time. We know stuff about each other. And one of those things is that neither of us is likely to turn the reins over to you often, baby."

She licked her lips. Her chest heaved. She was turned on.

Fuck yes.

Reid added, "What he's trying to say is that you'll find us to be far bossier than you can imagine in the bedroom." He leaned closer, his face inches from hers. "And you're going to love it."

Her flush rose higher on her cheeks, and the shade of red was deeper. Her arousal also heightened, filling the room with desire. She lifted her knees a few inches and clamped them around Reid's thighs. "Please..." That one word. Spoken so softly it gave away all her cards. Defeat. Heaven.

Nolan slid his hand from her chest to her pussy and dragged a finger through her moisture.

She moaned, her head tipping back and her mouth falling open.

He pressed one finger slowly into her tight warmth and dragged it back out across her G-spot.

Her breath hitched. "Oh, God. Don't make me wait any longer. Please."

Nolan smiled. "Don't worry, baby. We've got you." He was worried though. She was tight. And there were two of them. He glanced at Reid and communicated with him privately. *"You have a single clue how we're going to play this?"*

"With the utmost care, watching her closely. That's all I've got."

Nolan pulled his hand from Adriana's pussy and sucked her juices from his finger. "She's delicious. I'll never tire of her flavor."

Reid said nothing as he released her hands and lifted one knee over her leg to straddle it, pulling it wider.

Nolan took his cue and settled his opposite knee between her thighs next to Reid. He noted for the first time that their cocks—now lined up and bobbing in front of their sweet mate—were similar in size.

Adriana was staring back and forth at the two of them. She took a breath. "On second thought, maybe don't rush. I hate to sound cliché, but I'm pretty sure this isn't going to work."

Reid chuckled, his body vibrating all three of them. He slid a hand up her waist and cupped her breast. "Relax. We're going to figure it out."

"Well, you can't do it at the same time. That's for sure. So if you had anything like that in mind, wipe the thought away." She lowered her arms to grip both their outer thighs, white knuckling them to get their attention.

Nolan leaned toward her, setting his hand beside her head for balance. "Maybe someday, but not today. Relax," he repeated.

A new clarity filled his soul. Everything was going to work out fine. They just needed to have patience and a willingness to work together.

CHAPTER 24

Adriana stared up at both men. Her body and her soul insisted she have sex with them urgently. Her mind took in the size of their erections and thought otherwise.

In tandem, they both lowered themselves over her straddled thighs. They reached forward to stroke her cheeks, her neck, her shoulders, finally moving to her chest.

Goosebumps rose all over her body as they teased her nipples with gentle strokes of their fingertips.

"That's it, baby. Relax. Don't worry. We'll make it work." Nolan's voice. Soothing and deep.

Reid lifted a finger to his mouth, sucked it in, and returned it to her nipple. The cool air of the room hit the wetness on the swollen tip and made her shudder. He smiled.

She knew they had to be silently communicating to each other, and for once, she didn't care as long as they made love to her and figured out a way to do so without killing her.

Nolan was the first to return his attention to her sex,

tapping her clit lightly and then dipping his finger inside her.

She moaned, bucking her torso upward unsuccessfully. She was totally trapped by their legs.

"So wet," Nolan whispered. "I love how responsive you are. It makes my cock ten times harder." He added a second finger to the first.

She bit back the noise in the back of her throat.

Surprising her, Reid's fingers joined Nolan's between her legs. They jockeyed for position, both of them touching her everywhere. So many fingers. Circling her clit, pinching it, teasing the skin of her lower lips, spreading them wider, tapping the sensitive skin behind her opening. Even that last part felt good, dangerously close to her bottom, but shockingly arousing.

Suddenly both men pushed a finger into her at the same time.

She whimpered, partly because it felt so damn good, and partly because she was scared out of her mind. Watching the two of them worship her was heady.

At least one of them added a finger, stretching her. Too far. She winced. But in a moment the stiffness passed, and she once again felt nothing but desire. A driving desire to have them inside her.

Reid lifted his leg out from between hers and settled on one hip at her side, leaning his head against his palm. He stared down at her, taking her chin in his fingers. "You're so tight, baby. It's gonna hurt a bit, but only for a moment. Ride through it. Don't fight it."

She nodded, unable to speak. In fact, she was holding her breath as Nolan centered himself between her legs and slid down to line his thick length up with her opening. She didn't know what to expect, but him gripping his cock and stroking the tip across her lower lips wasn't it.

He was teasing her, and she liked it. Her nerves calmed with every pass of his penis over her sensitive flesh. Her clit pulsed with need. She jerked her gaze toward Reid and boldly asked, "Touch me. Please."

He smiled and splayed his hand on her belly, his middle finger stretching toward her clit and then stroking it until she thought she might come.

They must have realized how close she was by her expression or her pheromones because Nolan took that opportunity to line himself up with her opening and dip inside.

The stretch was shocking. She gasped. Did he intend to slowly ease inside? Because she hated that plan. "Do it. Please, Nolan. Now. Don't draw it out."

He swiped a lock of hair off her cheek, brushed Reid's hand out of the way, and lowered himself over her. And then he thrust into her without another word.

She didn't know who gasped louder, him or her, or perhaps even Reid, but sensation bombarded her. It was too tight. How did women do this? At the same time, the fullness made her feel consumed.

He didn't move, staring into her eyes while he waited patiently for her to accommodate him.

She was grateful, both for his intention and the fact that he didn't voice it out loud to mortify her. She finally took a breath, realizing she had been holding it back. The ache return, not from the tightness but from the driving need. She grabbed his waist with both hands and pushed. "Move, Nolan. Please. Oh God, I need..."

He did as she asked, slowly easing out and then thrusting back in. "That's it, baby. So damn sexy." He kissed her lips then, his elbows landing beside her ears. Again he retreated only to thrust back inside. Every time he entered her it felt better. Nerve endings came alive. Tingling climbed up her spine. She was going to come.

Reid had one hand cupping the top of her head, and the other one rested at her side, stroking the edge of her breast. She was aware of him in a way that bound them together, but her main focus was on Nolan.

Suddenly he pulled out, rising off her body and climbing over her to lean on his side next to her. She glanced around in confusion, but seconds later, she realized the plan when Reid replaced Nolan between her legs.

He lined himself up with her entrance and thrust forward without preamble. He groaned loudly, his eyes rolling back. He held himself aloft, leaving enough space for Nolan to stroke her breasts and her belly. When his fingers dipped lower and tagged her clit, she flew over the edge without warning.

She cried out, and then her vision blurred as her entire body rode the waves of her orgasm. It felt so much better with Reid inside her than the ones they'd given her without penetration.

She was still pulsing around Reid's cock when he stiffened above her, plunged deep one last time, and roared out his orgasm. Every pulse of his cock shoved her forward. Was that possible? Maybe she simply imagined it.

He lowered himself, breathing heavily, kissed her lips languidly, and then whispered against them. "You're amazing." And then he pulled out, his lips brushing over hers again. Instead of climbing off her as she expected, he tucked his hands under her shoulder blades and rolled them both over so that she was sprawled on top of him, her legs spread wide, her knees planted on the bed at the sides of his hips.

Reid flattened a palm on her back to hold her against

his chest when she started to lift up. "Stay still, baby. Let Nolan make you feel good."

Nolan's hands landed on her hips as he straddled Reid's legs and helped Adriana tuck her knees up closer to Reid's chest.

She was spread so wide open in this position she felt somehow more exposed. It was absurd. They'd both seen, touched, and tasted every inch of her skin in the last few days. Why would she feel more vulnerable? The emotion she saw in Reid's eyes melted her soul. He loved her so much. He didn't need to say a word for her to feel the intensity. She'd known both of them for only a week. It was crazy how she felt about them. But it was true all the same.

A restlessness took over.

Maybe it had something to do with Reid's hand on her back, holding her steady. Or maybe it was the way her knees were drawn high. It didn't matter. It made her squirm.

When Nolan reached between her legs to stroke her folds, she stilled. He set a hand on her lower back, pressing her against Reid's still-thick erection at her belly, and teased her clit with rapid flicks of his fingers.

She moaned, her breaths coming quickly. Unable to hold her head up, she set it on Reid's shoulder, her face against his neck.

Nolan lined his cock up with her entrance once again and eased into her. He took it slow, gripping her hip with one hand and reaching around her side to play with her clit with the other hand.

She was aware that his fingers were brushing against the base of Reid's erection, but neither man tensed. Thank God. She didn't want things to be weird for them. For as much as they'd both worried about something like this being too strange to consider, Nature had a way of making it perfect.

Her arousal rose, the need to come again right at the surface. She balled her fists at the sides of Reid's head and concentrated on the many powerful feelings overwhelming her.

When Nolan shuffled forward a few inches, changing the angle of his next thrust, she gasped. "Oh, yeah. God. Right there." He hit just the right spot.

She lifted her face, met Reid's gaze, and licked her lips.

He smiled and then urged her to close the gap with a firm press to her back.

And then their lips were locked, a deep kiss adding to her already emotional overload.

Nolan picked up the pace, thrusting in and out of her faster, every stroke of his cock against her G-spot sending her closer to the edge. His fingers worked her clit rapidly at the same time.

He grunted. Loud. Stiffening. "Adriana, come with me, baby. Now."

At his command, she flew apart, only half realizing he came at the same time. She released Reid's lips, dropping her forehead to his shoulder. The ability to hold her neck up was long gone. Her body seemed to literally become several pieces, scattered like a puzzle all over the room. The orgasm was so powerful it took her breath away.

Nolan held himself inside her for long moments, his fingers circling her clit in gentle strokes. Finally, he eased out of her and collapsed onto his side beside them both. He left one hand on her ass, stroking the skin, his fingers close to her crack.

She was shaking. Sated. So tired.

Reid kissed her temple and eased her onto her side so that she was spooned in Nolan's embrace.

She was marginally aware of Reid slipping from the bed and returning a few minutes later. She flinched when he gently lifted her top leg a few inches, set a warm wet cloth on her sex, and wiped away the evidence of their lovemaking.

Her eyes were too heavy to open. She heard the click of the light on the bedside table being turned off, Reid's body positioning to face her so close they were touching in several places. He kissed her forehead. "Sleep, baby."

That was the last thing she was aware of before she slid into dreamland.

Vinny had bided his time long enough. He didn't want to get so far away from Calgary that it would be time-consuming to return. However, he did want to be far enough away that no one was around when he made his move and could shift into bear form and make his way back toward the city.

Henry was concentrating on the road. He was also concentrating on a variety of telepathic conversations he'd been engaged in since they'd pulled away from Osborn's hotel in Calgary. He'd probably alerted the entire Arcadian Council, especially Eleanor—the council head.

Every time Vinny pondered his fate, he shuddered. No way in hell could he permit himself to be taken to the Northwest Territories. He would never be able to escape. He needed to make his move and fast while he was in the company of only one council member in the middle of nowhere.

He'd managed to extract his knife from his boot half an hour ago. It was time.

He glanced out the window. Every ounce of his energy

had been exerted blocking Henry from his thoughts. It was a tough job. The forty members of the Arcadian Council had powers far superior to regular grizzly shifters. Their ability to delve into the minds of their subordinates was uncanny under normal circumstances.

Either Vinny was doing a hell of a job blocking Henry, Henry was so distracted he wasn't paying attention, or—and this was the most likely scenario—Henry knew exactly what Vinny was plotting and could do nothing about it except alert his superiors.

If the latter was the case, all the more reason for Vinny to act quickly before reinforcements arrived. He'd hoped to wait until Henry stopped for gas, but the gauge showed the tank to be half full still.

Vinny let his gaze wander around the vicinity without moving his head more than necessary. He waited for the moment when no cars were coming toward them and no lights shone behind them. And that's when he jumped.

He lurched forward, wrapped his arm around Henry's forehead, and used his other hand to slit the man's throat in less than two seconds.

The SUV veered sharply into the other lane, but Vinny yanked Henry's body to the right, climbed over him and maneuvered himself into the driver's seat. It wasn't pretty. He had to keep one hand on the wheel at all times to keep from running off the road, but he managed to pull over and stop the car within seconds.

He reached over Henry's writhing body to jerk the glove compartment open. Bingo. He grabbed the gun. He only glanced back at Henry, just enough to see the man had wide eyes and his hand over his throat, gurgling through the final moments of his life.

Seconds after that, Vinny was out of the car, running for the tree line and shifting at the same time. It was the riskiest move he'd ever made. The Arcadian Council didn't need to use any unnecessary force when they picked someone up. No one in their right mind would challenge a council member or attempt to escape.

Which meant Vinny was now totally rogue. Capture would mean death. He would spend the rest of his life on the run. To Vinny, it was preferable to the alternative.

Before he took off for good, however, he needed to finish his current job and collect a hefty paycheck. If he slid off the grid before Nolan Osborn was dead, he would be leaving behind a fuck-ton of seed money.

Adriana had no idea how long she was unconscious, peacefully engulfed in both her mates' embrace, but something suddenly yanked her out of a deep sleep, and she jerked upright. Her heart was racing as Reid and Nolan came alert at her sides, each of them reaching for her.

She inhaled deeply, but her normal grizzly senses were too late this time. Bombarded with information she couldn't process fast enough, she was aware of several things at once.

There was a shifter nearby, in the house, approaching. Not just any shifter, but her cousin Vinson Tarben. What was Vinson doing in Reid's condo? He'd been on the run for months, missing ever since he had a role in meddling with the new product releases of both her hometown breweries.

And now he was rounding the doorway to stand in her line of sight before she could fully process how out of place that was, or that she was naked, or that she was in bed with two men.

To make matters worse, he held a gun aimed at her.

"What the fuck sort of sick twisted sex are you into, cousin?" he growled at the same time Reid and Nolan jerked fully awake next to her and sat up.

Vinson took a whiff of the air, and his face contorted grossly. "You bound yourself to both of them?"

She didn't answer. She stared dumbfounded at her cousin, whom she hadn't seen in months, not since he took off earlier that year after sabotaging the competitor's marketing plans for their brewery.

She took in several other facts. Vinson had blood all over him, even on his skin. His face was spattered. His clothes were a mess of dried blood. Bile rose in her throat from the stench of death.

Reid slid from the bed to stand beside it, positioning himself between Vinson and her body.

Nolan had grabbed the sheet tangled around their ankles, and he drew it up over her breasts. "This guy is your cousin?" he asked.

"Yes." She held the sheet tight and leaned around Reid's hip. Ignoring his questions, she asked one of her own. "What the hell are you doing here?"

He smirked. "Your bodyguard forgot to reset the alarm. It was too easy."

Reid swayed to one side to once again break contact between Vinson and Adriana.

How had all three of them slept through Vinson entering the home and then his ascent up the stairs? They must have been sleeping like the dead or else Vinson managed to block them better than the average shifter could accomplish.

"Lower the fucking gun, asshole." Reid's voice was menacing.

"Step out of the way, big guy. My beef isn't with you."

"It is now. You're in my home. In my bedroom. Threatening my woman."

Vinson growled. "If you don't want to get shot, I suggest you fucking move out of the way." The blood splatters on his cheeks and forehead were dry. He'd killed someone to get to them. Adriana's stomach revolted at the thought. Whose life had he taken? And why? Did Reid have men stationed outside to guard them? He hadn't mentioned it. Besides, this blood was older than a few minutes.

Reid subtly inched to the right.

Nolan wrapped an arm around Adriana and held her against his chest. *"Don't move, baby,"* he said into her mind.

She wanted to move. Hell, she wanted to leap off the bed and strangle her motherfucking cousin with her bare hands. But she also knew Reid was trained to handle things like this, and he had a gun, undoubtedly in the bedside table he was inching toward.

She held her breath while Reid continued to distract Vinson with his verbal volley. *"I don't understand what he's doing here,"* she said into Nolan's mind. *"Does he have something to do with the threat to your life?"*

"He has everything to do with it. I've scented him several times in the last week. He must be working for Rimouski."

She bit her lip. What a dick.

"I knew you two were shacking up, probably sharing a woman," Vinson hissed. "But I didn't realize she was my damn cousin and you'd bound her to you. Two of you. Gross. Sick fuckers."

Adriana flinched. Was this the reception they were going to get from everyone they ran into? She hoped not. The last few hours had been about binding and then consummating their union. She hadn't bothered to stop and think about the implications before now.

There was a possibility Vinson was right and many members of their community would not accept this union. But that wouldn't change anything. Nature selected this combination. The three of them had nothing to do with it. All they could do was heed Her call and follow Her desires.

Reid didn't go for the bedside table as Adriana expected. Instead, he took advantage of the next time Vinson leaned around to meet Adriana's gaze and lurched forward, smacking the gun out of Vinson's hands. It slid across the floor and slammed into the wall at the force.

Vinson rushed forward, plowing into Reid's enormous body as if he intended to tackle him.

Reid was much larger and stronger and luckily braced himself for the impact before it hit him. He grabbed Vinson by the arms and flipped him onto the floor. Vinson's head hit with a resounding thud. He screamed.

Adriana leaned over to see her stupid cousin struggling, flailing his arms and legs in an attempt to get up.

Nolan released Adriana to jump off the bed. He grabbed his discarded jeans from the floor and shrugged into them. Next, he snagged Reid's sleep pants and handed them to his friend. "I got it." He set a knee on Vinson's chest close to his neck and pressed so hard Vinson's eyes bugged out and he stopped squirming.

"Can't breathe," he mouthed.

"Shoulda thought of that before you came into my home waving a gun, asshole," Reid shouted as he pulled his pants on.

Adriana tugged the sheet free of the bed and worked her way off the other side, wrapping the cotton around her to keep her cousin from getting an even bigger eyeful.

Someone else was approaching. Rapidly.

George. He rushed into the room and quickly took in

the scene. "Son of a bitch. You do have a death wish, don't you, Vinson?"

Vinson growled against Nolan's knee, grabbing at it in an effort to free himself.

George set a foot on Vinson's forehead. "Stop moving, you piece of shit. You're in so much trouble, you'll never see the light of day."

"Fuck you," Vinson managed to hiss.

Two more shifters entered the room, approaching silently. They too had blocked their scents. Laurence and Charles.

Adriana was shocked that three members of the Arcadian Council had been so close they were able to rush in so fast. Where was Henry?

In a flurry of activity, Laurence kneeled beside Vinson, grabbed his arm, and then shoved a needle in it, emptying the contents.

Vinson jerked to try to escape, but it was too late. "What the fuck did you just shoot into me?"

Laurence stood, put the cap back on the syringe, and tucked it in his pocket. He ignored Vinson's question and turned toward Adriana. "You okay?"

She nodded, confused and speechless.

Charles and George each grabbed one of Vinson's arms and flipped him onto his belly. They used some serious handcuffs to secure his hands painfully tight. Moments later, Vinson passed out.

Nolan stepped back and lowered his butt to the bed, rubbing his forehead. He sighed as Adriana came around to step into his embrace. "What happened?" he asked George. "I thought you had him in custody."

George's face was firm, his lips pursed as he nodded.

Nolan stiffened. "Where's Henry?"

Adriana went totally still. Reid had told her Henry was

the one who took Vinson into custody. She hadn't realized who the shifter was that had been stalking Nolan with intent to kill, but she did know it was Henry who headed back to the Northwest Territories with his felon.

She glanced at Vinson. So much blood. *Oh, God…*

George rubbed his forehead with two fingers. "He's gonna make it."

Reid leaned on the bed next to Nolan, setting a hand on Adriana's and giving her fingers a squeeze. "This asshole escaped?"

"That's putting it mildly," Charles added. "He had a knife in his boot, and he slit Henry's throat while Henry was still driving."

Adriana gasped. "And he lived?"

"It was close. He'd lost a lot of blood when I got to him," George added. "But we council members are tough. He's gonna make it."

"How long did it take you to get there? And how did you know where to find this fucker next?" Nolan asked, pointing at the unconscious Vinson on the floor.

"Vinson miscalculated, as usual. I caught up with them after I dropped you at the hotel. I was following in my car. We would have stopped soon to combine and ditch the extra car, but before that could happen Vinson made his move. I wasn't able to capture Vinson, who ran into the trees at the side of the road, because I needed to save Henry's life first. But once I got Henry to shift and resume normal breathing, he started to heal quickly. I assumed Vinson would head straight for this condo. After all, he hadn't finished the job Rimouski was paying him for."

It was Nolan's turn to rub his temples with his fingers. He lowered his gaze toward the floor across the room.

Adriana felt his unease.

And then he spoke. "I never should have come here. I put my mates at risk. I lost my mind and let my guard down. There's still a threat to my life out there, and I took off like it wasn't happening. The police must be looking for me. I never even contacted Officer Schaefer before I left the hotel."

Adriana realized Nolan was right, and the pain that brought to her chest made her stop breathing. Nolan needed to get as far away from Calgary as possible. And there was no way he would take Reid or her with him. He would never take that kind of risk.

George cleared his throat, getting not only Adriana's attention but everyone's. He was smiling when she looked up. "There's a reason you haven't heard from Schaefer, oh and you won't have to worry about Rimouski anymore either. They're both dead."

Nolan gasped. So did Adriana and Reid.

"What? How?" Nolan asked.

"Schaefer was your mole. He was selling details to Vinson. Vinson's been working for Rimouski for months, ever since he left Silvertip, fleeing in the night. The little fuck has been right here under our noses." George stepped closer. "Schaefer knew he was caught when the rest of the department started putting the pieces together and figured out no one else knew the kind of information he shared about each hotel room and then the existence of Reid and Adriana."

"What did he do?" Adriana asked, her voice coming out weak.

"He went to the jail and used a silencer to shoot Rimouski between the eyes, and then he turned the gun on himself."

Holy shit.

Nolan shuddered, his arm tightening around her

middle. "So you knew Vinson was involved, and you knew he was Adriana's cousin. Why the secrecy?"

George nodded. "We didn't know who was involved until this evening. I didn't tell you it was Vinson because I knew it would be upsetting to Adriana, and this night didn't need any more surprises. I figured it could wait a few days." He glanced at Adriana apologetically.

"So it's over?" Nolan asked.

"Yes." George smiled. Charles and Laurence gathered Vinson's unconscious body off the floor and headed out the door.

"You're sure? Didn't Rimouski have other employees who might want revenge on me out of spite?"

George nodded. "The police are arresting several of them as we speak. Vinson wasn't too careful about covering his tracks. They were able to use his phone and other evidence in his car to find his apartment and track down his contacts, especially the man who seemed to be second in command under Rimouski."

Adriana started to ask the questions she knew all of them were thinking.

But George held up a hand and continued. "It was easy to leave Vinson's car open next to the park with his phone and other evidence visible to the police. Our cleanup on this only had once small glitch."

"Vinson's body." Reid sighed.

"Yes." He glanced at Adriana, cringing. "I'm so sorry."

Adriana was confused for a moment, and then Nolan gave her a squeeze, forcing her to meet his gaze. He communicated silently. *"There're going to have to leave his body for the police to find."*

For a moment she stared at her mate, and then it started to make sense. She knew the Arcadian Council did not exercise capital punishment often, but in this case

Vinson had attempted to murder one of their own members.

Reid touched her arm on the other side, and continued Nolan's line of thinking, projecting his thoughts. *"It won't be a stretch to assume another member of Rimouski's team took him out after he failed his mission. That will put everything about the case in the police's lap so the council no longer needs to interfere. Everyone else involved is human."*

It wasn't as though either of her mates were blocking George from hearing their thoughts, but no one in the room wanted to speak those words out loud. And it wouldn't have been prudent for George to verbalize the probable future decisions of the council.

Adriana held her breath. Vinson was her cousin. For a fleeting moment, she felt horrified, but her own cousin had been the cause of everything that had happened to her and her mates in the last week. He may not have known she was involved, but it didn't matter. It was inexcusable. He knew he was attacking his own kind. He deserved whatever the council decided.

George met her gaze. "I'm terribly sorry," he repeated. His sorrow and understanding flowed through her. He continued, "Since Rimouski is dead, I think you can safely say it's not only over, but as an added bonus the country doesn't have to deal with the expenses associated with his trial."

Nolan finally smiled. "Thank you."

George nodded, glanced at Adriana, and headed for the door. Before he stepped out of sight, he met Nolan's gaze dead on. "Like I told you in the car earlier, things might not be as bleak as they seem. Have faith."

Adriana felt the warmth coming from her mate. She had no idea what George was referring to, but she did know it pleased Nolan. And that's all that mattered.

CHAPTER 25

One week later...

"Adriana, you look fine. Stop fussing and come downstairs."

Adriana spun around from where she stood in the master bathroom and met Nolan's gaze. "Don't rush me." She resumed brushing through her hair even though she'd done so already for long enough that not one piece would dare get out of line for the entire day. For the last several days, she'd been coming back into herself, taking extra care with her hair and makeup and clothes. She'd even designed several new dresses, spending hours escaping into her work.

But Nolan was right. She was stalling. Her hands were shaking, though she tried to hide this fact by brushing more vigorously.

Nolan shoved off the door frame where he'd been leaning and came to her. He took the brush out of her hands and set it on the counter. She sighed as he wrapped his arms around her middle and set his chin on her shoulder, meeting her gaze in the mirror. "You're beautiful. Always. No matter what you do. And that dress is amazing."

She glanced down at her latest design, hoping others would see it the same way she did. It was floral with an array of pinks and blues and purples, and it had a fitted bodice with a filmy flowing skirt that hung to mid-calf. It accented her chest and her waist. "You have to say that."

He chuckled, his chin vibrating her entire body.

"In fact, it's worse. You're programmed to believe that even if it's not true." She wasn't lying. After binding together, mates were forever permanently attracted to each other for life. They could literally do no wrong. That's how bindings worked in her world.

He nudged her hair out of the way with his chin and kissed her neck, sending shivers down her spine.

Her nipples jumped to attention, which was absurd since they'd had sex twice that morning, and she was pretty sure between Nolan and Reid, they'd delivered about five orgasms. Her body was constantly aroused.

"What's bothering you, baby?" he whispered into her ear.

She blew out a breath.

Reid stepped into the room and came to her side. When he saw her look in the mirror, he turned to face her fully and slid into the space between her and the vanity, his ass against the granite. He cupped her chin opposite Nolan's cheek. "Everyone's here."

"I know." She could scent them and had before they each arrived at the door. Besides, the volume downstairs was loud enough to attest to the number of people in the condo. Her parents, Nolan's parents, Wyatt and Paige,

Alton and Joselyn. Eight guests. It was a tight fit in the condo, but no one would care.

The only people unable to come were Reid's parents. The trip from Ottawa was too far for them to come that weekend. Reid had promised them he would bring his new mates to visit in the near future.

"What if they don't accept this?" She didn't need to elaborate. Both her men knew she'd fretted all weekend over their arrangement. So far they hadn't had to confront anyone, human or shifter. She'd taken Monday off school, but returned Tuesday and had followed her normal schedule all week. Reid hadn't relented to let her drive on her own yet, but he would soon.

He was no longer worried about her safety so much as he didn't want her out of his sight yet. She understood because she felt the same way about him. And Nolan. In fact, Nolan tagged along two of the days also.

Perhaps it was insanely strange having two men wait outside for her, but no one seemed to notice, or they assumed one of them was her boyfriend and the other his friend. Humans wouldn't be tuned in to something like that, and there were no shifters in any of her classes.

She was calmer in her classroom having them nearby. Separating from them for even those few sporadic hours during the week was hard. It was true what people said, the binding was intense. It held them together like Super Glue. She had no idea when the magnetic pull would loosen, but as of yet, there had been no change.

Nolan had moved his computer and boxes of files to Reid's home office so he could work. He claimed he was actually ahead of the game with his workload since he'd had nothing to do the previous week in hotels but work. It helped keep his mind off Adriana. He'd had to cancel several client appointments and reschedule, but he was relieved this situation was no longer going to last for months.

Reid hadn't taken a new assignment yet, but he had enough people working for him that he was covered for a while. After his last assignment that ended just over a week ago, he'd been due for a vacation anyway.

According to both the police and the Arcadian Council, the threat was eliminated. With the kingpin taken out of the picture, no one cared if his witness was alive or not. Anyone employed by Stephen Rimouski needed to find another line of work and fast.

Adriana shuddered to imagine how many people that included.

Reid wrapped his fingers around her neck and tugged her face toward his, taking her lips. When he pulled back, he met her gaze. "The people downstairs are all family. Not a single one of them faults us for something that's totally out of our control. We're a unit. Unconventional perhaps, but united."

She nodded but still argued. "This has never happened before in the shifter population. Who's going to believe us?"

Reid smiled. "Actually, you're wrong."

She lifted a brow, glancing at Nolan.

"He's right," Nolan added. "We spoke to Wyatt Arthur yesterday. Remember, he and his brother Isaiah traveled to Montana a while back to help the wolf shifters with their strange weather problems."

"Yes." It was lore among the grizzlies. Everyone knew *of* the wolf shifters, but few of them had met any. She also knew Wyatt was downstairs right now.

"Turns out, we misunderstood what light Wyatt might share concerning the mating habits of wolves," Reid continued. "It's not simply that they meet more than one mate and choose like we assumed. They often mate in groups of threes."

She flinched. "Seriously?"

"Yes." Nolan kissed her cheek and lifted his head. "And, even more interesting, those ménages are always two men and one woman."

Her eyes grew wide. If what he was saying was true, then maybe they weren't as freaky as she thought.

"If you want," Reid suggested, "we could take a trip to Montana one of these days and meet some of the people Wyatt knows. Maybe it would ease your mind to speak with other women who live in arrangements like ours."

"That would be amazing." She stood taller, the weight of two weeks of fretting easing slightly from her shoulders. Hope. Something to look forward to.

Every time the three of them ventured out to places where they would be around other shifters, she would still feel nervous—probably for the rest of her life—but at least she now knew they weren't alone in the universe. They could fake anything while in human circles and pretend their relationship to each other was whatever they made up. But in shifter circles, that would be impossible. Any grizzly would scent their ménage and be shocked. They would never be able to hide what they were to each other.

Nolan squeezed her body where he still held her around the waist. "Yes, it's going to be weird for a while. When we run into shifters, they might do a double take when they catch the scent of us together and realize the sort of arrangement we have, but anyone who stops to think will realize we didn't choose this for ourselves. Fate chose it. We simply headed Her desires."

Reid added to that. "When we're out in pairs, we'll appear to be bound couples. No one will flinch."

"What about our human neighbors and people around us? How are we going to handle them?"

Reid smiled. "Nolan and I were discussing that earlier. We thought we should sell this condo. We can move into his house for a while until you finish school and then build something outside of Calgary. Maybe we could get some land where there aren't neighbors nearby. If we pool our resources, we can afford something with more acreage."

She liked that idea. It could work.

Nolan and Reid seemed to have adjusted to their ménage more seamlessly than her. Maybe because they'd been friends for years and she was the new common denominator. It still surprised her.

They'd been leery and reluctant around each other for the entire first week after she met them. Clearly, they'd had no interest in getting naked in front of each other or possibly brushing against each other while loving her, but after the binding, it was like a switch was flipped. Whatever concerns the two of them had vanished immediately. In fact, they were outwardly shocked to find they didn't care one bit for their cocks to sometimes touch or their mouths to share hers.

The three of them had spent more hours naked in the past week than clothed. They were constantly touching at all hours of the day and night. The sexual interest was clearly focused on her and not each other. It wasn't as though Reid and Nolan had any desire to have sex outside of their devotion to her, but the idea of brushing against each other in their efforts no longer made them cringe.

It just was. The world was perfect. Perfect in its own way.

Perfection came in many forms.

For Adriana, it came in the form of two men who loved

her unconditionally and intended to rock her world for as long as they lived.

She was blessed. Truly blessed.

With a deep breath, she smiled at them both and wiggled free of their grasp. "What are we doing standing in the bathroom? There're a lot of people downstairs waiting to congratulate us."

They both chuckled as they followed her out the door.

Yep. Having two men in her life was her perfect world. And it always would be.

EPILOGUE

Eight months later…

Adriana spun in a slow circle, her head tipped up toward the horizon, taking in every angle of the view from where she stood, the grin on her face growing.

"What do you think?" Nolan stopped her by grabbing her from behind and hauling her back against his front.

Reid blocked her view by pressing into her front, setting his hands on her hips. "You like it?"

She smiled up at him. "I love it."

Nolan kissed her neck. "I think the view is fantastic."

"Yes," she agreed, choking up. "You're sure about this? I don't want you two to feel pressured into buying a piece of land just for me."

Reid shook her hips. "Baby, I've never wanted anything more in my life, except you of course." He chuckled.

Nolan's lips tickled her skin again. "I agree. I can move my practice from Calgary to Silvertip easily."

"And it doesn't matter where my home base is. When

I'm on a job, I have to travel to it anyway." He cringed. She knew he hated it when he was gone for weeks at a time working, but he was right. It wouldn't matter where they lived.

Nolan inhaled deeply. "Clean fresh air. Your family is only a few miles from here. The view is fucking awesome. We can live together in our unconventional arrangement far more peacefully than in the city. It's a win win."

Reid nodded. "It will take almost a year to get a home built on this property. Gives you plenty of time to finish school. All you have to do is take a few hours out of your weekends to design and pick color schemes and shit." He smirked. "That won't be a hardship."

Understatement. She would love helping with the design. In fact, she could not wait.

"This property just needs to pass one more test," Nolan joked.

"What's that?" She tipped her head back to meet his teasing gaze.

"How's the location for shifting, of course." He winked, releasing her to step back. "Let's check out the perimeter." Before she knew what he intended, he was mid-shift, his body coming forward onto all fours, fir replacing clothes and skin, face elongating, paws on the ground.

Reid released her hips and followed right behind Nolan.

She watched his transformation with equal awe. Reid's fur was darker than Nolan's, but they were equal to each other in stature. And she giggled, backing up a few paces as they stalked toward her side by side.

They were huge. The last thing she needed was two grown grizzly bears bounding into her, so she jumped back a few more paces and let her own transformation take place. Thirty seconds later, she was on their heels, following them toward the tree line. She was smaller than them, but in her grizzly form she always felt invincible. So much sturdier and stronger than in her human form.

A deep inhale told her no other significant creatures were around, human or shifter. As Reid and Nolan rushed into the edge of the evergreens, she turned back to look at the clearing.

Yeah, this piece of land was just right. The view was incomparable. They would have privacy and fresh air and miles of mountains and forest as far as they could see. She was anxious to get started building. The past eight months had been the best of her life, and it was only going to get better from here.

She couldn't ask for more.

Perfection.

AUTHOR'S NOTE

I hope you've enjoyed this last book in the Arcadian Bears series. Please enjoy the following excerpt from the first book in the Wolf Gatherings series, *Tarnished.*

TARNISHED

WOLF GATHERINGS, BOOK ONE

"Have fun. Don't do anything I wouldn't do." Mackenzie Rogers snorted in her sister's direction and took another bite of her Lucky Charms. No matter how old she got, she'd never be too old for the perfect bite of marshmallows and cereal.

"You're kidding, right?" Kathleen stopped midstride between the fridge and the table. "You aren't really going to skip the gathering, are you? Mom and Dad will have a fit."

"They can fly a kite for all I care. That stupid bi-annual event makes me want to vomit. No way in hell am I going to participate in such a farce again this year." Mackenzie took another bite, crunching into the cereal and spooning up a balanced combo for her next bite.

Kath took a seat next to Kenzie and grabbed for the red box of sugary goodness. "Hey, you ate almost all of this."

Kenzie smiled through a mouthful. "Uh-huh." She swallowed. "And it's the last box too."

"Who peed in your cereal this morning?" Kath scowled.

"Nobody. I'm perfectly happy. I have a nice human boyfriend, a college degree, a job, and plenty of friends. I'm about as fantastic as a person can get." She smiled at her sister. "I sure don't need to attend some match festival to find some barbaric mate. Been there. Done that. Have the mental scars to prove it."

Kathleen narrowed her gaze at Kenzie. "I don't know what happened to you two years ago, but that was last time. How do you know this gathering will be the same? You were only twenty-one last festival. Now, you're more … mature … sometimes." Kath ducked when Kenzie swung at her sister's head, managing to swat her on the top.

"And now I'm wiser. Older. Less stupid. And in no need of a matchmaking service. Boyfriend, remember? Human boyfriend. Sexy, human boyfriend who has a job and likes me for who I am." Kath had no idea that Kenzie's mental scars went way deeper than just the last gathering. The events of two years ago paled in comparison to what happened four years ago. Mackenzie kept those details to herself, buried deep inside.

"Really? And who does he think you are exactly? Have you told him about your tendency to shift into a wolf now and then and run free in the forest?" Kath grinned big.

Of course Kenzie hadn't told him anything of the sort. And she never intended to. "What makes you such an expert? How many guys have you dated, smarty pants?" Kenzie knew her sister hadn't dated a single guy. She was just twenty-one herself.

"That's why I'm going to the gathering, smartass. Dating humans is a pain in the butt. It can't go anywhere long term. Sure, you have a degree and a pseudo-job, but your human boyfriend is a farce, and all those friends you claim to have are really his." Kathleen's honesty was over-the-top.

"When I need your opinion next time, I'll ask for it."

It was tough being a shapeshifter and living among

regular humans. Stressful at best. Downright annoying most of the time. Wolves could scent almost anything. Fear. Anxiety. Stress. Arousal... It gave them both an advantage and a disadvantage. It sucked royally when Kenzie was out with friends and realized one of them didn't like her. That was why wolves tended to mate with their own kind. It was so much easier than dealing with the nuances of the human world.

But Kenzie had no interest in following wolf tradition and allowing some supposed ruling of fate to determine who, where, and when she mated. It sickened her. She was in control of her own destiny. Definitely.

And lately, things were looking up. Darrell adored her. He was the first man she'd ever dated who truly enjoyed her company, didn't pressure her to have sex, and smelled fantastically of ... well, Darrell. Nothing was going to ruin the human high she was enjoying.

"Have you told Mom and Dad this decision yet?" Kath tipped her bowl and drank the rest of the sugary milk.

"Nope." She was putting it off.

"We're leaving in about an hour, ya know. For the opening day."

"Yep. And like I said, have fun." Kenzie scooted her chair back, letting it scrape against the floor with an annoying screech that always pissed her sister off.

"Mackenzie Renae, how many times have I asked you not to do that? It scratches the wood floor and..." Kenzie's mother, Carina, paused midsentence. "Why aren't you dressed?"

Kathleen chuckled. "'Cause she isn't going with us." She ran from the room. The bitch.

Their youngest sister, nineteen-year-old Cassidy, came in on her mother's heels. "What's going on? Why is Kath running?"

Kenzie's mother didn't look amused. As Kenzie deposited her bowl in the sink, her mother stared her down. "Tell me this is some sort of joke? What, are you sick?"

"Nope. But I would be if I let you drag me to the mating event of the year." Kenzie skirted her mother and hoped to escape the room before World War III broke out.

"Sit down." Her mother was taking prisoners today. *Great.*

"Mom, I'm twenty-three. Don't you think I should be allowed to make my own choices by now?" Kenzie worked hard to keep a whine out of her voice as she plopped back into the chair she'd vacated, careful not to scrape the floor. That wouldn't make her sound as grown up as she insisted, and it sure wouldn't help her case.

"As the oldest in this family, don't you think you owe it to your sisters to attend with them? They're counting on you for guidance. Reassurance." Her mother sat in the chair Kath had vacated while Cassidy grabbed the orange juice and joined the bantering.

"Mom, they're both grown adults themselves. They do not need me for anything. That's ridiculous and you know it."

"It's typical for the oldest child to pave the way, so to speak." Her mom lowered her voice to übercalm, as though it would change Kenzie's mind. "Besides, we are so fortunate to live only fifteen minutes from the gathering. People come from all over the country to this event, and you take it for granted. You're not getting any younger."

"Good grief. Are we seriously having this conversation? Do you realize how absurd you sound? By human standards, I'm young."

"You aren't human, Mackenzie." Her mother eyed her over the top of her glasses after she lowered them from her hair. They were a constant hairband when she wasn't reading. Forever stuck in the soft brown curls all the women in the family sported.

"I don't have any interest in playing nice with the other wolves in the mating dance, Mom. Sniffing each other out in that stupid replica of the one-minute dating game is barbaric." She shivered as the thought and memories of the disaster from two years ago assaulted her. That event had not been kind to her.

No one knew what had happened when Kenzie was only nineteen, either. And she intended to keep it that way. Suffice it to say, she had no interest in the mating ritual.

"You do realize we live in the middle of Oklahoma, right? This isn't exactly a prime area for finding a mate. If you don't attend the gathering, you're just blowing another opportunity." Her mother shook her head in dismay.

Kenzie sighed. "I have a boyfriend. He's perfect. I don't need a wolf sticking his nose all up in my business."

"Darrell's gay," Cassidy interjected. "And you know it. If you would stop spreading your feathers like a peacock for one minute, you'd see the truth of it."

What the fuck? Sweet innocent Cassidy weighs in, and this is what she has to say? And what is this, gang up on Kenzie's boyfriend day?

"Cassidy," her mother admonished. "Watch your language."

Cassidy smirked. "Gay? Mom, what's wrong with the word gay?"

Her mother chose to ignore the comment.

Kenzie did not. "Why on earth would you say that?" Kathleen had implied something similar.

"Come on, Kenz. I have excellent gaydar, and you apparently do not." Cassidy rolled her eyes.

"Stop it, girls. Listen, your father is going to be

downstairs any minute. Please go get ready." Her mother stood and turned toward the sink.

Kenzie narrowed her gaze at her mother's back and fumed. She crossed her arms over her chest. She still wore a simple T-shirt and cotton shorts, the same thing she'd worn to bed last night. She'd have a longer leg to stand on if she didn't still live with her parents. As it was, her degree in early childhood development had landed her a job at the local YMCA working with disabled children. She loved the work, but it didn't pay well enough for her to move out of the house.

Her mother turned and leaned warily against the counter. "Why, Kenzie? Why can't you just go along with the family and try to enjoy yourself?"

Because the stupid thing is a farce, and I can't stand men pawing at me like I'm some kind of candy. It unnerved her. Especially after that crazy he-wolf had tried to corner her in the hall and make out with her, insisting she was "the one." His breath had been revolting, and she'd had no feelings for him whatsoever. And she wasn't even going to dip further back in the memory bank to the gathering before that one. A wise woman would seal that experience off eternally. She shivered. "I have a date with Darrell this evening."

"Doing what?" Cass asked. "Hanging out with his friends, most of whom are girls, none of whom are really your friends. Just his. Don't you realize why he has so many girl friends?"

"No, Cass. But do tell me," Kenzie mocked.

"Because girls like to hang out with gay guys. They're safe." Cass ducked and fled the room when Kenzie threw the empty box of cereal at her.

Kenzie's cell phone vibrated on the table. She glanced at the text from Darrell.

Kenz, sorry, can't make it tonight, family plans. Rain check?

Shit. She groaned and glanced back at her mother. "One day. I'm not attending tomorrow. Just today. And only so long as nobody tries to claim me. If they do, I'm out of there."

Her mother smiled. "Agreed."

Reviving Zeke

Reviving Graham

Reviving Bianca

Reviving Olivia

Project DEEP Box Set One

Project DEEP Box Set Two

SEALs in Paradise:

Hot SEAL, Red Wine

Hot SEAL, Australian Nights

Hot SEAL, Cold Feet

Dark Falls:

Dark Nightmares

Club Zodiac:

Training Sasha

Obeying Rowen

Collaring Brooke

Mastering Rayne

Trusting Aaron

Claiming London

Sharing Charlotte

Taming Rex

Tempting Elizabeth

Club Zodiac Box Set One

Club Zodiac Box Set Two

The Art of Kink:

Pose

Paint

Sculpt

Arcadian Bears:

Grizzly Mountain

Grizzly Beginning

Grizzly Secret

Grizzly Promise

Grizzly Survival

Grizzly Perfection

Arcadian Bears Box Set One

Arcadian Bears Box Set Two

Sleeper SEALs:

Saving Zola

Spring Training:

Catching Zia

Catching Lily

Catching Ava

Spring Training Box Set

The Underground series:

Force

Clinch

Guard

Submit

Thrust

Torque

The Underground Box Set One

The Underground Box Set Two

Saving Sofia (Special Forces: Operations Alpha)

Wolf Masters series:

Kara's Wolves

Lindsey's Wolves

Jessica's Wolves

Alyssa's Wolves

Tessa's Wolf

Rebecca's Wolves

Melinda's Wolves

Laurie's Wolves

Amanda's Wolves

Sharon's Wolves

Wolf Masters Box Set One

Wolf Masters Box Set Two

Claiming Her series:

The Rules

The Game

The Prize

Emergence series:

Bound to be Taken

Bound to be Tamed

Bound to be Tested

Bound to be Tempted

Emergence Box Set

The Fight Club series:

Come

Perv

Need

Hers

Want

Lust

The Fight Club Box Set One

The Fight Club Box Set Two

Wolf Gatherings series:

Tarnished

Dominated

Completed

Redeemed

Abandoned

Betrayed

Wolf Gatherings Box Set One

Wolf Gathering Box Set Two

Durham Wolves series:

Rescue in the Smokies

Fire in the Smokies

Freedom in the Smokies

Stand Alone Books:

Blind with Love

Guarding the Truth

Out of the Smoke

Abducting His Mate

Three's a Cruise

Wolf Trinity

Frostbitten

A Princess for Cale/A Princess for Cain

ABOUT THE AUTHOR

Becca Jameson is a USA Today best-selling author of over 100 books. She is well-known for her Wolf Masters series, her Fight Club series, and her Club Zodiac series. She currently lives in Houston, Texas, with her husband and her Goldendoodle. Two grown kids pop in every once in a while too! She is loving this journey and has dabbled in a variety of genres, including paranormal, sports romance, military, and BDSM.

A total night owl, Becca writes late at night, sequestering herself in her office with a glass of red wine and a bar of dark chocolate, her fingers flying across the keyboard as her characters weave their own stories.

During the day--which never starts before ten in the morning!--she can be found jogging, running errands, or reading in her favorite hammock chair!

…where Alphas dominate…

Becca's Newsletter Sign-up

Join my Facebook fan group, Becca's Bibliomaniacs, for the most up-to-date information, random excerpts while I work, giveaways, and fun release parties!

Facebook Fan Group:
Becca's Bibliomaniacs

Contact Becca:

www.beccajameson.com
beccajameson4@aol.com

facebook.com/becca.jameson.18
twitter.com/beccajameson
instagram.com/becca.jameson
bookbub.com/authors/becca-jameson
goodreads.com/beccajameson
amazon.com/author/beccajameson

Printed in Great Britain
by Amazon